Praise for *The Christ[mas...]*

"A heartwarming story."                    —*Publishers Weekly*

"Heart-tugging . . . an inspiring Christmas story."
                                            —*BookPage*

"Has precious gifts for all of us."
                                            —*The Washington Times*


Praise for *The Christmas Blessing*

"Sweet and emotional . . . A perfect holiday gift."
                                            —*BookReporter*

"A story of tragedy and, of course, ultimate triumph."
                                            —*New York Daily News*

# Christmas Keepsakes

Two Books in One:
## The Christmas Shoes &
## The Christmas Blessing

DONNA VANLIERE

ST. MARTIN'S GRIFFIN
NEW YORK

This is a work of fiction. All of the characters, organizations, and events portrayed in this novel are either products of the author's imagination or are used fictitiously.

www.stmartins.com

ISBN 978-1-250-04170-8 (trade paperback)
ISBN 978-1-4668-3867-3 (e-book)

St. Martin's Griffin books may be purchased for educational, business, or promotional use. For information on bulk purchases, please contact Macmillan Corporate and Premium Sales Department at 1-800-221-7945, extension 5442, or write specialmarkets@macmillan.com.

First Edition: October 2013

10  9  8  7  6  5  4  3  2  1

# The Christmas Shoes

For Troy,
who always encourages, always inspires, always believes

## ACKNOWLEDGMENTS

Troy, thank you for continuing to challenge and inspire me to new heights. I love you for giving me the courage to follow my dreams.

Eddie Carswell, Billy Goodwin, and the members of NewSong for inspiring this book. Your beautiful song has—and will—continue to touch millions of hearts around the world.

Helga Schmidt provided the beautiful true inspiration behind NewSong's lyrics. Helga, thank you for your tender heart and for sharing your moving story. You have left all of us forever changed.

From its earliest form, Jennifer Gates has shown nothing but unwavering belief in this book and given me constant guidance and encouragement. It wouldn't have happened without you. . . . I hope we can do it again!

Jennifer Enderlin and the staff at St. Martin's Press, thank you for your enthusiasm and for going the extra mile to get this book out quickly!

Esmond Harmsworth (and the Zachary Shuster

Harmsworth Agency), Mark Maxwell and Don Zachary, thank you for your countless hours and incredible insight.

Deborah Chiel read the story again and again and provided invaluable input. Thank you.

It's a blessing to know that there are still people like Eddie and Terri Carswell in the world. We hope to grow up to be just like you . . . really.

To other supporters, family, and friends: my parents, my mother- and father-in-law, Dave and Vicki, who have always loved me like one of their own, the ladies of Monday night, Vince Wilcox, Brian Smith and the Turning Point staff, Bob and Dannah Gresh, Paul Grimshaw, and George King, Dean Diehl, Jimmy Wheeler, Jackie Marushka, Benjie Gentry, and all of the Reunion Records, Provident, and Jive Records staffs. Thank you for your tremendous help.

And finally, thank you to Bailey, my faithful writing companion, for keeping me company and providing nothing but positive feedback.

# PREFACE

## *Today*

Some people go their entire lives missing the small miracles that happen throughout the day—those small blessings God sends from heaven to make us smile, laugh, or to break our hearts, and gently nudge us closer to His side.

I used to miss those tiny miracles: my children's giggles, their first awkward steps—their little hands wrapped gingerly around my fingers for support. I missed the sense of renewal as one season changed into the next: our dogwoods' scrawny limbs exploding into magnificent blossoms each spring, and summers when the giant oaks in our backyard dressed themselves in thick foliage, shading our home. I never noticed my wife's warm glances and easy laugh. I missed the blessing of her love for me.

One night, when joy was far away, God's grace touched me and opened my eyes. That same grace has inspired me to write this story, to share with you some of the things I have learned, though it's true, no one could have told me any of this then.

We all have questions in this life. It's taken me a long

time to figure out what the really important questions are, the ones that matter. Not *How am I going to make enough money?* or *What can I do to get promoted?* No, more like *What are the flowers thinking beneath the snow? When do birds make reservations to fly south? What is God's plan for my life? What are my wife's dreams?*

A year ago I was finally able to connect all of the pieces. I met a young man who told me how it all happened. Now I know the truth, because now I know how God's hand guided my life.

Some people, perhaps someone like you, may write off this story as coincidence—a chance encounter, the random crossing of two lives. There was a time, just a few years ago, when I would have said the same. Back then you could not have convinced me that God would use a pair of shoes to change someone's life. But now I believe.

I most definitely believe.

God gave us the greatest proof of love that
the world has ever seen.
—Andrew Murray

Christmas Day, 2000

That winter, Christmas arrived without snow, which for our town was quite unusual. The fall had been beautiful, sunny and mild. People were in shirtsleeves at Thanksgiving. However, as the holiday season approached, nature turned, bringing, instead of blizzards, some of the worst ice storms of the century, coating everything with ice and knocking down trees and power lines. Then the weather turned bitterly cold, and stayed dark and grim, as everyone waited for the White Christmas Bing Crosby was dreaming of on all the local jukeboxes.

The sedan's tires spun on the ice, groping for solid ground. I put the car in reverse, backed up, turned the wheels at a different angle, put the car in drive, and attempted the hill into the cemetery a second time. This time the car climbed halfway up, but then the tires began to hum loudly, spinning again. I gave the car more gas but to no avail. Shifting into neutral, I released the clutch and let the car ease backward to the base of the hill, where I parked and turned off the engine.

From where I sat, I could see that the tombstone was

covered with a brilliant sheen of ice. Icicles hung off the sides, and brown leaves sat in frozen clusters on the cold stone. I would have to clean it off before I could decorate. I decided to leave everything in the trunk until I cleared the site.

As I got out of the car, the wind shrieked, cutting at my face. I pulled my wool overcoat tightly around me and picked up my gloves from the front seat. Realizing I'd left my hat at home, I pulled up my coat collar as high around my neck as I could and closed the car door behind me. I shivered and began the short climb up the hill.

Walking the hill was not much easier than driving it. I had to place my steps carefully to avoid slipping on the ice. As I entered the park, I could see that most of the pathways that wove throughout the grounds were clear and sparkling. I reached the gravesite I was in the habit of decorating every Christmas. Frost clung to the lettering, shielding the name. I pushed away the leaves and ice, working hard with my gloves, until a ray of sunlight il-luminated the date of death: 1985.

It had been fifteen years. . . .

# ONE

December 1985

We did not dare to breathe a prayer,
Or give our anguish scope.
Something was dead within each of us,
And what was dead was Hope.
—Oscar Wilde

The first big snowstorm of the winter of 1985 fell on Thanksgiving. After that, another massive storm seemed to enter the area every few weeks and drop inches, or even a foot, blanketing the landscape and making the town look like a Christmas card, long before the holiday arrived.

Schools were closed more times that winter than in the previous five years combined. Nearly every week, Doris Patterson finalized the lesson plan for her second-grade class, only to have to change it entirely due to yet another snow day.

After twenty-nine years of teaching, Doris was accustomed to the unexpected. Where some saw chaos, she saw opportunity. When the principal announced an early dismissal over the PA system, Doris tried to think up a fun, new assignment for her students, to accompany the traditional spelling and math homework. Assignments like

*What are the flowers thinking beneath the snow?* or *When do birds make reservations to fly south?* Though simple assignments, she'd seen them stir her students' imaginations, creating wonderful memories for her scrapbook.

In the last couple of years, Doris had considered retiring but, for whatever reason, had always felt she wasn't ready. Until now. She'd recently informed the principal that this would be her last school year. Her husband had retired four years earlier from the post office. He was anxious to hit the wide-open roads with her in a brand-new RV he'd purchased, with "Herb and Doris" airbrushed in blue and pink on the spare-tire cover. Maybe it was all the snow there had been that year, but warm winters in the Southwest had begun to sound good to her.

Doris never showed favoritism outwardly, but every year there was one child in her classroom who captured her heart. In 1985 that child was Nathan Andrews. Nathan was quiet and introspective. He had sandy hair, huge blue eyes, and a shy smile. Doris noticed that his gentle nature was lacking the spark she'd seen in his previous two years at the school. While other students interrupted her with "Um, Mrs. Patterson, Charity just sneezed on my head" or "Hey, Mrs. Patterson, Jacob just hit me with a spitball," Nathan made his way to her desk without calling attention to himself and whispered, "Excuse me, Mrs. Patterson." He'd then wait patiently until she turned to him. Compared with the boisterous natures of the twenty-five other eight-year-olds in her class, Nathan's measured, serious disposition was, almost in a sad way, beyond his years.

Some of her colleagues maintained that children from poorer homes were harder to teach, had more disciplinary problems, and were generally mouthier than those students who came from middle- to upper-class homes. Doris disagreed. She knew Nathan's family could be considered lower income. Mr. Andrews worked at a local auto-repair shop and, people said, could barely make ends meet. Yet in all her years of teaching, Nathan was one of the most polite children she'd ever met. Doris had learned that it wasn't the size or cost of a home that created kind, well-adjusted children, but the love and attention that filled that home.

Nathan's mother had often volunteered at the school in the early fall. She had helped out in Doris's classroom, cutting out shapes and numbers for a math lesson, sounding out words for a student struggling with phonics, or stapling paper flowers and trees on the bulletin board. Nathan would beam with pride at the sight of his mother. But Doris hadn't seen Maggie Andrews in many weeks.

One day her husband, Jack, had come to school to tell Doris that his wife was seriously ill. Maggie Andrews had cancer, and the prognosis wasn't good. No wonder Nathan often seemed distracted. He was not old enough to fully understand the situation and probably didn't know that his mother was dying. But some days Doris could see it in the boy's eyes, a terrible sadness she recognized.

Her own mother had died of cancer when Doris was only twenty, and that single event had indelibly changed her. Her heart broke for the little boy as she watched him erase a hole into his paper, smoothing the tear with the back of his small hand as he continued with his work. She'd never had a student in her class who had lost a parent, and she found herself at a loss for words or actions. Somehow the gentle hug or extra playtime she'd given over the years to children who had lost a precious pet or extended family member seemed inadequate, even inappropriate. She still remembered that after her mother's death, she had wished that people would say nothing at all, rather than the trite, though well-meaning words they'd offered in sympathy. Sometimes being quiet is the greatest gift you can give someone, Doris thought, as she watched the boy sharpen his pencil, something terribly heartbreaking in the way he struggled to turn the handle. She whispered a silent prayer for God to draw near and wrap the little boy in His arms.

I slammed the phone down in my office. For the umpteenth time, I had tried to make a call, only to hear a busy signal in my ear. The day was short on hours, and I was feeling even shorter on patience.

"Would somebody tell me how these new phones are supposed to work?" I shouted out my office door to my secretary.

Gwen Sturdivant, my assistant for the past ten years, hurried in to help me.

"First, make sure you select a line that isn't lit up," she explained.

"I know that, Gwen," I said, exasperated. "I'm thirty-eight years old. I'm familiar with the general uses of a telephone. I want to know why I hear that stupid busy signal every time I make a call."

"Once you dial, you need to wait for the tone and then punch in one of these codes for the client you're billing to." Gwen calmly demonstrated.

When I had started with the firm, the phone bill, along with the electric bill and office expenses, had been paid from the firm's general receipts. Now everything—the fax machine, the photocopier, the office phones—all had a code. As soon as someone could figure out how to program it, my pager would have a code too. Ordinary tasks like dialing the phone had been made more frustrating so the firm could bill our clients right down to the penny.

"Just get Doug Crenshaw on the phone for me!" I groaned.

I had been at Mathers, Williams & Hurst for thirteen years. Like many young attorneys, I had walked in the door a bright-eyed, naively optimistic law-school graduate. We were a small firm at the time, sixteen lawyers, but the location was perfect—only a few miles from my mother's home. My father had died of a heart attack five years earlier, and I wanted to move closer to my mother so I could keep an eye on her, in case she needed anything. My wife Kate's family lived only three hours away, so she couldn't have been more pleased when I took the job.

I spent the first day at MW&H in conference, a conference that had lasted thirteen years: conferences with clients, conferences with other associates, conferences with the firm's partners, conferences with secretaries, conferences with paralegals, conferences at lunch, conferences over the phone. The visions of wowing a courtroom with my verbal prowess faded as the firm's partners shifted many of their bankruptcy cases onto my desk. I had not minded the work at first. It was challenging and fun in the beginning, helping owners of small businesses and corporations liquidate their assets, seeing so many zeroes on a page reduced to one lone goose egg. Somehow my position within the firm as "the associate who helped with bankruptcy cases" changed over the years to "our bankruptcy associate." After I got over my initial disappointment and accepted that my dream of becoming a hotshot courtroom brawler was not going to play out (the bankruptcy cases that made it as far as the courtroom were invariably simple presentations of fact, never the in-your-face litigating tours de force I'd always dreamed of performing), I buried myself in the bankruptcy files to impress the partners. My position within the firm established, I concentrated on every young law student's goal: to become partner in just seven years.

I found that once I put my mind to a task and worked at it diligently, things came together as I had planned. Even with my wife, this seemed true.

I met Kate Abbott during my last year of law school. From the moment I saw her, I was smitten. She had recently moved into the neighborhood where I was sharing a small apartment with five roommates. My parents had paid for my books and tuition, on the condition that I support myself by taking on odd jobs to pay for food, rent, clothes, and whatever car I could afford. Meals in those days consisted of macaroni and cheese, Ramen noodles, and the rare special of Five Burgers for a Buck at the local Burger Castle. I owned one suit that my parents had bought me for my college graduation, three pairs of jeans, several ratty sweatshirts, two button-down shirts, a pair of loafers with a hole in the sole, and a pair of old running shoes. I would have felt my wardrobe was pathetic had not my roommates' clothes looked exactly the same.

I first saw Kate unloading boxes and secondhand furniture from the back of a U-Haul van. I set out to meet her, and then, once I met her, I set out to marry her. She was raven-haired and lovely. A certain melody filled the air when she laughed. We married a week after I finished law school.

Like most new law graduates, I was poor and saddled with debt. Kate continued her work in the marketing department of a small local hospital while I looked for a job. Though her salary was paltry, it paid the rent on our tiny one-bedroom apartment and put gas and the occasional spark plug in our beat up Plymouth Champ. We both knew we would struggle for a few years but that once my career took off, we'd live comfortably.

With my job secure at Mathers, Williams & Hurst, the money started rolling in. Kate suggested that we stay on in our apartment, or maybe move to a small condo for a few years, so we could sock away savings for our future. I disagreed; we couldn't entertain my colleagues in cramped quarters decorated with hand-me-down furniture from our parents or the Goodwill store. Like it or not, part of being an effective attorney is looking the part, and I felt that extended to our home.

We bought a large brick house in a respectable neighborhood and filled it with furniture. My old wardrobe was quickly replaced with freshly starched Polo shirts, Hart Schaffner and Marx suits, and Johnston and Murphy shoes. I considered the Plymouth Champ beneath Kate's status and sold it for $500, buying her what she called a "no-personality" used Volvo sedan, to sit beside my new BMW in our new two-car garage.

Both cars, like the home and the furniture, were financed. Kate had grown up in a home where nothing was purchased on credit. Her parents hadn't even owned a credit card until she was in college, and the card was used only for absolute necessities; the balance was paid off at the beginning of every month. As hard as she tried, Kate couldn't see as crucial to our well-being a Carver CD player, tape deck, amp, and preamp, a Thorens turntable, B&W speakers, hi-fi Mitsubishi VCR, or 27-inch Proton monitor. But I always prevailed. Each item was the best our money could buy, and I justified the purchases by reasoning "We have the money, and we're not tied down with kids yet. Let's have some fun with it while we can." When Kate complained that the house was too large, as she often did, I reminded her that we would need extra room after the children were born.

We were just about to celebrate our fifth wedding anniversary when Kate got pregnant. I had imagined that we would wait a couple more years to start a family. A few months into the pregnancy, I wanted to put the house on the market to move to a neighborhood with better schools.

"Robert, the baby won't be in school for years," Kate protested.

"Once the baby comes, we'll have twice as much stuff, and the move will be twice the headache," I said. "This is the right time."

We put our place on the market and began the search for a new house. Several of my colleagues lived in what was called the Adams Hill section of town, an older neighborhood that boasted of even older money. The area was named for Thomas Adams, one of the area's founding residents, who claimed to be related to President John Quincy Adams, though none of the locals had ever bothered to research his genealogy.

People of affluence and influence have lived in Adams Hill since before the turn of the twentieth century. The streets were lined with red maple and giant oak trees older than the oldest resident of Adams Hill. The lawns were professionally manicured; the shrubs were trimmed and clipped. The well-kept homes were all built of brick, wood, and stone, with not a panel of vinyl siding in sight. Great Victorian homes with enormous wraparound porches nestled among the oak trees, next to brick colonials with huge antebellum columns out front. Each home had a story. Many even had placards positioned next to the front door stating the year the home was built and any other information deemed worthy of sharing with those fortunate enough to ring the doorbell. Finding a residence that was actually for sale, as opposed to handed down from one generation to the next, was nearly impossible.

When the new listing popped up on our real-estate agent's computer, she couldn't reach for the phone quickly enough to call us. My palms began to sweat as I anticipated walking through what could be my dream home. Even Kate couldn't suppress a smile when the Realtor led us into the drive. The front was gray stone and yellow wood, with a beautiful double-tiered wraparound deck. It was a big house and, of course, that meant a big mortgage, but I wanted Kate to have lots of space to create a lovely home for our family. A home, like my mother's, that would come alive at Christmas with a roaring fire and a tall, sparkling tree.

Though the firm was pleased with my work, there were times I wished I'd opened a private practice, the way so many of my law-school buddies did, hiring two or three associates, their names painted in gold letters on doors (Gerald Greenlaw & Associates), on lawn signs, (Curtis Howard & Associates), or on parking-garage walls (Thomas Michelson & Associates). Instead of working eighty hours a week for someone else, I could have been working for myself—Robert Layton & Associates. It was too late to start over now, however, and our brand-new mortgage confirmed it. What I lost in freedom, I made up for in the security of working for a larger firm.

In the seventh year of my service with them, the partners at Mathers, Williams & Hurst unanimously made me a partner. They called me into the conference room, each partner seated in a leather chair at the cherry table that ran the length of the room. They made their announcement, clapped me on the back with congratulations, promised to get together with the wives very soon, and went back to work. The celebration lasted all of two minutes. I sat alone at the table as they filed out, thinking that this moment hadn't lived up to my expectations. Then I slowly walked back to my office, shut the door, and began sifting through the bankruptcy files Gwen had placed on my desk that morning.

I was so busy for the rest of the day that I completely forgot to call Kate and tell her the news. By the time I pulled into the driveway, the house was dark. Kate, in her seventh month of her second pregnancy, was no doubt exhausted chasing after our two-year-old daughter, Hannah. Like the first, this pregnancy was unplanned. To be honest, I had wanted to wait a few years before we had another child. I was so busy, I hardly had time to see Hannah. I worried that I would not be able to be a proper father to baby number two . . . and if I was, would it be at Hannah's expense?

Kate, of course, was ecstatic. Hannah had brought a joy into her life that I hadn't seen in a long time, and I knew this baby would do the same. Kate loved being a mother. I can admit that she was much more adept at being a mom than I was at being a dad. I had to work to understand what my daughter was saying, whereas Kate could carry on a full conversation with her without missing a beat.

I pushed open Hannah's door, her Winnie the Pooh night-light smiling at me from across the room. I walked softly to her bed. She looked so much like Kate when she was asleep, but when her eyes were open they blazed, as my mother said, with the same fire she'd seen in mine when I was young. I kissed her on the head, picking Bobo, her one-eyed stuffed bunny, off the floor, and put him back under the blankets before leaving the room. Peeking into our bedroom I saw that Kate was asleep. I heard her slight snoring, which had gotten louder as her pregnancy progressed, one of the side effects, as was fatigue, but even so, during the first pregnancy, she used to wait up for me. I closed the door and made my way down the stairs into the kitchen for something to eat.

In the refrigerator I found a cold, wrapped hamburger patty and some macaroni and cheese. As I put the plate in the microwave, I wondered when we would ever be able to eat food again that didn't come in colors, shapes, numbers, or that wasn't smothered in processed cheese. I'd come too far to be eating macaroni again, the way I did when I was single. Finding a hamburger bun or condiments was too much hassle, so when my food popped and splattered in the microwave, I took it out and let it cool as I poured myself a glass of milk. The recessed lighting I had had installed under the kitchen cabinets burned dimly as I sat down at the kitchen counter and toasted myself, "To Partner Layton," I said, raising the glass. And as the clock struck ten, I ate my rubbery hamburger and my macaroni and cheese, alone.

One night, shortly before Christmas, I came home to find the house dark, save a blue light glowing in the living-room window. Hannah, now eight, and her six-year-old sister, Lily, were long asleep. It was the third time that week I'd gotten home late, though the holiday season was always busy. Everyone was putting in eighty-hour weeks, and I couldn't expect special treatment. To top it off, Gwen had been crying in my office that morning. The long hours were "ripping her apart" and "wearing her down." She threatened to quit, as she had for the last eight holiday seasons, so I gave her the rest of the day off, with pay, knowing she would be back the next morning good as new and telling me how relieved she was to have gotten her shopping done.

I put the Mercedes in the garage, dropped my briefcase heavily on the dining-room table, and went to the living room, expecting to find Kate asleep in front of an *I Love Lucy* rerun. Instead, she was awake.

"Girls asleep?" I asked, flipping through the stack of bills.

"Yep."

"Everybody have a good day?" I asked, uninterested.

"Yeah. You?"

"Busy. You know. I let Gwen have the day off. Had her holiday cry," I said as I walked into the kitchen. I opened the refrigerator door and began my nightly rummaging for dinner leftovers.

Kate moved to the dining-room table and watched for a long time before she finally spoke.

"I'm tired, Robert," she said evenly.

"Go to bed. You didn't have to wait up for me," I told her halfheartedly.

"No, Robert. I'm tired of this. Of us."

I stood frozen, my head still in the refrigerator. In my heart, I'd known the marriage had been over for nearly a year, but I had never imagined either one of us would have the courage to bring it up. I should have known it would be Kate. She'd always been the stronger one. The year before she had accused me of having an affair. I wasn't. She never believed me, but there had never been another woman. Frankly, there'd never been enough time for Kate, let alone another woman. Some nights, I knew, I worked late because it was the one thing I knew I could do for my family, one concrete step I could take to make sure that they had the things that they needed, that the girls' college tuitions were taken care of, that there was a roof over their heads. Some nights I worked late because I didn't know what else to do, and because I didn't want to go home and face the fact that we were in trouble.

I dragged some sort of casserole from the top shelf of the refrigerator and silently pulled a plate down from the cabinet. I couldn't seem to find the words I wanted to say.

"I'm sorry, Robert, but I just can't do this anymore," Kate continued. "I can't go on pretending that everything's all right. It's not all right. It hasn't been for some time. Living under the same roof doesn't mean we're living together. I need more than this."

I stared blankly at the casserole in front of me. She needs more, I thought to myself. Well, I don't have any more. I have given everything, I reasoned. I can't work harder. I can't do more. But I didn't say any of that.

"Let's face it, you left this family a long time ago. We'll stay together through the holidays," Kate explained unemotionally. This all seemed too easy for her, almost as if she'd rehearsed it several times.

"I don't want to ruin my family's Christmas or your mother's, and it'd absolutely kill the girls if we split up right now. But as soon as the holidays are over, you'll have to find another place to live."

There. It was over. She paused briefly to see if I would respond in any way, but, as expected, I didn't, so she softly wandered back upstairs and closed the bedroom door.

## TWO

The more I think it over, the more I feel that there is nothing
more truly artistic than to love people.
—Vincent van Gogh

Doris Patterson loved dressing her classroom for Christmas. She and her giggling, excited students had cut out paper snowflakes and Christmas trees, snowmen and Santas, from brightly colored construction paper, then decorated them with glitter and cotton and yarn. She brought in a four-foot artificial tree to adorn with popcorn and cranberry strands, gingerbread men, and candy canes. Her students chattered loudly as they worked, until the room reached a raucous din with the anticipation of Christmas.

Doris always had her students prepare a Christmas wish list of the things they wanted Santa to bring them, but this year, she had broken with tradition. She knew what Nathan would wish for. She couldn't ask him to stand up in front of his classmates to say out loud what he wanted so badly. She knew that Nathan would give back all the toys he'd ever received at Christmas if his mother could just get better. This year, Doris had asked her students to focus on their favorite Christmas memories and to write them into a story. She hoped the assignment would help Nathan concentrate on the happy times he'd shared with his mother, instead of the time that would never be.

When Nathan's father told her how sick Maggie was, Doris volunteered to drive the boy home from school each day. With all of the stops it made, the school bus took forty-five minutes to bring him to his driveway, and she could get there in fifteen.

"I can't have you do that, Mrs. Patterson," Jack said adamantly.

But Doris insisted. She remembered how she would have given anything for a few more moments with her mother. Other teachers felt Doris was going beyond the call of duty, but if driving five extra miles a day meant a little boy could spend thirty extra minutes with his mother, she would more than gladly make the trip.

The car ride was usually quiet. Doris didn't force conversation, although she often wondered what the child was thinking about. Perhaps his thoughts weren't sorrowful at all, but were instead of his mother being miraculously healed. Doris had had the same dreams when she was young—that God would simply touch her mother and destroy the disease that had viciously eaten away at her, yet there were times, she knew, that miracles didn't happen, that people didn't recover. Sometimes they never get better. In the silence of the car rides Doris would pray for her small passenger. For peace . . . for hope . . . for comfort.

Nathan slammed his teacher's car door and ran up the gravel drive to his home. The beginnings of a snowman stood in the yard, but whoever started it had quit, leaving a single large ball with stick arms and pinecone eyes and a soda bottle for a nose. Neither the driveway nor the sidewalks had been shoveled; footpaths were beaten down in the snow. Today, Nathan and his mother were going to make Santa cookies for relatives and neighbors. Each year they worked for hours on the cookies, decorating them just right with food coloring and silver sugar balls before wrapping them and presenting them as gifts. He ran in the front door to find his grandma Evelyn preparing the butter and eggs and mixing bowls they were going to use. His mother lay propped on the hospital bed in the living room, smiling as he threw open the door.

"Are we making them?" he shouted.

"We're making them," Maggie laughed. "We've just been waiting for you!"

"Well, come on!" he said, tugging on the sleeve of her bathrobe.

"I'm watching Rachel right now," she said, indicating the playpen, "but I'll help in a minute."

Maggie's eyes filled with tears as she watched Nathan jump into the kitchen. She wasn't strong enough to help in a minute, and both she and her mother knew it.

Evelyn had moved in the previous Thursday, the same day Sylvia, the visiting hospice nurse, arrived and the medical-supplies truck delivered the hospital bed. Evelyn had been coming in every day, but Jack asked her if she could stay around the clock, explaining that Maggie no longer had the energy to take care of Rachel.

Evelyn was an active sixty-year-old widow, and the death of her husband four years earlier was easier for her to deal with than the impending death of her youngest child. It wasn't supposed to be this way. Parents were supposed to go first. It was the logical progression of life. Sometimes, when Evelyn was alone in the shower or in the car, she would weep until she was certain her heart would burst. She wept for her grandchildren, for Jack, for her beautiful daughter, and for the ache that was growing sharper with each passing day.

Maggie listened as her mother cracked the eggs into the cookie batter, each flourish producing a giggle from her son. Maggie loved to hear him laugh. Nathan had grown quiet during the last few months, though they hadn't yet told him of the severity of her illness. Evelyn craned her neck and winked at Maggie, then dabbed the end of Nathan's nose with the gooey concoction, causing a belly laugh that shook his small frame from head to toe. Rachel stretched herself to see over the playpen and laughed with delight. Maggie struggled to sit up, listening as her mother and Nathan cut out each cookie with precision. These were the last smells of Christmas, the last smiles of her little boy, the last squeals of her baby girl, that she would ever experience. She didn't want to commit them to memory, but, rather, she wanted to be fully present in the here and now, and love with all her soul.

Maggie had met Jack Andrews when she was twenty-three. Her new 1974 Ford Escort, her pride and joy, was making weird braking noises, so she took it into City Auto Service. A girl she worked with in the bakery at Ferguson's Supermarket recommended City Auto as an honest garage. A young man, wiping grease from his hands, came over as she drove into the shop. Maggie was immediately taken with his intensely blue eyes. She read the name stitched on his green overalls: Jack. A nice, hardworking name.

"What can we do for you?" he asked, and then smiled the most genuine smile she'd ever seen. Jack seldom took notice of the people who came in to drop off their cars for repairs. When the slender Maggie stepped out of her Escort, tucked her dark bobbed hair neatly behind her ears, and smiled, he was immediately interested in more than just her car.

"I think it's my brakes," she said.

"I do," she said six months later.

When Nathan was born, Maggie cut her hours at Ferguson's to part-time. She and Jack did not want to drop their kids at day care, for strangers to take care of them.

If they couldn't rearrange their schedules so one of them could watch Nathan, they'd agreed that Maggie would quit working. It might mean that, on a single income, they'd never live in a big house on Adams Hill or afford better furniture, but it was worth the sacrifice to know that their child was being raised by his parents.

Nathan was two when Maggie and Jack moved into a small, aluminum-sided ranch house on 14th Street in a quiet neighborhood of older homes. The house needed some work. The roof leaked in what would be Nathan's bedroom, the subflooring was rotten where the sink leaked in the kitchen, there was termite damage in the foundation, the carpeting needed replacing throughout the entire house, and much of the plumbing was rusting and needed new copper pipes. The prospect of buying a home in such disrepair might have daunted other couples, but Jack was an all-around handyman, a true "Jack" of all trades, Maggie called him, and she loved helping him. She could rip up floorboards and subflooring as good as any man, or hold a flashlight lying on her stomach under the kitchen sink for hours without complaining as Jack twisted and yanked and soldered the pipes. She loved to watch Jack work, and working together on the house gave them hours of uninterrupted time together. Whereas other couples struggled to find something to talk about, Jack and Maggie never wanted for conversation. When friends wanted to go out after work, Jack went home, even though they teased him and told him he was getting soft, but if that was true he didn't mind. He enjoyed being with Maggie more than anything else in the world. He loved to come home and find out what new improvement she'd made in the house, which gradually they had transformed from the shabbiest dwelling on the block to the nicest.

Two large elm trees guarded the front of the house, and an oak and a maple stood in the back. Maggie thought they were the most beautiful trees she'd ever seen. All her life, she wanted to live in a home surrounded by enormous shade trees, and now her dream had come true. She began tearing up the earth around the bases of her shade trees and prepared the soil for what would be a circle of tulips or daffodils. She dug up the soil by the tiny front porch and planted creeping phlox by the sidewalk, dianthus around the shrubs, daylilies between the shrubs, shasta daisies and Victoria salvia near the house, and pansies to fill in the rest of the bed with splashes of purples, reds, and yellows. Each afternoon when Jack arrived home, she'd take him and Nathan by the hand and describe what flower she had planted where, and in which month it would bloom.

When Maggie discovered she was pregnant a second time, Jack's eyes welled with tears. At such moments, Maggie was humbled by the love she felt for her husband, overwhelmed that God had sent him to her. Maggie had gone back to the bakery part-time, once Nathan started kindergarten, but when the baby came, she would quit her job and stay home. Money would be tight, but they knew they could make it. Jack made a modest but honest living at City Auto Service, and he'd already been there five years. He'd be up for another raise soon, and that would help.

The owners of City Auto were three brothers—Carl, Mike, and Ted Shaver. The shop was originally called Three Brothers, until they decided that the name made it sound as if it was owned by the Mafia. They then changed the name to the more respectable City Auto Service. They were a small operation with two full-time employees— Jack in the shop and Jeannie in the office—and one part-timer who worked in the garage on Saturdays. Mike ran the business end of the shop (he was always the first to claim he couldn't charge a battery to save his life), and Carl and Ted both worked in the garage. The Shavers were good, decent men to work for, and in his time there, Jack had learned more from them than he ever had in school. They provided insurance for their full-time employees, and each Christmas they'd give a Butterball turkey and a fifty-dollar bonus.

When Jack tossed and turned at night, worrying about money, Maggie always told him, "There's a difference between needs and wants, and we have everything we need." When Jack's spirits sagged, wishing his wife could shop at department stores like other women she knew instead of at yard sales and thrift shops, Maggie would hold his face in her hands and say, "It doesn't matter,

Jack. None of it matters. We're healthy. We're happy. All that other stuff is just extras. Maybe one day we'll have it, but right now, we don't need it." That was always enough to keep Jack going. Maggie reached his soul in a way no one else could.

Years earlier, he figured he'd probably live his life as a single man. Now, when he thought back to those days, he thanked God again and again for directing Maggie to City Auto Service.

During her second pregnancy, Maggie often felt as if her belly was bloated but passed it off as the woes of pregnancy. After the smallest of meals, she'd feel terribly full. It was so unlike her pregnancy with Nathan, when she'd craved everything in sight. After Rachel was born, Maggie noticed the discomfort again yet disregarded it as a postpartum side effect. She mentioned her problem to the pediatrician at Rachel's four-month follow-up visit. The doctor agreed it was probably associated with the pregnancy but suggested Maggie get it checked out. Another month went by before Maggie relented and made an appointment to see her gynecologist, who ran a series of tests and told her he wanted to see her again in another two weeks to go over the results.

Maggie arrived for her appointment with Rachel on her hip.

"I'm sorry," the receptionist said. "The doctor was in

the delivery room all morning, so he's behind schedule. Have a seat—it could be a while."

A woman dressed in a navy-blue tailored suit, carrying a rich Italian-leather briefcase, approached the appointment desk as Maggie sat down.

"I'm here to see Dr. Nylander," the woman in the blue suit said.

"He's with patients right now," the receptionist droned, barely lifting her eyes from her computer.

"I'll just wait for him then," the woman said, turning her attention to the nearly full waiting room.

"He's going to be a while," she replied in a pinched voice. "He's got three other patients ahead of you."

"That's okay," she said. "He's expecting me."

She spotted an empty seat next to Maggie. She slid into the chair and set the briefcase on her lap. Rachel made a loud gurgling noise that sounded like a sink backing up, then smiled.

The receptionist slid open her glass window: "Maggie Andrews."

"That was fast," Maggie exclaimed as she approached the desk.

"Mrs. Andrews," the receptionist continued. "Your insurance is only going to cover a portion of your tests, which means you will be responsible for the remainder of the charges," she said, handing her the printout of expenses.

"Do I have to pay them today?" Maggie asked, jiggling and shifting the baby.

"Charges are expected to be met on the day of service," the receptionist answered, typing feverishly into her computer.

Maggie scanned the bill and asked hesitantly, "Is there a way that we could be set up on a payment plan where we could pay off a little of the bill each month?"

"Services are supposed to be paid for on the day of service," the receptionist reiterated loudly enough for everyone in the waiting area to hear.

"I understand," Maggie whispered, "but it would be helpful if we could pay monthly on the bill."

"I'll see who I can talk to," the receptionist snapped, closing her window.

Embarrassed, Maggie sat back down in her seat, bouncing Rachel, who had begun to slightly whimper.

"She must have charmed her way into the job," the woman next to her said with a smile. "I work here, and I'd like to say she's just having a bad day, but if that's the case, I've unfortunately never caught her on a good one."

Maggie chuckled, relaxing, and said, "What do you do here?"

"Freelance marketing. I'm on a team that creates the annual reports, so we interview doctors and patients in each department and review the new medical equipment, look at procedures, and compile the report . . . I'm Kate," she said, extending her hand.

"Maggie Andrews."

Rachel hiccupped and squirmed on her mother's lap.

"She's beautiful," Kate said, admiring the infant's wide, bright eyes.

"She is when she's not mad," Maggie laughed.

"What's her name?" Kate asked.

"Rachel."

"Oh! I was going to have a Rachel," Kate gushed. "It was between Hannah and Rachel, and on the day she was born, I looked at her and decided on Hannah."

"I love that name," Maggie replied, smiling at the wriggling baby on her lap. "It's a beautiful name she can grow into."

"Exactly!" Kate exclaimed. "How old is she?"

"Five and a half months," Maggie answered sweetly. "And I have a seven-year-old in first grade. How about you?"

"Two girls," Kate smiled. "My youngest started kindergarten this year. I thought it would kill me," she laughed.

"When I put Nathan on the school bus for his first day in kindergarten, I cried the rest of the morning," Maggie agreed. "That's why I take this one with me wherever I go." Rachel whimpered and coughed before straightening her body into a full-blown crying jag.

"I'm so sorry." Maggie apologized, lifting the baby onto her shoulder. "She's had an upset stomach."

"I understand," Kate comforted. "Both of mine had colic."

"Did you want to have any more?" Maggie asked, thumping the baby's back.

"Oh, I would have loved to. I don't think my husband would have loved it, though."

Maggie liked this stylish woman. She wasn't self-absorbed, the way she'd always assumed rich people would be. "What does your husband do?" Maggie asked, shushing the baby's cries.

"He's in law," Kate replied. There was an odd sadness in her voice. It made Maggie suddenly feel sorry for her.

"What does yours do?" Kate asked.

"He's a mechanic," she answered.

"Maggie Andrews," the nurse said, standing in the doorway.

"Oh, that's me, again," she said, patting Rachel's back.

"I can watch her if you'd like," Kate offered, smiling. "I can't see the doctor until he finishes with his patients anyway."

Maggie would never leave her baby with a complete stranger, regardless of how kind she thought she was. She looked uncomfortably toward the nurse waiting for her in the doorway. "I could never ask you to do that," Maggie said, inching toward the nurse.

"We can all vouch for Kate around here, Maggie," the nurse smiled. "She's been around here a long time. If you'd like, we can leave Rachel with her in Dr. Nylander's office while he sees you. Might make your appointment a little easier. It's up to you."

"Dr. Nylander wouldn't mind?" Maggie asked.

"Not a bit. He has to meet with Kate in his office anyway."

The look in the nurse's eyes told Maggie her baby would most definitely be safe. "Thank you so much," she said, feeling reassured, and handed the child to Kate.

"Not a problem," Kate cooed at the baby. "It's been way too long since I've held one this small."

Kate patted the baby's back and walked her into the doctor's office. She loved the flexibility of her job. It paid well, and she was able to drop Hannah and Lily off at school, work a few hours, and be done in time to pick them up. She was completely at ease interviewing doctors and medical experts from around the world and was thoroughly proficient writing about medical issues, technology, and the latest research findings. People found her sharp and engaging, always the consummate professional, which is why the hospital continued to hire her year after year. Kate continued to walk the baby around, bouncing, patting, and rubbing her until Rachel burped.

When she came out of the examining room, Maggie found Rachel asleep in Kate's arms. She weakly thanked her new friend.

"Oh, I loved it," Kate smiled. "Are you all right?"

"Thank you again," Maggie managed, sliding the baby bag over her shoulder.

"Good-bye, my little Gerber baby," Kate whispered, squeezing the child's tiny hand.

Maggie buried her face into Rachel's warm body, kissing her belly, and left quickly. She heard Kate ask her if she wanted to go to the coffee shop and talk, but she didn't answer. Her visit to the doctor had left her stunned and shaken. Maggie had barely sat down in his office when he told her he'd sent her blood work for oncological testing. Several tests confirmed she had ovarian cancer.

"Do you know if your grandmother had it?" the doctor asked.

"No. Not that I know of."

"Anyone else in your family—aunt or a sister, perhaps?"

"No. No one."

He wanted to start aggressive treatments right away. The cancer had gone undetected for so long that he feared it had already spread more than they would have liked. He picked up the phone and scheduled her an appointment with a surgeon. In all likelihood, he continued, she would need a total abdominal hysterectomy and two other procedures she'd never heard of before. He explained that the procedures would detect if the cancer had spread.

When she came home, Jack held Rachel in his arms as Maggie told him the news. He sat silent for several minutes, holding the baby close to him, listening to her tiny breaths, breathing in her milky-powdery smell. He squeezed her tight. She was as beautiful as her mother. Her face looked exactly like Maggie's. His heart pounded anxiously. Could this disease take her from him? Could he lose her?

"What did they say exactly?"

"They've scheduled surgery for Monday."

Jack could feel the pounding of his heart.

"Then they'll start chemotherapy right away."

"Did they say anything about any sort of prognosis?"

"No."

"Did they say if the chances were good with this type of cancer?"

"They didn't say."

Jack couldn't help thinking that if they didn't say it, the chances, then, were not good—not good at all.

Maggie opened her eyes and realized she'd drifted off, lost in memory. She strained to sit up, listening as her mother and Nathan chattered and worked in the kitchen. As Evelyn opened the oven door to bring out another batch of cookies, an aroma of vanilla wafted into the living room. Maggie shut her eyes. What she would give to be covered in flour right now, watching her son's eyes gleam as she pulled tray after tray of hot Santa cookies from the oven. She threw her arm over her face.

"Oh God, help me," she prayed. "I don't want to leave my children. I don't want to leave my babies." She could stand the pain of the disease, but the pain in her heart was nearly unbearable. Then Nathan ran to her, holding a tray full of freshly frosted Santas, and plopped them clumsily down onto her lap.

"Ooh, look at this. What a baker you are," Maggie exclaimed. She wiped her eyes and hoped he hadn't seen her. Nathan moved excitedly to the head of her bed and expertly cranked it into a sitting position.

"Time for his beard," Nathan yelled, running back into the kitchen for a bowl full of coconut. Together they sprinkled coconut across the smiling Santas, pressing the white flakes into each beard, talking and laughing as they worked.

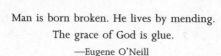

## THREE

Man is born broken. He lives by mending.
The grace of God is glue.
—Eugene O'Neill

My mother, Ellen Layton, had thrown a tree-decorating party at Christmas for as long as I could remember. When my brother, Hugh, and I were small, the party would begin first thing on a Saturday morning. Mom would rouse us out of bed with the smells of bacon, and pancakes in the shape of snowmen. Then the entire family would load into the station wagon and head to Hurley's Farm—John Hurley was an old friend of my father's— for a trek deep into the woods. My father, Albert, wielded the ax, occasionally letting one of us take a careful whack at the prized tree. Even later, when he'd acquired a small, gasoline-powered chain saw, my father insisted that the Christmas tree be hewn by ax, an antique double-bladed tool passed down by my grandfather, because it was tradition. Once home, Dad and I positioned the tree while Mom and Hugh braved the cold attic for the abundance of Christmas ornaments and decorations Mom had collected over the years. Mom sang and danced with Dad to Bing Crosby's "White Christmas" while Hugh and I busily continued with the tree, pretending not to see our parents' silliness.

I cannot ever recall seeing my mother happier than she was on those tree-decorating days. A joy radiated from her, and even from my father, who routinely conked out at six-thirty every evening, after getting up at five every morning to go to work. The whole family would get caught up in Mom's ecstasy, and would sing and decorate until every last ornament had a limb to call home. After we were grown, and my father had died, Mom continued her tree-decorating parties with another widow in the neighborhood. Just because they were alone didn't mean they couldn't enjoy the beauty of Christmas. When the grandchildren came along, the parties regained some of their traditional momentum, with the exception that we'd buy a tree from a supermarket parking lot instead of cutting one down from Hurley's farm, which saved time, and besides, the trees were invariably fuller and more symmetrical than the scruffier wild trees my father used to drag home.

A few weeks before Christmas, Kate and I loaded the girls into the Mercedes and drove the short distance to my mother's house. Mom had lived in the same brick Tudor house for more than forty years, and even though she was sixty-eight and lived alone, she insisted on decorating the outside of her home as a winter wonderland.

Garlands of holly and ivy draped over the doorway, and a huge evergreen wreath hung prominently in the center of the door and on each of the front windows, tied with wide red-velvet ribbons. Bright electric candles threw off a brilliant light in the center of each window. Strands of small twinkling lights wrapped each yew and juniper and evergreen shrub, as well as each tree in the front lawn that could be reached with a ladder. The bigger trees provided the backdrop for the Nativity scene, complete with lighting.

When we were little boys, Hugh and I helped my mother set up the Nativity. She had bought the hand-crafted Nativity years ago at a yard sale. Though my mother's home was filled with magnificent antiques, she always claimed the twenty-dollar Nativity was one of her most prized possessions. As kids, my brother and I saw the set as little more than a collection of large wooden dolls, but each year Mom would explain the meaning of the Nativity to us. "This is the most miraculous thing about Christ's life, boys," she'd say. "The most miraculous thing isn't that He rose from the grave. He's the Son of God—you'd expect God to be able to raise His own son from the grave. Don't you think?" And we would eagerly nod our heads in agreement. "But that's not the most spectacular thing at all. What's spectacular and mind-boggling is that God would want to leave the beauty of heaven to come to live here as a man. And you'd think that since Jesus was the King of Kings that he'd at least be born in a castle somewhere, not in some dirty barn. That's what's amazing!" she'd exclaim, turning Joseph ever so slightly toward Mary. "That's why Christmas is so special. Jesus came as a baby to Bethlehem—a baby that would grow up to live as a servant, not as a king." Plugging in the floodlights that beamed over the back of the shepherds onto the baby in the manger, she'd continue, "That's the beauty and wonder of Christmas, and that's why we'll set up the Nativity for as long as we can—to remind us. Isn't it a nice reminder, boys?" And we'd earnestly nod our heads again.

Since my father died, Dalton Gregory, Mom's neighbor of twenty years, had helped haul, hang, and string the outdoor decorations. He also shoveled her walk and drive when it snowed, though she never asked him to, no small commitment in the winter of 1985. Dalton and his family were the first black family to move to the neighborhood, arriving in 1965, and when the moving trucks backed into the driveway, my mother stood ready to work, holding a platter full of sandwiches and chips. When they moved in, Dalton worked as a high school history teacher and his wife, Heddy, worked in the intensive care unit of the hospital as a nurse. In 1976, Dalton was made superintendent of schools, and even though his job kept him busier than ever before, he still marked on his calendar the day he would help my mother decorate her house. Twenty years separated them, but Mom, Dalton, and Heddy were more than just neighbors. They were friends. Dalton was hunched over, stringing his own simple strand of lights along the porch rails, when I got out of the car.

"Merry Christmas, Dalton! The house is award-winning. As usual."

"It better be. Your mother about worked me to death out here in the freezing cold."

"Why do you do it every year, Dalton?"

"Because there are three things I'm afraid of in life: my mother, my wife, and your mother. And at Christmas, I reverse the order!"

My mother swung open the front door and shouted "Merry Christmas" loud enough to wake Heddy's patients in the ICU. Hannah and Lily ran to their grandmother, wrapping their tiny arms around her waist. "Here are my Christmas babies!" Mom cried, kissing and squeezing them until they pulled away, giggling. Walking to the edge of her driveway, she teased, "Where are your Christmas babies, Dalton?"

"Just give my kids time," he said wearily, shaking his head. "One day they'll figure out how to make babies and you won't be the only obnoxious grandparent in the neighborhood!"

"Maybe not, but I'll still hold the title of being the first!"

"The first and the loudest," he laughed.

"Are you and Heddy coming over for lunch tomorrow?" she asked, rocking Lily back and forth on the top of her feet.

"I didn't know we were invited."

"I just invited you!" she said.

"Then we're coming," he replied waving his arm to shoo her away.

Mom led her brood into the house, which was very much like a Christmas botanical garden, with poinsettias, holly, and a garland of pine boughs filling the huge foyer. As Kate and I entered through the heavy cherry door, Mom playfully pointed out the mistletoe hanging just above us. Trying to avoid any awkwardness, we clumsily kissed Mom on both sides of her face.

"Not me," Mom joked, pointing at the mistletoe. "You're supposed to kiss each other." But Kate and I were already taking off our coats, preparing for a day of decorating. Mom promptly slid my coat back on, sending me out with a handful of money for the tree.

"Ferguson's, on the other side of town, has the prettiest ones, but they're more expensive," she instructed. "Maybe you should try the Daly's lot first. The trees there are smaller, but they're priced better."

"Where do you want me to go, Mother?" I sighed.

"Better get it at Daly's. It's closer."

"I'll be back in a minute."

"No! Wait!" she screamed. "Go to Ferguson's. I can't stand the idea of a small tree at Christmas. Get a great big pretty one at Ferguson's."

"You're sure?"

She paused for a moment and thought over the advantages and disadvantages of each lot.

"Yes," she finally sputtered. "Get a big, beautiful one at Ferguson's."

As I closed the front door behind me, Mom led Kate, Hannah, and Lily to the attic to retrieve the decorations. As they unwrapped each ornament, Mom would say "Your grandfather gave this to me on our first Christmas together" or "Your father made this for me when he was your age." Downstairs, in the living room, the girls presented their grandmother with the ornaments they'd made with Kate's help. I'd come home the night they'd made them, asking Kate the next morning about the mess left on the dining-room table. Kate always knew I hated cluttered, messy rooms and I accused her of leaving things in disarray on purpose.

I think my mother sensed something was wrong between us from the moment we walked in the door, but she also knew that neither one of us would want to talk about it, so she made as much small talk as possible.

"What are you doing in school, Lily?" she asked our dark-haired six-year-old.

"Learning about bugs," she said, squirming. Tugging at her sweater, she claimed, "Itched like the dickens."

"Ew. I don't think I'd want to learn about bugs," Mom said, scrunching up her face.

"I don't either, but they make you, anyway." Lily shrugged.

"How's Robert's work, Kate?" The two women had always had a good relationship. Mom knew not to meddle, and Kate always appreciated her mother-in-law's "What-I-don't-know-isn't-my-business-anyway" approach to her marriage.

"It's the same. Busy," Kate replied, head deep in a box of decorations.

"Has Gwen had her Christmas cry yet?"

"I guess so," Kate laughed.

"Will he be taking any time off for the holidays?"

"Christmas Day," Kate answered, without looking at her. "I don't know if he has any others scheduled. You know how busy he is."

"Daddy says he has a stack of work this high on his desk," Hannah exclaimed, standing on tiptoes and holding her hand far above her head.

Mom would withhold judgment until later, but she intended to wring my arrogant, ambitious, and selfish neck when I got back.


Although she could easily afford someone to cook and clean for her, Mom absolutely refused to have someone do this. "Why would I want someone to clean my home when I could get it cleaner?" she'd say to me. My father's salary as an insurance executive had afforded the best of everything in the home and had kept Mom comfortable since his death. I often wondered if she insisted on doing her own chores because it kept her busy, and that kept her from missing my father so much.

The girls buzzed around the tree while the dinner cooked, and my mother handed out popcorn strings, ornaments, and tinsel. Everyone scattered their treasures on the tall, dark spruce, while Bing Crosby, Nat King Cole, and Ella Fitzgerald entertained. When the last of the tinsel was hung, Kate set the table for dinner, and Mom carried in the platter of pot roast surrounded by potatoes, carrots, and rings of onions. A steaming bowl of green beans was set out, along with gravy, broccoli salad, fresh rolls, and iced tea. I couldn't remember why, but my mother had always served pot roast on tree-decorating day, probably for no better reason than that it had been on sale at Daly's twenty-five years ago—not much to base a family tradition on, if you thought about it. We made small talk around the table, most of it focusing on the girls and school and dance classes. Hannah proudly told her grandmother that she was first understudy to Clara in The Nutcracker. I promised that next year she'd get the starring role. Kate said we'd be just as proud of her if she didn't get the lead. Mom played along with us, pretending that everything was okay. Despite the fact that I felt like a fraud inside, I was pleased I hadn't spoiled my mother's holiday tradition. As Lily swallowed her last bite of German chocolate cake, Kate stood and began to clear the table.

"Kate, I'll get those," Mom insisted.

"No, Mom. Let me wash up."

"No, not today. Take the girls into the living room and enjoy the tree. Play that game they've been begging us to play with them all day. Robert will help me."

Kate slipped away from the dining-room table, thankful, no doubt, that she wouldn't be cornered in the same room with me, and ushered Hannah and Lily into the living room.

I stacked the dirty dishes and carried them into the kitchen. Mom began to scrape what was left on the plates into the garbage disposal as I continued to bring in bowls and dishes from the table. Then she asked me point-blank, "What's going on with you and Kate?"

I looked at her, shocked, stunned even. "Going on?" I stammered, trying to act nonchalant. "Nothing's going on."

"Robert, how old do I look?" she asked loading the dishwasher.

"Is this where I say you don't look a day over forty-five?"

"How old do I look, Robert?" she said impatiently.

"Mother, what is the point of the question, because I know how old you are. You're sixty-eight."

"And in sixty-eight years, don't you think I've picked up a little discernment? A smidge of perception?"

"We're in the middle of an argument," I sighed. "You remember what those are. You and dad had them. Every couple has them."

"I've seen you two argue before," she said, turning on the garbage disposal.

"Well, I don't know what to tell you, Mom," I answered sarcastically.

"Sit down, Robert."

"I'm helping you clean up."

"I don't want you to help. I want you to sit."

I sat at the kitchen table as my mother put on a pot of coffee. She continued to load the dishwasher as she confronted me. "I know Kate. She's been in this family for a long time now. I know when there's something more than an argument going on between you two."

I swished a Christmas card around on the table as I pondered how to tell her. This wasn't going to be easy. She loved Kate like a daughter. I knew my mother wouldn't naturally take my side in the matter. She was too honest for that. I'd have to tell her the truth and be done with it.

"The marriage is over, Mom," I said bluntly, staring at the Christmas card.

"Why?" she questioned, dumping leftover broccoli salad into a Pyrex dish.

Why? I didn't know why.

"I'm not sure."

"You're not sure of what?"

I knew my mother wasn't going to make this easy.

"I'm not sure why the marriage is over."

"Well you're in it, so surely you must have some idea as to why it's over," she said, stacking Pyrex dishes full of leftover food into the refrigerator.

"Mom, I've done everything I can," I stammered. "I've worked hard. I've provided a good living. A great home. I've given Kate and the girls everything they could ever want, but it's never good enough." I paused, waiting for my mother to interject, but her back remained to me as she cleaned. "Over the last couple of years we've just kind of grown apart."

I sat and waited for her response. She pulled out a soft-scrubbing cleanser from beneath the sink and rubbed diligently at a stubborn stain on the countertop. She held her tongue and simply listened. I shifted uncomfortably in the silence. I almost wished she would just let me have it rather than leaving me hanging.

"We just have different interests," I continued awkwardly. "I guess when we first got married we were both on the same page, so to speak. We wanted the same things. Shared a lot of the same goals. But somehow over the years all that shifted. I don't know how. Same as it does for a lot of marriages, I guess."

She reached into a cabinet for two coffee cups and poured a cup, sitting it in front of me. She quietly poured herself a cup and sat across from me, staring into my eyes. She always told me I looked so much like my father around the eyes—I'm sure she wondered why I wasn't acting like him.

"If you had to pinpoint what the number-one problem of the marriage is, would you be able to do that?" she asked.

I thought for a moment. This really wasn't the conversation I wanted to be having right now. "Um . . ."

"You don't know what the number-one problem is?" she pressed. "Because I do."

I looked up at her. This was exactly the conversation I wanted to avoid. My mother was never one to beat around the bush. I couldn't even begin to recall the times in my youth that I heard "Do you know what your problem is?" as she would continue to lay bare everything before me. In the same way, I always knew that if I approached her with any problem, she would be honest and open with me. It was the only approach she knew.

"Your marriage isn't working because you're too selfish to live with," she stated matter-of-factly.

"Thanks for the cup of Christmas cheer, Mother," I said, toasting her with my coffee.

"You've grown apart? I get so sick of hearing floundering couples say they've grown apart! I always want to say, 'Well, dingbats—what have you done to try to stay together?' "

"We've tried everything, Mom."

"And what is everything? You come home at eight or nine o'clock at night. You work on weekends. What exactly have you done to keep the marriage together?"

It was funny. For as long as I had been a lawyer, no judge or opposing attorney had ever been able to fluster me the way my mother could. I shook my head, watching the dark liquid swirl and slosh up the sides of the cup in my hands.

"What, Robert? What have you personally contributed to the marriage to hold it together?"

"I don't know, Mom. How about I've provided Kate with everything she could ever want."

"You've never given her yourself."

"I've given her . . ."

"You've given her things," she interrupted. "Never yourself. There's a huge difference. You've tried to finance your happiness, and that doesn't work. Kate never wanted to live in a huge house or . . ."

"Mom, you've always lived in a huge house, and you're happy."

"Because your father made me happy," she said with sting. "I'd have lived in a shoe box with him. It had nothing to do with the house. Kate never asked you for a new BMW, or for a big house, or for expensive clothes, because those weren't things that she wanted."

"She never had to ask for them because I gave them to her *before* she asked," I said triumphantly.

"Exactly!" she agreed. "Because those were all things

you wanted her to have. Giving Kate things was so much easier for you than ever giving one minute of yourself. Piling stuff in front of her and the kids was a great way to block them from you. Women don't want stuff, Robert. They want your attention. Kids don't want things. They can only play with so many toys at one time. What they want is their daddy to pay attention to them and hold them and laugh with them. That's what everybody has ever wanted from the beginning of time!"

I looked around the kitchen, hoping my mother would finish soon.

"You said you have different interests now? How would you even know what Kate's interests or dreams are? Tell me—what are her dreams?"

"I don't know," I said. "The usual things, to have a healthy family, and see the girls finish school and . . ."

"Those are hopes," my mother said. "Everybody has them. I'm talking about dreams. What are they? What are Kate's dreams?" She waited. I didn't answer, because I couldn't. Whatever they were, they were Kate's dreams, her business—she was free to pursue them, just as I was free to pursue mine.

"You don't know, do you? You're never there long enough to ask her. Maybe it's your interests that have changed," she said slowly. "Maybe other women are a little more interesting these days."

I rolled my eyes and groaned.

"There is no other woman, Mother. There never has

been. Why do women always assume there's another woman?"

"Maybe because a wife figures that if you're not seeking attention from her, then you must naturally be looking for it somewhere else."

This was really an area I did not want to talk about with my mother!

"Mom. Believe me on this. There has never been another woman. Never." Oh how I wished she would release me from this conversation. "Even if I wanted to, which I don't, I'm too busy to even think about taking on another woman in my life."

"You're right," she said, nodding her head. "I apologize. I should have put a little more thought into that. You're way too busy to have a mistress when work is your mistress."

I buried my face in my hands. "You are making my head hurt, Mother."

She ignored me and forged ahead. "Sexual conquests make some men feel more powerful," she said, as if reading from the latest *Ladies' Home Journal*.

"Mother, can we please stop talking about this?" I begged.

"But your conquests aren't made in bed." I put my head down on the table. "Your conquests are at work. You're only as good as your last victory—but the little victories at home never count—the first steps, the crayon drawings on the refrigerator door, the first visit from the

Tooth Fairy. None of that matters to you. Those little moments—those simple everyday victories—don't mean anything to you, but they mean everything in the world to Kate." I buried my head into my arms, bringing my hands over the top of my head. Despite my attempts to quiet my mother, she continued anyway. "Those everyday successes are never enough for you. It's the wins at work that make you feel like a man, not the little girls who wrap their arms around your legs and call you Daddy. It's the power high at work that charges your batteries, not the power you have in helping mold and shape another person's life." She stopped, exasperated. Sighing heavily, she added, "I just don't think I understand how you could so easily give up those precious little babies for something that's never going to matter on your deathbed."

I looked at my watch. It felt as if her verbal lashing had gone on for hours. The thought that I was giving up easily was preposterous. I was merely trying to be realistic.

"Are you in a hurry?" she lovingly snipped.

"No, Mother, I was just checking to see if you beat the record for talking the longest without taking a breath."

She laughed and poured me another cup of coffee, slicing off another piece of German chocolate cake.

"I don't want that, Mom," I said, but it was no use.

"Dalton and Heddy won't be able to finish up all that cake. I need to get rid of it."

As she turned her back to pour more coffee into her cup, I picked up my fork and began to separate the sweet, gooey coconut icing from the rest of the cake. "Eat all of it, Robert. Not just the topping," she said, scolding, without looking. Resigned, I pushed the frosting back to the cake and took a bite.

"Things are a lot different now than when you were married, Mom," I said with a mouth full of cake. "People go through more complicated things than they did back when you and Dad married."

"And what are those things?" she asked, interested. "Power? Prestige? Jockeying for top position on the corporate ladder?" Her brow raised and crinkled after each question, seeking a response from me. "Those things have been around for centuries," she stated with certainty. "There's nothing new under the sun—just the same mistakes made time and time again, but the thing is, we're actually getting worse at figuring out what those mistakes are. Why do you think your divorce-lawyer colleagues are so busy?"

I sipped the coffee and swallowed hard, looking at my mother. "Mom, at this point Kate and I are past the mending stage. Things have gone broken for so long that they would be too hard to fix now. I know that's not what you want to hear, but it's the truth. We were going to tell you after the holidays because we didn't want to spoil Christmas for you or for her parents."

"How very grown up of you," she offered acerbically.

"But I have thought about trying to fix things. I really have. The bottom line is, making the effort wouldn't be worth it because Kate doesn't love me anymore." Somehow those words hurt more than I expected. "I'm sorry, Mom, but it's true."

She set her cup down with a thump.

"Nonsense," she blurted. "I know Kate. I know women. I know she still loves you, but she doesn't feel loved, Robert. All she wants is to feel that you love and need her and can't live without her. You make her feel like you're living with her because you have to, not because you want to. Women want to feel cherished, and that they're the most important thing in your life. You've made Kate feel as if she's the third or fourth most important thing, and the girls don't feel anything at all. You're just some guy who pays the cable bill and wanders through the living room from time to time." Her voice softened. "But I know she loves you, Robert. I know it wouldn't take Kate long to remember why she fell in love with you in the first place, and if you'd give up some of the things you're holding tight in your claws, you'd remember why you fell in love with her."

"Sounds easy, doesn't it?" I mocked.

"No," she retorted, defensively. "As a matter of fact, it doesn't sound easy at all. That's why divorce is skyrocketing—because it's much easier than actually working at the marriage. But there isn't a book anywhere that says marriage is easy." Her eyes blazed. "Never in the history of marriage ceremonies has any minister ever said, 'You may kiss the bride and be on your way to an easy life.' Whoever said 'Life's a breeze' should be smacked! That person didn't have a clue. Life isn't easy. Just when you get close to having it figured out, they haul you away in a hearse."

I leaned back in the chair, interlocking my fingers on top of my head. "Things sure did seem a lot easier for you and Dad."

She burst into laughter. "Oh, my goodness. Your father and I were like Ralph Kramden and Lucy Ricardo the first ten years of our marriage. He always wanted his way, and I always wanted mine, and we'd roll up our sleeves, jump into the ring, and duke it out till one of us got tired," she laughed. "If one person in a marriage expects to always get his or her way, they're going to be mighty disappointed."

"Ralph Kramden and Lucy Ricardo weren't even on the same show," I said.

"Exactly!"

"But you always worked things out. Kate and I have never been able to do that." I looked deep into the empty coffee cup. "When Dad died, you didn't have any regrets."

She thought for a moment and then scooted her chair away from the table. "Come with me," she motioned.

I followed as she led me upstairs and into the bedroom she'd shared with my father for over thirty years. She removed the hand-stitched quilt from atop the cedar chest her mother had given them on their wedding day and opened the cherry lid, the familiar piney fragrance I remembered from childhood filling the room. Rummaging through the chest, she lifted out a small box and opened the lid. She folded open the tissue paper and pulled out a long, straight-stemmed pipe made of burly briar and handed it to me.

"What's this?" I asked.

"This is my regret," she answered softly. "This is a Dunhill Billiard from England. Your father always wanted one. I was saving it for a special occasion." She took it back from me. "You know what I thought about as I held your father's hand when he lay dying in that coma after his heart attack? I thought about this Dunhill Billiard pipe, buried up here in this stupid chest." She stared at it for a moment and then re-wrapped the pipe in the tissue paper. "I don't know what sort of occasion I was waiting for," she said quietly, her voice trailing off, "because every day was a special occasion with your father. Every single day." She tucked the box back into the chest and closed the lid. Taking my hands, she pulled me down on top of it, sitting next to me.

"Don't treat your wife or your kids like they're not special, Robert," she whispered, her eyes glistening. "They should be the most special people in the world to you."

"I know, Mom," I said squeezing her arm.

"No. You don't. Maybe once you've lost them, you

will. But don't lose them Robert." She grabbed my face and spoke plainly to me, "You and Kate can still make it," she said sincerely. "It's still fixable. But you have to work on fixing yourself first. It's too easy to want to fix someone else but the hard part is fixing yourself. Instead of demanding more from her, you need to give more of yourself." She dropped her hands and folded them around mine. "No man ever really lives, Robert," she said softly, "until he gives himself away to others. That's what you need to do. What did I always tell you and your brother at Christmas?"

I rolled it off my tongue as if on tape. "That that's why Jesus was born in a manger. He humbled Himself to give His life away for mankind. That's the meaning of Christmas." I then spoke in a high voice to imitate my mother, "Isn't that right, boys?"

She laughed and smacked my leg. "Finally, you've remembered something I've said over the years. Now why don't you ever put any of that good advice to practice?"

She turned off the lights in her bedroom and was heading back to the kitchen when Lily greeted us on the stairs. "Grandma, I need a treat," she giggled. My mother raced her downstairs and cut slices of cake for everyone except me. (I just couldn't stomach the thought of one more piece.) She poured milk into tall Santa glasses for the girls and sat down at the table with them for the final snack of the day. When they finished eating, Mom took one more picture of Hannah and Lily by the tree, and then it was time for everyone to gather up their coats and hats and mittens, the great swishing of Gore-Tex and nylon ending with hugs at the front door. It was snowing again. Three inches had collected on top of the car since dinner. My mother told me to drive carefully and to call and let her know we were safe.

She went back to the kitchen and finished washing the dishes. She wrapped the leftover cake for Dalton and Heddy. Then, shutting off all the lights in the kitchen and living room, my mother fell into her favorite winged chair, the one she and my father purchased years ago at an auction, and stared into the lights of the uneven, magnificent mess of a Christmas tree her granddaughters had decorated, and closed her eyes. A few minutes later, the phone rang once, my signal that we were home safely. Only then could she fall asleep.

## FOUR

> Life must be lived forwards, but it can be
> understood only backwards.
> —Sören Kierkegaard

Monday was a day when nothing was going my way.
I had scheduled an early meeting with one of my more
important clients and was rushing out the door when Kate
reminded me I'd promised to drop Hannah off at school
that morning. Kate had to be at the hospital by eight and
had asked me last week to take Hannah. I'd completely
forgotten.

With traffic, I'd kept my client waiting for twenty-five
minutes. He was none too pleased. As if that weren't bad
enough, I'd recently taken my car in to have the brakes
worked on. Gwen had recommended a place on the edge
of town that was supposed to do good work, and they'd
quite cheerily told me to bring the car back if there were
any problems. The car was running fine, but I'd just received the bill. Now, I had a problem, and they were
going to hear about it. You drive an expensive car and
people think you have money to burn. They assume you

won't notice if they pad the bill. On my lunch hour, I headed to the shop. I had better things to do with my time. I asked the receptionist if I could speak to whoever had worked on my car. She summoned a man with the name Jack embroidered on his overalls.

"Jack," the receptionist began, "this is Robert Layton, and he has some questions about the work done on his car."

"Thank you, Jeannie. What can I help you with, Mr. Layton?" Jack asked politely. By the look on my face, he appeared to be dreading the answer.

"Did you work on my car . . . Jack, is it?"

"Yes. Jack. I worked on your car along with Carl."

"Who's Carl?" I snipped.

"He's one of the owners. He's been doing Mercedes work for over twenty years."

"Well, you'd think he'd know how to fix them then, wouldn't you, Jack?" Jack winced every time I said his name. I was having a bad day, but, I reasoned, I pay good money for service, and I will make sure I get it. I won't let anyone take me for a ride.

"If your car still isn't running right, Mr. Layton, we'd be glad to fix it for you."

"By looking at this bill, Jack, I don't think I can afford to have you guys fix it again." I threw the bill on the counter. Jeannie turned her head to her desk, looking as if she wished the phone would ring. "Do you mind explaining this bill?"

Jack carefully looked over the work done and all the specific charges. "Mr. Layton, everything seems to be in order here."

"Everything seems to be in order, Jack?" I mocked. "Look at the total!"

"Our prices have always been below our competitors'," Jack assured me.

"Below your competitors'?" I said, amazed, reading from the bill. "Two hundred and seventy dollars for front-brake work? You're telling me that's below your competitors prices? I should have just taken it to the dealership."

Jack shifted from one foot to the other as Jeannie began rummaging through her desk drawers.

"You had warped discs on both front sides," Jack explained. "We took the old ones off, cleaned everything up inside, and then put on brand-new rotors. Sometimes we can just rotate the rotors, but yours were too warped to do that. We even rotated and balanced your tires at no charge."

"Oh, well," I said, throwing my arms in the air. "If I'd known you'd done that, I never would have complained."

Jeannie dug deeper into a drawer as Jack took a deep breath before attempting once again to appease me. "If your car's still shaking when you brake, you can leave it with us and we'll look at it again."

"No, thanks," I said sharply, yanking the bill away from

him. "Like I said, I can't afford to leave my car here anymore. I guess since it's Christmas, you guys think you can jack up the prices on guys like me . . . no pun intended, Jack." Throwing open the office door, I added, "Oh, Jack, be sure to tell Carl that he shouldn't expect my business anymore," and slammed the door behind me.

Sylvia was checking Maggie's vital signs and gently caressing the thin arm resting on the bed. She glanced at the picture of Maggie up on the mantel and silently compared the image to the frail, gaunt shell of a woman lying before her. She changed the IV drip that administered medication through Maggie's arm and gently massaged her hands and feet. That wasn't part of her job description, but Sylvia felt that in more ways than one, tender touches were the most important part of her work. The redheaded nurse was ten or fifteen years Maggie's senior and had a sweet, sensitive spirit. Maggie liked her very much.

"Thank you, Sylvia," Maggie said, smiling. Sylvia had seen some of her patients fight the dying process all the way to the end, kicking and screaming until the sheet was pulled over their heads. Then there were others who somehow managed to face death without fear, despite the sorrow they felt for those they would leave behind, people who could somehow meet death with a strange confidence . . . a knowing. People like Maggie.

"You're welcome, baby. You feeling all right?" But Sylvia already knew what Maggie would say.

"I feel good."

Sylvia had seen other ovarian-cancer patients die, and she knew they didn't feel well.

"You're not lying to me, are you?" she teased. "Because Sylvia does not like to be lied to."

"I'm all right. Really."

"Oh," Sylvia exclaimed, running to the sofa. "I nearly forgot. I found this tucked away in one of my drawers last night," she said, pulling a beautiful red and green scarf from her purse. "The colors of Christmas." She pulled the blue scarf off Maggie's bald head and tied the new one on, fashioning it into a knot so the tails hung down her neck. "Oh, my. This one makes your eyes pop. Let me get you the mirror."

"Thank you, Sylvia," Maggie said. She smiled as she examined her image in the glass. "Last night I dreamed I had hair."

"You did?" Sylvia laughed. This wasn't the first time a patient had dreamed of having hair.

"And this time it was long and red, just like yours," Maggie said. Sylvia chuckled, adjusting the pillows behind Maggie's head. "I was driving a convertible, and my long red hair was blowing in the wind." Maggie stopped, realizing she would never have long hair again, knowing she would never get behind the wheel of a convertible. Sylvia brushed her cheek and squeezed her hand.

Rachel toddled to the bed and reached for her mother. "Up," she ordered Sylvia.

The little girl would often want to get up into the bed with her mother to snuggle. Maggie would scratch her back or tickle her arms. When Evelyn first realized Rachel wanted to be in the bed with her mother, she worried that the child would squirm too much and somehow hurt Maggie. When Sylvia set up the IV drip, Evelyn worried Rachel might rip the needle from Maggie's arm. Evelyn tried several ways to discourage the baby from wanting to climb into the bed, but she would only persist, "Up," she'd scold, her little fists thumping her chubby thighs. Maggie would say, "It's all right, Mom. Set her up here," and Rachel would burrow close to her mother, never fidgeting for a moment.

"All right, baby girl," Sylvia said lifting the child onto the bed. "Get up there and love on your mama." Maggie wrapped her arms around Rachel, proceeding with the story of Cinderella and her handsome prince.

Sylvia marked some things on Maggie's chart, tucking it under her arm as she gathered her things to leave. "I'll be back tomorrow," she told Evelyn.

"Thank you, Sylvia," Evelyn replied, showing her to the door.

"I'll see you tomorrow, Maggie," Sylvia yelled. "And you too, Little Miss Rachel!"

Evelyn closed the door behind Sylvia, wishing that they wouldn't see her tomorrow or the next day or the next, because her frequent visits meant Maggie was getting sicker and sicker. One day Evelyn wouldn't be able to care for her alone during the day, and Sylvia would be brought in for long shifts to help with Maggie's medications, bathe her, and take her to the bathroom. Evelyn pushed such thoughts out of her head and busied herself cleaning the bathroom. Through the open door, she listened to Maggie tell one story after another to Rachel, her enraptured audience. As each tale ended, Rachel would touch her mother's face and say, "More Mama," and Maggie would launch into Snow White or Rudolph or Joseph and Mary, each story more intriguing than the last. Rachel sat up in the bed when she heard her daddy's car in the driveway.

Jack had started going home on his lunch break as soon as Maggie told him she was ill. By the time he got home, ate, and went back to work, it was usually longer than an hour, but Carl, Ted, and Mike had all told him he should eat lunch at home, and if it took an hour and a half or two hours, it wasn't a problem. Back when City Auto first opened, a large part of its winter business was putting snow tires on people's cars, but now that everyone was driving four-wheel-drive vehicles, there was less of that. He was grateful for the extra hours at home.

Jack was untying his boots in the front hall when Rachel called out, "Daddy!" from the bed where she was lying next to her mother. Jack lifted her up from the bed as she reached for him, kissing her forehead. He sat her down and leaned over to kiss Maggie. "How do you feel?"

"Good. Not bad at all."

Evelyn emerged from the bathroom, whisking Rachel into her arms. "Who wants lunch?" she announced.

"Me!" the little girl shouted, pointing to her chest.

Evelyn set Rachel down, donned a pair of oven mitts, and took out the meat loaf she had been keeping warm in the oven. She put thick slabs of meat loaf between two slices of wheat bread spread with mustard, placed two large spoonfuls of potato salad beside the sandwich, poured a glass of iced tea, and handed it to Jack on the sofa. Evelyn managed to get a few bites of leftover mashed potatoes and applesauce into Rachel before laying her down for her nap, something Rachel always objected to vehemently.

"She always fights a nap," Evelyn sighed once the child was down. "Wonder who she gets that from?" she said, eyeballing Maggie. When Maggie was Rachel's age, Evelyn would practically have to tie her down for her naps. Humming, Evelyn had started cleaning up what little mess there was in the kitchen when Maggie called for her.

"Mom, what are you doing?"

"Just cleaning up a little."

"Could you come here for a second?"

Evelyn threw down the dishcloth, dashing into the living room. She had learned to act quickly over the last several weeks. Sometimes the pain left Maggie curled into a ball, begging for medication, but that was usually before one of Sylvia's visits, not after.

"What is it?" she asked.

"I just want to talk to both of you while we're alone."

Evelyn sat next to Jack, and they looked uneasily at Maggie.

"I have something very important that I want both of you to hear," she began.

Jack set aside his lunch and stood up to be closer to his wife's side. "What is it, Maggie?"

"As I was telling Rachel stories today this popped into my head, and I knew you'd both have to hear it because if just one of you heard it, you'd tell the other one someday that I never said any such thing."

"Well, what is it?" Evelyn asked, sitting up.

"I don't ever want you to force Rachel to wear my wedding gown."

Jack and Evelyn looked at each other.

"What?" Jack asked.

"I don't want you to force Rachel to wear my wedding gown."

"You got me all upset inside for that?" Evelyn protested.

"Yes!" Maggie laughed. "It's important to me. Twenty-two years from now, I don't want either one of you forcing her to wear my gown out of sympathy. She may not like that gown, and I don't want her to wear it just to make one of you happy. I want her to wear what will make her happy on her wedding day. Now, promise me."

"I promise," Jack chuckled.

"Mom?"

Evelyn crossed her arms. She could barely think of Maggie's death, let alone talk about it. And she would never consider laughing about it.

"You know, I don't like talking about these things," Evelyn said. "I may not even be around when Rachel gets married."

"Well, I know I won't be around, and that's why I want to make sure one of you two won't be forcing her to wear some old, ratty gown from the seventies."

"Fine! I won't make her wear it. You didn't wear mine—why would I expect her to wear yours?"

"Well, I'm glad we got that cleared up." Maggie laughed, noticing her mother had found no amusement in the conversation at all.

"For a minute there, I thought I was going to have to break you two up," Jack said, taking his plate into the kitchen. He didn't like to laugh about these things either, but if making light of them helped Maggie, then he was going to try his best to find the lighter side as well.

Maggie observed that her mother was obviously bothered by something. Evelyn stood up to follow Jack into the kitchen when Maggie stopped her.

"Mom, wait," she begged. "I didn't know that would upset you."

Evelyn patted her daughter's hand.

"I'm not upset. I just want to make sure Jack's had enough to eat." She attempted to make her getaway again.

"Mom, come on. Look at me. I can't chase you down. What's wrong?"

Evelyn sighed, trying her best to maintain control.

"It's just one of those things that I never imagined I'd ever have to think about," she said slowly. "I wish that Rachel would wear your dress. I wish that she'd want to wear it." Evelyn felt her emotions swelling, but she held them back. Jack leaned on the stove. This was a moment he knew would come, but he was not prepared for talking about the reality of Maggie not being with them for track races or football games, cheerleading tryouts or senior proms, graduations or wedding days. He braced himself as he walked into the living room and sat on the chair next to Maggie.

"Listen," Maggie started, looking at Jack and her mother. "We all know that Rachel's too young to remember me." A tear rolled slowly down Evelyn's face. "It's true, Mom. She is. But my things aren't going to make me alive to her. I want her to know things about my personality. I want her to know why I fell in love with her daddy. I want her to know that I would nearly burst into tears when I'd carry her through Ferguson's and people would stop me and say what a beautiful baby she was. And I want her to know that I thanked God every single day of her life for her. Those are the things I want to be kept alive in Rachel."

Jack stared at the floor, wondering if there would ever be an easy conversation in his life again.

"Can you do that for me, Mom? Can you keep me alive that way?"

Evelyn wiped her face and nodded.

"I can do that," she said convincingly. "I would love to do that." Yet there was nothing inside of Evelyn that would ever want to talk about her daughter in the past tense. She wanted to wrap her in her arms as she did when Maggie was the child who pleaded "Up. . . . Up" and simply make it all better.


Six inches of snow fell the last week of school before Christmas break. Doris had learned over the years that there was no point in expecting her students to concentrate on anything when the holidays loomed tantalizingly near. As red- and green-frosted cupcakes were passed out, Doris asked the students to stand and each read their story of their favorite Christmas memory.

Joshua told the story of making the biggest snowman on his block, and how some crazy neighbor came over in the middle of the night and knocked its head off, smashing it into a bazillion snowy pieces and making his little sister cry for three whole days. Alyssa related a tale about the year she got a brand-new puppy and how it went potty on her mother's brand-new sofa. Visiting Santa's workshop was Patrick's favorite memory. He got to see how all the toys were made and loaded into Santa's sled. He even got to pet a reindeer, which, he announced to the class, smelled like doo-doo, and that produced a chorus of giggles from the audience of eight-year-olds. Desmond loved visiting his Grandma and Grandpa, and eating fudge till he got sick. Tyler liked the year he stayed awake until four in the morning and caught Santa sneaking in through the kitchen door instead of coming down the chimney. He even claimed he'd taken a picture with his camera but couldn't find it to show the class. Of course, everyone was terribly disappointed. Nathan read a short tale about going sledding with his mom and dad, and then eating chicken and dumplings while his mom and dad danced around the house. When he was done, he quietly took his seat, licking the remainder of red frosting from the crinkled paper cupcake wrapper. Doris laughed and clapped after each student finished. Then it was her turn.

She recalled when she was also a child of eight, and on Christmas, her grandmother gave her a pair of shoes adorned with sparkly, pink beads. She put them on and twirled and curtsied and danced around the house, she said, feeling like a beautiful fairy princess until she fell asleep on her grandfather's lap. When she woke up the next morning, she was in her own bed . . . but was still wearing her beaded shoes. "So I got out of bed and danced and twirled and curtsied some more!" she exclaimed, as her students giggled. "I had never felt so special in all my life."

She led her students in choruses of "Jingle Bells," "Frosty the Snowman," and "Rudolph the Red-Nosed Reindeer," even popping in Rudolph's famous story in the VCR for a last-day-of-class treat. At the end of the day the students screamed in frenzied joy as they scurried to their locker cubbies at the back of the classroom to gather the things they'd crammed inside when they had arrived. Doris helped bundle them into their snow jackets, hats, scarves, boots, and gloves, each child looking like a plump, colorful goose when fully dressed. As the children embarked onto buses and into the waiting cars of parents, Doris couldn't remember having more fun with one of her classes. There was an electricity, a joy, that buzzed through the classroom unlike any Doris had experienced before. Maybe it was because it was her last year of teaching and she was letting go. Or maybe it was because God had filled the room with incredible laughter and song to help one of His smallest children through the greatest sadness of his life.

Whatever the reason, Doris was grateful. It had been a wonderful day.

## FIVE

Faith is not intelligent understanding, faith is deliberate
commitment to a Person where I see no way.
—Oswald Chambers

Jack had been installing a carburetor he'd rebuilt when
Carl and Ted approached him.

"How's everything going, Jack," Ted began, sliding his
hands in his pockets.

"Almost finished here, Ted. What d'ya need?"

"Nothing," Carl answered, folding his hands across his
wide belly, then opting for his pockets as well. "We just
wanted to let you know that we've talked about it and
would like you to take as much time as you need right
now." Carl scratched his bald head, slipped his hand back
into his pocket, and continued, "Ted's son is back from
college and can help us out here until he heads back to
school in January. It'll do him good to get his hands dirty
after all that readin.' " When Carl said "we've talked
about it," he meant he and his brothers.

Jack stared into the engine, trying to think of the right
thing to say. Every now and then in life there were those

people who couldn't take away the load you carry but they sure could make it easier. In their own quiet way, the Shaver brothers were making his load easier.

"I'll make up the work," Jack said to the carburetor, feeling too awkward to make eye contact.

"We know you would," Carl replied, talking to the same carburetor. "But there's no need to do that."

"You don't have to come into the shop to pick up your check," Ted added. "Mike will send it to you every week."

Jack fumbled for words. He would be receiving a check for work he wouldn't be doing.

"Now let me take over that carburetor," Ted said, stepping in beside him, "and you head on home."

Jack tried to speak, but Ted already had his head under the hood, and Carl had quietly disappeared. Jack washed his hands, grabbed his coat, and drove home for the last holiday season he would spend with his wife.

When Nathan arrived home, he was surprised to see his father there so early. Nathan showered his family with chocolate snowmen and hard-candy snowflakes. He hung a construction-paper Christmas tree at the foot of his mother's bed and lined the bed rails with the snowflakes he had cut out with his class that morning, using a roll of Scotch tape he got from the kitchen table, where Evelyn had started wrapping presents. When he stuck a crisp, white crafted paper snowflake onto the bed, Rachel ripped it off, laughing merrily at her crime.

"Rachel. No!" Nathan screamed, grabbing the torn snowflake from his sister's sticky clutch. "Leave those alone." Rachel ran to the other side, ripped off another flake, and giggled endlessly as her brother fumed and hollered.

"You're ruining them," he yelled, pushing her down. "Stop it."

Jack picked up his crying daughter and turned her upside down, which led to shrieks of delight.

"That's enough, Nathan," Jack scolded.

"She was ruining them!" Nathan shouted.

"Well, now it looks perfect," Maggie affirmed. "I feel like I've been plopped down right in the middle of a winter wonderland."

Evelyn looked at her watch and scooted Nathan and Rachel out the door to go grocery shopping with her. She knew Sylvia would be there soon to administer some much needed pain medication. Maggie's pain had grown worse over the last several days, and she didn't want the children to see her in discomfort. The children never seemed to catch on, and if they complained about going somewhere, Jack would merely say, "But who's going to help your grandma if you don't go?" and Nathan would scurry to put his boots on as Rachel tumbled after.

When the dinner dishes were washed and put away, Jack helped Maggie into the bathroom. There were times nausea from the medications overwhelmed her, and after hours of queasiness she would finally vomit, which left her even weaker than before. She had motioned to Jack that she was not feeling well in the sign language they had developed between the two of them. He swung her legs over the side of the bed and eased her onto the floor. She'd lost a lot of strength, but she was still able to walk if Jack helped her. Turning on the fan, Jack supported her body as Maggie retched into the sink. He wrapped his arm around his wife, rinsed out the sink, and helped her back, gently tucking her into bed. With Jack's arm around her, Maggie felt as if he was the strongest man she'd ever known.

When Maggie was comfortable in her bed again, the family sat down together to watch *A Charlie Brown Christmas* before Evelyn laid Rachel down for the night. They laughed as the whole Peanuts gang prepared for the Christmas pageant Charlie Brown was directing. Rachel laughed particularly loudly while watching Snoopy dance with his nose sticking straight up in the air.

"That's one of my favorite Christmas stories," Evelyn said, scooping Rachel up in her arms. Nathan bolted upright, realizing he'd left his very own Christmas story in his backpack. Evelyn ran water in the bathtub for Rachel's bath as Nathan plopped down in the seat by his mother to read her his favorite Christmas memory.

"Mrs. Patterson had everybody stand up in class and read their stories," Nathan eagerly told his parents. "Tyler took a picture of Santa coming in his kitchen door, and somebody hacked Joshua's snowman to death."

"Oh, that sounds awful," Maggie said, smiling.

Nathan read from his paper: "My favorite Christmas memory was when my mom and dad and me went sledding all day long at Whitman's Farm. My dad fell off the back of the sled because we had too many people on it, and my mom laughed the whole way down the hill. Then we ate chicken and dumplings and drank hot chocolate, and my mom and dad danced around the Christmas tree." Maggie admired the story and smiled at the backward *d*'s, the *g*'s that looked like *j*'s, and the *m*'s with one too many humps. She complimented Nathan for having such a good memory. It was hard to believe that it had been only three years ago. Maggie could see it all as if it had just happened yesterday. She and Jack had sandwiched Nathan on the sled, and just a quarter of the way down the hill, Jack fell off and Maggie howled with laughter, watching him tumble and roll down the hill before coming to a complete halt, spread-eagle on his belly.

"That would definitely have to be my favorite Christmas memory too," she said, holding the story.

"Mine too," Jack offered. "Even though I couldn't walk straight for two weeks afterward."

"Then remember you and Daddy dancing around the tree?" Nathan teased.

Maggie's eyes blurred. Jack always loved to dance, even though he wasn't very good, but what he lacked in grace, he made up for in reckless abandon.

"Your mother is a fabulous dancer," Jack told his son.

"Mrs. Patterson told us her Christmas story about how she danced in a special pair of pink shoes her grandma gave her. She even slept in them," Nathan exclaimed.

"Oh my, they do sound very special," Maggie agreed, smiling.

Evelyn pulled Rachel from the tub and wrapped her in her favorite snuggly towel, then took her into her room, closing the door behind them. Maggie looked at her son's handsome face. He was his father's child, blue eyes and all. In the quietness of the moment, she knew she had to talk with Nathan about the upcoming days. She knew this might be one of her last chances to spend some quality alone time with her baby boy, but she struggled with how to begin.

"Honey, would you mind making me something warm to drink?" she asked Jack, her eyes imploring him to leave the room.

Jack jumped from his seat, knowing what his wife was about to say. They had talked about it the previous days, how and what and when to tell Nathan. Maggie's condition was rapidly worsening. Neither Jack nor Maggie talked about time, but they both knew it was running out.

"Sure," he said, exiting to the kitchen.

"Mrs. Patterson always thinks up such fun things for you to do," Maggie said to Nathan. "What was the story you had to write a few weeks ago that I liked so much?"

"About the frogs?"

"No. I liked that one a lot, but wasn't there one about flowers?"

"Oh yeah!" his eyes beamed. "What are flowers thinking underneath all the snow."

Maggie smiled at her son's enthusiasm. He had always loved helping her in the flower beds. When he was just a toddler, she would point to the smallest dot of green in the ground and say "Look, Nathan, here it comes," and then day by day they'd watch the flowers grow and bloom throughout the spring and summer.

Maggie repositioned herself, fighting back tears as she spoke to her son.

"You know, a lot of things are going to be happening over the next few weeks," she began slowly. "And a lot of it might be confusing to you."

Nathan was already confused, and his look told her so.

"Nathan," she soothed. "One day when you're older you might want to blame God for making me sick, but I don't want you to do that." Nathan frowned, bewildered. Why was his mother talking about being sick? He had always assumed that she would get better because really sick people were the ones who were in the hospital. "I want you to always know that God didn't make me sick, He helped me through this sickness," she comforted. "He gave me strength to play with you and Rachel and held me on my really horrible days."

Nathan put his head down. He didn't like talking about his mother's sickness. Maggie struggled to find the right words to say to her eight-year-old son.

"In a little while," she said slowly, "you may hear grown-ups say things like, 'Isn't it a pity? God took her so young.' But they're wrong, Nathan. They're wrong, and I don't want you to listen to them. When they say things like that, I want you to remember what I'm telling you now. God didn't take me, He received me."

Nathan's forehead crinkled as he looked at his mother. Maggie looked into her son's frightened eyes. Maybe what she was telling him was too much for him to understand.

"You mean in heaven, Mama?" he asked in nearly a whisper.

It broke Maggie's heart to hear him say it.

"Yes, sweetie, in heaven."

Nathan paused. Jack listened from the kitchen.

"God's going to take you to heaven?" Nathan asked, confused.

"No," Maggie assured. "He's not going to take me, Nathan. He's going to open His arms and receive me. There's a big difference, and I always want you to remember that."

Nathan fidgeted with the story in his hands and quietly asked, "What will you do there?"

"I can't even imagine," Maggie said, her voice faltering. "I know for the longest time I'll just be looking at God and thanking Him over and over for sending Jesus at Christmas and for the life He gave me here with you. It's going to be so beautiful there Nathan that I can't even begin to think what I'll be doing, but I know I won't be sick anymore." Nathan looked up at his mother. Maggie smiled. "I'll be completely healthy and I'll be running and jumping and playing and dancing just like I used to do with you before I got sick."

Nathan studied the paper in his hands for a long time. He didn't like talking to his mother about this. He didn't like how it made him feel.

"Will there be animals there?" he finally asked curiously.

"The most beautiful animals I've ever seen," Maggie answered, to the amazement of her son. "The animals that God created here for us on earth aren't anything compared to the animals in heaven. The zebra and giraffe? They'll look like common house cats compared to the animals in heaven."

"And none of them will be mean, right?" Nathan inquired anxiously.

"No. None of them will be mean. They'll be gentle and beautiful, and you can ride them and play with them all day long."

"Will the streets really be gold?"

Maggie smiled.

"The streets will be gold, and there will be beautiful rivers and waterfalls and the most beautiful landscaping I've ever seen."

"The flowers will be prettier than yours?" he asked, surprised.

"Much prettier than mine," Maggie laughed. "The flowers and trees will be much more beautiful than anything God ever created on earth." She stopped and allowed Nathan to process what she was saying.

"Will you see Grandpa there?" he finally asked, staring at his swinging legs.

"Yes," she smiled. "He'll be at the gate waiting for me." Her eyes filled with tears, and she turned her head away.

Nathan thought for a few moments, stopped swinging his legs, and then asked faintly, staring at his feet, "Why do you have to go?"

In the kitchen, Jack buried his head in his arms.

"Because Mommy's sick, and I just can't get better," Maggie answered softly.

"Will I be able to go with you?" he asked, his voice frightened at what his mother was telling him. Maggie clenched the bed sheet and twisted it, tears rimming her eyes.

"No, sweetie, you can't go with Mommy."

Tears ran down Nathan's face as he sprang to his mother's side, holding onto her. "I don't want you to go there without me," he sobbed. She wrapped her arms around his small back. In a short time she wouldn't have the strength to do that anymore. She hugged him tighter to her.

"I don't want to go without you either," she said, tears streaming down her face. "I'd give anything in the world to stay here with you, but I can't. I have to go."

"No, Mama—no!" the little boy implored, his tiny fingers digging into his mother. "I don't want you to leave me."

Maggie wiped her face and pulled Nathan from her, wiping his tears away.

"Just because I'm leaving doesn't mean I'm not always going to be with you," she soothed. Maggie knew Nathan clearly didn't understand what she was saying, as his bottom lip began to quiver. She cupped his face gently in her hands. "I may not be around but I'm always going to be alive right in here," she said touching his chest. "That's where my dad lived after he went to heaven and that's where I'll always live in you, right inside your heart." He laid his head on his mother's chest, and she softly scratched his back.

"I want you to always know," she said, whispering to him, "that the greatest joy in my life is being your mommy." She turned his face toward hers and kissed his forehead. Looking into his eyes, she prayed that he would remember this night. That one day it would give him peace—that it would give him hope at Christmas.

She hugged him tightly, kissing every part of his face

as the boy squirmed and started giggling in her arms. "You'd better get ready for bed, Little Man."

Jack stood in the kitchen, wiping his eyes with a dishtowel before heading into the living room. He didn't want his son to see him crying, then thought twice about that. Maybe it would be good to let Nathan see him crying, to show him that it was allowed, that everyone did.

"Go on back to your room, Nathan," Jack said, "and I'll be back to tuck you in in a minute."

"Love you," Maggie said, kissing the little boy again.

"I love you too, Mama," he replied, kissing her good night.

Nathan made his way down the hall, unaware of how the conversation would one day affect him. A flood of emotion washed over Maggie's face. Jack sweetly kissed her eyes and wiped her tears. He would try to explain it all to Nathan, someday when he was older. He would explain it again and again until Nathan understood.

## SIX

Every happening, great or small, is a parable whereby God speaks
to us, and the art of life is to get the message.
—Malcolm Muggeridge

Gwen!" I shouted out my door. "Did you reschedule
the Alberto Diaz conference?" I waited for her to answer
before impatiently getting up from my desk to look for
her. When I saw her empty chair, I remembered that I'd
let her leave three hours ago. It was Christmas Eve, and
she had relatives to pick up at the airport. I sighed, looking at my watch.

"Seven o'clock," I said aloud to the empty office. I
looked at my desk and groaned at the stack of files that
had been sitting there since morning. I shoved a couple
of the more important ones into my briefcase. I'd meant
to knock off at five because I still hadn't done any Christmas shopping. Sometimes when I worked, I was in the
habit of concentrating so hard that I occasionally failed to
notice the passage of time.

After flipping off the office lights, I locked the door
and rushed down the hall for the elevators. Aggravated, I

pushed the button and wrestled with my coat as I stepped inside the doors. I rode to the ground floor alone, stewing in my thoughts. "This is just great," I grumbled. "Where can I find a store open so late on Christmas Eve?"

Just two days earlier I had driven to my mother's after work. Since Kate had asked me to leave, my life felt as if it was spinning out of control, and I had no idea of how to get it back on track. Mom was always a good sounding board. I pulled up in front of her house, but all the lights were off inside. Of course they were. It was 10:45. How could I ever expect to get my life back on track when I couldn't even leave the office at a decent hour? I sat in my car and marveled at my mother's house, twinkling with white lights, the Nativity shining brilliantly. She and my father had made our home a magical place to live. Birthdays were magical. Thanksgiving and Easter and Christmas were all magical. I used to joke with Kate that I believed in the Tooth Fairy till I was twenty-one because I never caught my mother sliding a quarter under my pillow. Mom and Dad wanted our home to be the most exciting place on earth for Hugh and me. Not a place of bickering, bitterness, and strife. They wanted to create magical memories, and they did. I leaned on the steering wheel and stared at the house. What magical memories would my girls remember of me? I shook my head and drove home, wondering how I could ever get the magic back.

Now I jumped into the Mercedes and wound my way

through the brightly lit streets, heading downtown. Store windows sparkled with brilliant lights and decorations, but they were all closed. It was, no surprise, snowing again—large fat flakes filled the air. The streets were nearly empty, and I felt like the only person in the world who wasn't already home with his family. Even the tinkling of bells had stopped, as the Salvation Army ringers had already turned in their bright red pots for the night.

As I'd hoped, Wilson's department store was open. I'd tried to make a list at lunch, but I didn't know what anybody wanted.

I rushed, shouldering my way past other last-minute shoppers, to the toy department, where I found a large selection of Barbie dolls. Was Lily too young for Barbies? Was Hannah too old? How could you go wrong with a Barbie doll? I threw one in the shopping cart, trusting that Kate would be able to tell me which one of my daughters would like it more. In the electronics department, I picked up a Walkman for Hannah, who, I figured, had to be about the right age to be discovering music, though who knew what kind of music she might like? In women's apparel I found a red cashmere sweater for my mother, then remembered that she already had a red sweater. I moaned and threw the sweater back on the pile without folding it, then picked it up again, thinking Kate might like it. A year ago I'd bought her a diamond necklace that cost me nearly five thousand dollars, because she'd been complaining that I didn't make her feel important, and I wanted to show her how much I cared. It hadn't changed a thing between us. I wasn't going to make the same mistake this year. I threw the sweater back down. I heard so many voices in my head. One said, "How could she?" One said, "What took her so long?" Another said, "If it's over, put it behind you as quickly as you can and move on—don't sit around moping." Yet another said, "But you love her, and she loves you—why isn't that enough?" Maybe separating would do us good, give us space to see clearly again. Maybe, I thought, she'd even miss me and come to her senses.

As I made my way through the store, I observed a little boy running through the aisles, touching every item on racks and shelves, much to the chagrin of the nearby store clerks. He ran straight into me as I was holding up a knit scarf for my mother. "Sorry, sir," he said breathlessly without looking up. I shook my head. I despised parents who let their children run unsupervised through stores. The little boy continued sifting through racks of clothing, moving around the circular stands, pulling out blouses, shirts, and jackets. I watched him. A rack toppled forward as he brushed it from behind. I looked around again for the kid's parents.

"Please watch what you're doing," I scolded the child, irritated.

Feeling aggravated and exhausted, I had thrown a few more items into the basket when I passed the little boy again, now nervously bounding into the women's-shoes department. I watched as the anxious boy touched or picked up nearly every boot, pump, and loafer in the department. Then a pair of shoes seemed to catch his eye on an overcrowded sales rack. He picked up the pair and, for a moment, he was still. The shoes were shiny silver, aglow with red, blue, and green rhinestones and shimmering sequins. The boy tucked them under his arm and hurried in the direction of the register. "Just my luck," I thought as I made my way to the checkout line, my shopping done, taking my place behind him. The boy fidgeted, shifting his weight from one foot to the other, as the cashier took forever to ring out the customers ahead of us. Again, I glanced sideways to see if the child's parents were nearby.

As the boy swung the glittery shoes, I finally had to smile. The child obviously didn't want his mother to see him buy the shoes for her. He began to pace.

I looked down at the items in my basket and wondered when was the last time I had anxiously raced around a department store looking for the perfect gift for someone.

When my brother and I were young, our arms would ache from shaking every last cent out of our piggy banks. We'd stuff our pockets until they bulged with the heavy coins and walk excitedly to the local five-and-dime. Rummaging through trays of pins, we would earnestly look for the one with the biggest fake diamonds for our mother, and then we'd run to the men's aisle for the adventure of finding the ideal Christmas tie for our father. One year we skipped getting him a tie and got him a three-foot-long shoehorn instead, one he wouldn't have to bend over to use. It used to be so exciting, Hugh and myself scurrying, stumbling, and fumbling through the store, nearly bursting from the thought of Mom and Dad opening their presents on Christmas Day.

The little boy moved forward and placed the shoes down for the cashier to scan the price—$14.25. The child dug into the pockets of his worn jeans and pulled out a small crumpled wad of bills and scattered change. The cashier straightened out the mess of currency.

"There's only $4.60 here, son," he said.

"How much are the shoes?" the child inquired, concerned.

"They're $14.25," the cashier replied. "You'll need to get some more money from your mom or dad."

Visibly upset, the boy asked, "Can I bring the rest of the money tomorrow?"

The cashier smiled and shook his head no, scooping up the change.

Tears pooled in the child's eyes.

He turned around and said, "Sir, I need to buy those shoes for my mother," his voice shaking. I was startled to see that the child was talking to me. I felt the hairs stand up on the back of my neck. "She's not been feeling very good, and when we were eating dinner my dad said that Mama might leave to see Jesus tonight."

I stood unmoving, holding the basket.

I didn't know what to say.

"I want her to look beautiful when she meets Jesus," he said, his eyes beseeching me.

Why is he asking me? I thought. Do I look like an easy target—the rich man with money to throw around? I instantly felt annoyed. Was this some sort of con, parents sending their children out to take advantage of people's emotions at Christmas? Yet, why did the child tell the cashier he'd bring the rest of the money tomorrow?

I didn't know what to say or how to react. All I knew was it was suddenly more than I could take. This kid was no scam artist, somehow I knew that. I looked into his wide eyes and something happened to me in that moment. A pair of shoes to meet Jesus in. This child is losing his mother.

Without thinking or saying a word, I pulled out my wallet and handed the cashier a fifty-dollar bill to pay the remainder of the cost of the shoes.

The little boy lifted onto his tiptoes and watched as the last of the money was distributed into the drawer. Eagerly, he grabbed the package, then turned and stopped for a moment, looking at me again.

"Thank you," was all he said.

I watched as the child ran out the door and disappeared into the streets.

"Are you ready, sir?" the cashier asked. I didn't hear

what he was saying. "Sir?" he asked again. "Are you ready to cash out?"

I looked at the items in my basket and shook my head.

"No," I answered. "I think I need to start over."

I left the full basket on the cashier's counter and slowly walked out the front doors. I put the Mercedes into gear and drove through the streets of town to Adams Hill, where, through the heavily falling snow, I could see Kate's bedroom light on upstairs.

The whole drive home I didn't know what I would say or how to say it. I just knew that I had to get there. I had to get the magic back. Suddenly, my life depended on it. Kate was right. My family wasn't leaving me, I'd left them. When did that happen? How did I get so lost? Home. The word all at once felt new. What had once been a place of emptiness was now one of joy, a place of refuge from life's unpredictable sorrow. A place of hope. I was going home at last.

I couldn't help it. I knew it was late, but the minute I entered the door I shouted, "Kate! Kate!"

Kate ran down the stairs, heatedly shushing me not to wake the girls, who were already in bed. Without saying a word, I guided Kate onto the sofa and knelt in front of her.

"What is wrong with you?" she asked.

"Listen to me," I began slowly. "I didn't get you or the girls anything for Christmas."

"I didn't expect you to get me anything," she answered hotly, throwing my hands from her shoulders. "But I thought you'd at least want to get your own children something." She attempted to push herself off the sofa and away from me, but I pressed her firmly back into the cushions.

"What are you doing, Robert?" she demanded, her cheeks flushed.

"Kate, I'm begging you. I don't really know what to say, but I need you to listen to me." She yanked her arms from me, crossing them in front of her.

"What?" she snapped.

I gathered my thoughts and began slowly.

"I didn't buy anything because I didn't know what to buy." She set her chin and stared at me, but she was listening, and that's all I wanted. "I didn't know what to buy because I don't know any of you," I continued. "I have let all of you slip away from me, to the point of where you're actually strangers now." Kate sat unmoved by my words or emotions.

"What?" she asked, bewildered.

I rose and sat square in front of her on the coffee table.

"Kate," I pleaded. "I went to the store. I went there to buy things for you and Mom and the girls. I was even in line to cash out when it hit me. . . ." I wasn't sure how to put any of my feelings into words. Kate arched her eyebrows for me to continue. "You all are the greatest gifts in the world," I said, selecting my words carefully, "but I don't treat you like a gift. I don't treat the girls like gifts."

She shifted uncomfortably, not sure how she should react to what I was saying.

"The greatest possible gift I could give to you or the girls would be myself," I went on. "I need to give you the respect and love you deserve, and I need to give the girls time and attention and piggyback rides and trips to the zoo and amusement parks and I don't know what else," I said, clasping my head in my hands. "I need to give them a dad. They've had a provider," I continued. "They've had some guy in the house who they've told people was their father, but they've never had a dad. I want to be with them, not just in the same room with them. I want to be with them and share in everything that makes them happy. I want to be there when they fail. I want us to be there," I said, looking at her. I peered into Kate's eyes, looking for the smallest glint of hope or acceptance. She was understandably skeptical—we'd logged a lot of years of hurt and anger together.

"Kate," I said, then stopped. "I don't know how you feel." I leaned on my knees and rubbed my hands together, thinking. "I don't know if you're really ready for us to end because . . . because I don't think I am."

"Why the sudden change of heart?" she asked, her tone still doubtful.

"I don't know, Kate," I replied, shaking my head. "All

I know is it's Christmas." She looked at me, confused. "It's Christmas, Kate, and I realized that nobody could give me a greater gift than that of my family."

She shook her head and looked away. I gently took hold of her arms and turned her toward me. She looked anxiously into my eyes.

"Nothing matters to me, Kate," I said, slightly squeezing her arms in my grip. "Nothing. The job, the cars, the house. None of it. The only thing that matters to me is you and Hannah and Lily because . . ." I stopped, concerned that she would never believe me, but I knew I had to say it. "Because I love all of you." I stopped to watch her face. Her expression was one of puzzled wonderment. It was the same look she used to give me when we were dating, when I'd say something that she thought was crazy. It was the exact same look, and I was warmed by the fact that I recognized it.

"I do, Kate," I whispered. "I love you and I don't want to lose you."

Kate searched my eyes. What was in them tonight? Hope? Forgiveness? Peace? I released my hold and she fell back into the sofa, still watching me. I wasn't burying myself in the mail or running away from her to go to the office but, instead, I felt filled to the very brim with some sort of joy. Joy. I wasn't anxious or restless or upset about anything. I was truly calm and serene, in an inexplicably strange, peaceful way. I hadn't been calm and serene in years.

She crossed her legs and asked slowly, "What happened to you tonight?"

"It's a long story," I said, smiling, and then we talked into the night.

Maggie's breathing was labored, but she was coherent. Sylvia prepared to switch the IV bag, but Maggie lifted her hand weakly to stop her. Sylvia had hooked up a new bag that morning, yet throughout the day it had slowly drained empty, and she needed to replace it with a full bag that would take Maggie through the evening.

"Maggie," Sylvia whispered, "this will help with your pain."

"No," Maggie mouthed.

"It's okay, Sylvia," Jack said. "She wants to watch the kids unwrap their presents. She knows she won't be able to if you give her that."

Sylvia stroked Maggie's cheek and straightened the scarf on her head.

"All right, baby doll," she comforted. "I'm going to leave this right here," she added, hooking the bag on the pole beside Maggie's bed. "If you want some medicine, just have somebody open up the drip, all right?" Maggie nodded and Sylvia smiled, squeezing her arm. "You just yell if you need me," she said to Jack, slipping to Rachel's room, where she would work on a needlepoint stocking or read when she wanted to give Jack and Maggie as much uninterrupted time as she could. She had been with them ten to twelve hours a day for the last two weeks, going home some time in the evening. Sylvia held the needlework in her hands and rested her head against the wall. She would be finishing up her shift in another thirty minutes, leaving the Andrews family to spend Christmas Eve alone.

Normally, Jack and Maggie would retrieve presents from the attic once Nathan had gone to bed, but this year Jack suggested they unwrap their gifts on Christmas Eve instead of waiting for Christmas morning. He and Evelyn had wrapped what few presents they had for the children and placed them under the tree days ago.

Evelyn went into the bathroom and brought out some blush, eye shadow, powder, and lipstick to Maggie's bedside. When Maggie was no longer strong enough to put on her own makeup, Evelyn did it for her. Evelyn gently freshened the colors she had applied that morning—a soft taupe to Maggie's eyelids, dusty mauve to her sunken cheeks, and rosewood to her lips. She finished by dusting Maggie's face with some fresh powder, then held up a mirror for Maggie to see herself.

"Thanks, Mom," she whispered feebly.

Nathan tiptoed in through the backdoor and into his room, unnoticed. After dinner he had told his father he needed to run to a neighbor's house down the street. Jack assumed Nathan and his little friend had made gifts for everyone and didn't question him any further. After a few minutes, Nathan carefully opened his bedroom door and tiptoed down the hall and into the living room, depositing the gift under the tree.

Jack had tried to get ready for this evening, hoping it would never come. As hard as he prayed, he just wasn't ready for this to be his last Christmas with Maggie. He sat by her bed earlier in the day and watched her sleep. How could she be so sick and still be so beautiful? How could he ever wake up in a house without her in it? He watched as she drew in small, shallow breaths. The look in Sylvia's eyes told him it wouldn't be long, that she'd started to let go. Two days ago Sylvia sat Jack down and talked to him about helping Maggie go—letting her know that it was okay, that she didn't have to hold on anymore.

Maggie woke to the same eyes she'd fallen in love with nearly twelve years earlier. "I love you," she whispered. There weren't enough hours in the day for them to say those words, but they said them as often as they could.

"I love you, Maggie," Jack answered softly. "I always have and I always will."

She smiled and moved her fingers toward him.

He stood up, holding the fragile hand in his and kissed her lightly.

"That broken down Ford Escort was the greatest thing that ever happened to me," he said slowly. Her eyes twinkled. How fortunate she was to have had someone who loved her so completely for so long. They talked about her mother and the kids and about taking care of her flowers in the spring. Jack talked about everything he could think of, rambling and groping for words as Maggie nodded and smiled. He caressed her face and held her hand, repeatedly saying "I love you" until she fell back to sleep, listening to his voice.

For dinner, Evelyn warmed up some turkey someone from church had dropped off, complete with gravy and stuffing and cranberry sauce. After the dinner dishes were set aside, Jack started pulling the few presents from under the tree and handed one to Nathan to unwrap. Rachel sat on Evelyn's lap, squirming and clapping her hands.

"Hurry up and hand this child a present before she bursts," Evelyn laughed. Maggie smiled as Rachel tightly squeezed the stuffed Pooh bear with the big, fat, soft tummy. Nathan's eyes lit up when he saw the new Matchbox cars he'd been wanting.

"I'm taking these to show-and-tell," he cried.

Jack winked at Maggie and held her hand as Rachel screamed, "Oh my! Oh my!" when she unwrapped a pink baby doll whose eyes actually moved. Nathan beamed with excitement at the package of ten different colored markers he held in his hands.

Evelyn unwrapped a beautiful purple and black scarf to go with her winter coat that Nathan and Rachel picked out themselves.

"It's so warm and toasty," she said, kissing her grandchildren.

Bending over, Evelyn pulled out a skinny box and handed it to Jack.

"We weren't supposed to exchange gifts," he said, feeling terribly sorry that there wasn't one under the tree for her.

"I know," Evelyn replied. "It's just something I thought you might like," she said, smiling at Maggie.

He opened it and pulled out a framed crayon drawing of a little girl with big circles of red on her cheeks and hair that flipped up at the ends. She was wearing a blue dress with big yellow flowers on it and holding a red balloon. Her arms were long and straight and both feet turned in the same direction, one clearly bigger than the other. Beside her stood a puffy white dog with a smile on its face, its four legs long and spider-like, all of them facing the same direction. By the dog's paws in big, red letters, the drawing was signed *Maggie*. Jack smiled broadly and thanked Evelyn, holding up the artwork for Maggie to see.

"She was in kindergarten when she drew that," Evelyn explained. "I found it in my things a while ago and told Maggie I'd get it framed for you."

Jack held the picture and imagined Maggie drawing it, wishing he could have seen her as a little girl rummaging through her crayons strewn all around her and carefully selecting the perfect one to color in the flowers or the right shade of blue for the dress. He clutched the drawing and leaned over to kiss Maggie.

"I'll hang it right next to the da Vinci," he said, holding her hand.

Nathan anxiously waited for his mother to open his present, the anticipation giving him butterflies. He scurried under the tree and pulled out a small box. There were only two more presents under the tree—he'd counted. Jack stood by Maggie and gently tore into the wrapping paper for her. It was a small jewelry box. Jack lifted the lid. In the center of the blue velvet padding was a delicate gold locket with a rose etched into the front of it. Jack opened the locket to reveal a picture of Rachel laughing at the camera in her red Christmas dress on one side and Nathan sitting on the front porch when all the flowers were in bloom on the other side.

"Oh," Maggie said, smiling.

"I know you've always wanted one of these with pictures of the kids," Jack said, putting it around her neck.

"This," Evelyn explained holding a present in her hand, "is something else she has always wanted."

Maggie looked at her mother quizzically as Evelyn softly tore the tissue wrapping paper around the gift. Evelyn lifted the lid to reveal her crimson satin wrap, the one Maggie had always adored. Evelyn had received it as a present from her own mother and had worn it draped over her shoulders in her wedding picture. She was wearing a skirt, a soft blouse, a corsage, a hat, and the beautiful wrap. Maggie's eyes lit up.

"She has always had her eye on this," Evelyn teased,

draping it around Maggie's shoulders. "Thank you," Maggie mouthed. Evelyn kissed her forehead and fussed with the wrap till it was tied elegantly in front.

Nathan crawled under the tree again. It was finally time for his present. Reaching toward the back, he pulled out the haphazardly wrapped package he'd shoved under the tree just minutes earlier. He placed the package on his mother's lap, and Evelyn and Jack exchanged glances as Nathan helped his mother tear the wrapping. Together they ripped into the plain brown paper. Nathan eagerly helped his mother lift the lid off the box. Nathan reached in and pulled out the sparkly shoes for his mother. Her eyes gleamed as she held the shoes on her chest, admiring them. Nathan hurried excitedly to the foot of the bed, uncovering Maggie's legs, triumphantly slipping the shoes onto his mother's feet.

"They're the prettiest shoes they had," he told her.

"They're so beautiful," she whispered, smiling at her proud son.

We arrived at my mother's house early Christmas Day. "Merry Christmas!" Mom yelled as she flung open the door. The air was filled with aromas of roast turkey, mulled cider, pecan pie, evergreen, and aged oak logs burning in the fireplace. Hannah and Lily ran screaming into their grandmother's arms, falling over each other to get to their presents under the tree.

"Merry Christmas, Mom!" Kate laughed as Hannah frantically dragged her to the tree.

"Merry Christmas, Mom," I said leaning in to kiss her. I was eager to tell her about what had happened last night.

"Come on!" Lily shouted as she threw herself against my legs.

"Okay, okay," I relented. "Let's get things started here."

Lily banged her tiny hands together as I handed her a present that she swore was bigger than anything she'd ever seen. Hannah gasped when a beautiful gold box with gold lace ribbon was given to her. I passed out the gifts until everyone had their very own pile in front of them—sweaters, earrings, cookware, and books for Kate; baby dolls, coloring books, clothes, and more baby dolls for Lily; then a beautiful grown-up necklace for Hannah, along with games, elegant paper dolls and the latest Barbie accessories. Kate had shopped weeks earlier for Mom. She unwrapped a gorgeous brooch with the birthstones of all her grandchildren embedded in a circle of gold.

"I have always wanted one of these!" she shouted. "I'm going to wear it everywhere," she exclaimed, proudly pinning it to her sweater. The new pin would also fit nicely on the lapel of her brand-new periwinkle blazer and red silk blouse. "Oh, how beautiful," she cried, squeezing Lily's cheeks. "What a fashionable granny I'll be."

I set aside my new aftershave, books, socks, and underwear. Why, after so many years, did my mother insist on buying me underwear?

"I assumed you were running low on boxers," she teased, to the infectious giggles of her granddaughters.

"I was, Mother. Thank you," I said, grinning, ripping into the last present from my pile. I tore back the paper and ran my thumbnail across the tape holding the small box shut. Lifting the lid, I carefully opened the edges of the tissue paper and looked at Mother in surprise. I pulled out the Dunhill Billiard and held it up, reading the card she had slipped into the box. "No regrets," it stated simply.

"What's that?" Kate asked, surprised.

"This," I said, pushing the end of the pipe proudly into my mouth with the flare of a British statesman, "is a reminder."

Mom was bent over, opening the oven door, when I snuck up on her.

"Mom," I said anxiously.

Startled, she snapped upright, slamming the door with a bang. "Don't scare me, Robert," she scolded.

"I didn't mean to," I said, ushering her to the kitchen table.

"I didn't check on my turkey," she claimed, spinning on her heels.

"Wait," I urged. "Sit down." She sat. "Mom, last night Kate and I talked till four-thirty in the morning."

"About what?" she exclaimed. "My word, you must be exhausted."

"I am," I said, rubbing my temples. "I'm dog tired. I could throw up, I'm so tired."

"Well, don't stand over me!" she shouted, laughing.

I sat down, my eyes flashing.

"Mom, the most incredible thing happened last night." She sat forward, listening. "It was like an epiphany, like a lightning bolt hit me or something. I was shopping for all of you when I decided not to get anybody anything. Oh, by the way—Kate bought you the brooch and stuff," I offered as an aside. "I didn't know anything about it."

"Thanks a lot," she roared.

"Really long story short—we're going to try to work it out."

She banged on the table, "I knew she still loved you."

"I think she does," I said shyly. "And I know I love her."

"Well, go," she commanded, shooing me toward the door. "Go, go, go! Go play with your girls on Christmas. I'll keep things going in here and will be out in a minute." She playfully shoved me out the door and moved to the oven.

"Thank you, Lord!" I could hear her whoop from the living room. I heard the oven door creak open and then the metallic swish of a carving knife being sharpened against steel. "Thank you," echoed from the kitchen, amid the clamoring of pots and pans. "Thank you! Thank you! Thank you!"

## SEVEN

We are not necessarily doubting that God will do the best for us;
we are wondering how painful the best will turn out to be.
—C. S. Lewis

It was nearing midnight. The lights on the tree blazed
faithfully. The children were sound asleep. Nathan was
probably too old to dream of Santa Claus, and Rachel was
too young. Jack looked into his wife's blue eyes for as
long as she could hold them open.

"I love you, Maggie," he said over and over. "Thank
you for being my wife. Thank you for loving me." She
was unable to speak but held Jack's gaze. "We're going
to be okay, Maggie," he said, holding her face. "We all
love you, and we're going to be okay, so it's all right if
you want to go now."

Evelyn stroked Maggie's arms and held her hand.

"You don't have to hold on anymore," Jack comforted.

"Your daddy's waiting for you," Evelyn added. "You
can go be with your daddy, and we'll all be okay here."

Maggie's eyes eventually closed, and for the next two
hours, Evelyn and Jack continued to talk to her, watching

as each breath became shallower, a low rattle building in her chest. Evelyn read the Christmas story from Luke. "So Joseph also went up from the town of Nazareth in Galilee to Judea, to Bethlehem the town of David," she read. Jack straightened the wrap around Maggie's shoulders and positioned the locket in the center of her chest. "He went there to register with Mary," Evelyn continued, "who was pledged to be married to him and was expecting a child. While they were there, the time came for the baby to be born, and she gave birth to her firstborn, a son." Evelyn paused, stroking Maggie's hand as she read on. "She wrapped him in cloths and placed him in a manger, because there was no room for them in the inn." Evelyn continued to read about the shepherds in their fields and realized the Book of Luke didn't include the Wise Men. Flipping back to the Book of Matthew, she quickly found the passage she was looking for.

"Here it is, Maggie," she said holding the Bible up toward her daughter. "After Jesus was born in Bethlehem in Judea, during the time of King Herod, Magi from the east came to Jerusalem and asked, 'Where is the one who has been born king of the Jews? We saw his star in the east and have come to worship him.' " Evelyn laid the Bible on her lap. "When she was little, Maggie would always say that she couldn't believe no one else even bothered to notice that huge star in the sky. Remember that, Maggie?" Evelyn asked, caressing her face. "Look for that star now, Maggie. We're all okay here. Nathan and

Rachel are warm and asleep in their beds. We're all going to be okay, so look for the star and follow it. Follow it till you find Jesus. He's waiting for you, baby."

Jack and Evelyn recalled sweet memories for another hour. They talked about Maggie on her wedding day, and of Nathan's and Rachel's births. Jack told Maggie over and over again how beautiful she was, and how she had completed his life, and at 2:43 A.M., as he uttered once more how much he loved her, she took one final breath and died. There was no more pain. No more suffering. No more labored breaths.

Evelyn stood motionless beside the bed, her hand trembling over her mouth.

"Oh God, no," she moaned, burying her head into Maggie's shoulder. "I'm not ready for her to go." Jack crumpled beside the bed, still holding Maggie's hand, his heaving shoulders shaking the bed with each broken sob.

"Oh, my sweet angel," Evelyn wailed, kissing Maggie's face and hands. "My sweet, sweet angel."

Jack pulled Maggie into his arms and rocked her back and forth, the bright colored scarf slipping from her head. "I thought I was ready to let you go, Maggie, but I'm not," he sobbed into her neck. "I'm just not."

It was shortly after 3 A.M. when Jack awakened Nathan and explained that Mommy had stepped into heaven. Nathan ran, frightened, into the living room, where he saw his mother lying peacefully. His grandmother was holding and stroking his mother's hand. Evelyn's face was red and wet with tears. Nathan stood by his mother's bed and tenderly touched her hand. It didn't reach out for him, or draw him close to her, but lay motionless on the bed. Nathan felt his father's hand on his shoulder as he looked into his mother's face. She looked as if she was sleeping.

"Is she already in heaven?" he asked softly, closely watching for his mother's chest to rise and fall in breath.

"She is, darlin'," his grandmother said, smiling, tears falling from her chin. "She's already there."

Before the men from the funeral-home arrived, they each said good-bye, kissing Maggie's face and her hands, stroking her arms, and caressing her cheek. "I love you, Mama," Nathan sobbed, falling into his father. It was more than his eight-year-old mind could comprehend, that he would never see his mother again.

There would be those in town who would say it was cruel for Jack to wake Nathan the night his mother died, but one day Nathan would be thankful for the time he had had with his father and grandmother as they each, in their own special way, said good-bye to her. He saw the peace on his mother's face and knew that what she had told him was true. That even at that very moment she was in heaven.

Although they were expecting it, the soft knock on the door startled them all. Jack moved to the entryway, feeling as if he were moving in slow motion. He opened the door. Two men spoke softly to Jack as he motioned them in. Evelyn pulled Nathan to her as they watched the men work in silence, gently placing Maggie's sheeted body on a collapsible stretcher. Jack kept a hand on his wife as the men wheeled her out into the cold and into the back of the hearse. Nathan stood beside the empty bed as his grandmother fell broken into the chair beside it, pulling him down on her lap, wrapping her arms tightly around him, sobbing. Beyond the window, snow gracefully fell to earth. Nathan's father stayed outside in the cold and watched the hearse back out onto the street and drive away.

The phone rang at eleven o'clock on Christmas morning. Doris had been busily chatting away with her son and daughter-in-law, everyone making their way through the great pile of gifts on the floor under the tree. Doris hurried into the kitchen and picked up the receiver. Her face fell as she listened to the voice on the other end of the line. She didn't know the person calling, an aunt, she thought she heard her say, or maybe it was a neighbor— she couldn't recall. The only thing she heard was that Maggie Andrews had died peacefully at home last night. Jack and her mother were by her side.

.   .   .

By one o'clock that afternoon, Nathan's home swelled with friends, relatives, and neighbors, and the countertops overflowed with food—turkey, gravy, dressing, green beans, peas, corn, and every potato imaginable: mashed potatoes, scalloped potatoes, cheesy potatoes, sweet potatoes, sweet potato casserole.

Nathan pulled a Santa cookie from a Tupperware container his grandmother kept them in and sat quietly on the floor in the corner. His father and grandmother emerged from the bedroom carrying everything his mother would be buried in, the favorite dress she often wore to church and weddings, along with the beautiful wrap his grandmother had given her, and the sparkly shoes Nathan had purchased. He observed quietly as the grown-ups consoled his father and grandmother, clasping Jack on the back or squeezing his arm and whispering in his ear. He recognized the men his father worked with in the crowd, and the people from church. Rachel toddled through the forest of long legs, swinging Pooh bear in her hand as she crawled onto her father's lap. A small group of women shook their heads somberly and patted his grandmother's arm.

Nathan recognized some neighbors. He wasn't sure who a lot of the adults were, maybe people from Ferguson's, where his mother used to work. Many of them slipped quietly in, leaving food or gifts on the kitchen table and then slipped back out without saying a word. The faces would blur, but Nathan would always remember their quiet acts of generosity. One elderly woman wearing a Christmas Is Love sweatshirt washed every dish, scrubbed every pan, emptied the garbage, and straightened and tidied the kitchen unnoticed. Drying her hands, she moved stealthily to the living room, where, when Nathan craned his neck, he could see her gathering cups, saucers, and plates, and taking them to the kitchen, where she promptly washed them, dried them, and put them away. She tackled the refrigerator next, dumping moldy dishes, wiping down shelves and making room for the many casserole and Corning Ware dishes of food that were sitting on the countertops and the table. When the food was in order and her work was done, she slid on her coat and left.

Another couple appeared in the front door, said a few words to Jack and Evelyn, and quietly bundled Rachel up, gathering Pooh, her new pink baby doll, and some clothes, and shuffled out the door as Jack planted a kiss on one of his daughter's plump, red cheeks. Nathan was glad that no one was whisking him away. Although his mother was not here, he knew, even then, that these moments were part of her and something he needed to share in.

He looked toward the front door when he heard the familiar voice of his teacher, Mrs. Patterson, saying hello in the entryway. He hadn't expected to see her until after Christmas break. When he saw her gentle face, his throat tightened. They hadn't said much to each other all those days she'd driven him home from school, but he'd come to look forward to the time they'd spent together in the car. A kind-looking man Nathan had never seen before was with her. Nathan watched as the couple spoke with his father and grandmother, Mrs. Patterson's arm around his grandmother's shoulders. Nathan sprung to his feet and walked toward his teacher.

"Hello, Nathan," Doris said warmly. She looked to Nathan as though she may have been crying.

"Hi, Mrs. Patterson," he said quietly, waving the Santa cookie in his hand.

"Nathan, this is Mr. Patterson," she said, holding her husband's hand.

"Very nice to meet you, Nathan," the man with the gentle face said.

Nathan was glad that his teacher and her nice husband came to visit today.

Doris guided Nathan to the kitchen table and sat down. He carefully placed his Santa cookie on the table in front of him.

"Nathan," Doris began. "I forgot all about the roll of film this picture was on. I found it when I was tidying my desk drawers for Christmas break. I thought you might like to have this." She pulled out a framed photo of Maggie and Nathan taken the first week of school, when they'd helped decorate the classroom bulletin board. Before the picture was snapped, Maggie held up two yellow pipe cleaners behind Nathan's head, laughing gleefully when the flash went off.

From an envelope, Doris pulled out two other pictures. In one, Maggie was sitting at a tiny table in the school hallway, holding up a flash card to a student intently studying it. As the school photographer had walked toward them, Maggie turned and grinned. In the second picture, she had leaned over the table, pressing her face, cheek to cheek, into the student's, as if they were crammed into a photo booth at the mall, her arm extended over her head, a broad smile running the width of her face.

"Those two were taken last year," Doris said, smiling.

Nathan stared at the photos, shuffling through the three of them like a deck of cards, the framed one to the top, then the top to the bottom, carefully examining and reexamining each one. His mom looked different in the pictures . . . and then he realized why. They had been taken before she got sick, when she was still the mom who could jump in the leaves with him and dance around the house to the music on the radio and come to help out at his school. That's how he would always remember her, just as she was in the pictures.

They sat together quietly for several minutes before Doris stood and turned to leave.

"Thank you, Mrs. Patterson," Nathan said softly, fumbling the pictures in his hands.

Doris turned to him, wishing she had something to say, but she didn't know what that was. She and her husband were saying good-bye to Jack and Evelyn when Doris noticed the shiny, beaded shoes lying among a small pile of clothing near the front door. She turned toward Nathan, who smiled shyly.

"I wanted her to feel special and beautiful," was all he said. Doris's eyes were wet with tears.

"Oh, darling, she did. I'm certain she did." She let go of her husband's hand and bent down and hugged Nathan tightly to her before closing the door behind her.

Nathan walked to the storm door and watched his teacher as she and her husband got into their car. He heard hushed fragments of a conversation in the hallway. He couldn't hear exactly what was being said, but heard enough to know that his mother wouldn't want him to listen. So he tuned out the voices, gazed at his mother's laughing face in the photo, and squinted into the sky, looking for her in the clouds.


The sun was rising in the sky, shimmering along the snowbanks and shining down on trees bending under the weight of the snow, when the phone rang. I had already completed a rousing game of hide-and-seek with Hannah and Lily when Kate called me from downstairs.

"It's Dalton," she said, handing me the receiver.

Dalton and Heddy were standing on the front porch waiting for Kate and me as I maneuvered the Mercedes into
the driveway. I threw open the car door and stumbled
past them into the house. I spun around the living room,
frantically searching for Mother, bursting through the
kitchen door, only to find it empty. I ran back into the
living room, where I was met by the wet, grave faces of
Dalton, Heddy, and Kate.

"Don't tell me, Dalton," I begged, falling in stunned
silence to the sofa, my voice breaking. "Don't tell me
she's not here." Kate sat beside me, wrapping her arms
around me, leaning her head on my shoulder.

"She'd invited us over for breakfast," Dalton said so-
berly. "When she didn't answer the door, we let ourselves
in with our own key and found her in her chair by the
tree. The ambulance got here right away but. . . ." He
stopped. This was heartbreaking for Dalton. He loved my
mother very much. He stepped toward me and handed
me a letter. "This was in her hand." I stuffed the paper
into my pocket.


Nathan stood at the front door, watching as the hospital
bed was wheeled out of the living room and loaded into
the back of a medical-supplies truck parked in the drive-

way. He'd felt nervous and scared as the men loaded it, his heart beating faster and faster as the truck door slammed shut with a clang. As the truck backed out of the drive, his body filled with emotion. He shut the door against the cold winter air, pressing his nose against its wood, and wept softly.

He took a deep breath. He thought about all of the times he'd sat in school wondering where his mother or father was at that exact moment. What kind of car was Dad working on? What was Mom doing? Was she playing with Rachel? Maybe she was in the kitchen baking cookies for when he got home from school. Perhaps she was wheeling Rachel around in a shopping cart, buying groceries at Ferguson's. He often pictured what his mother was doing throughout the day, but now he'd no longer wonder. He knew exactly where she was and what she was doing. She was running and jumping and playing, just like she used to do with him before she ever had to get into that hospital bed. And in some peaceful, inexplicable way, that vision wrapped him in hope as he stood by the window and cried.

The coroner's office called later that evening. My mother had died of a brain aneurysm. The voice on the line explained that my mother had gone very quickly and felt no pain. I'd called Hugh and made a number of other calls to relatives and friends before kissing Hannah and Lily goodnight, holding them tightly in my arms.

Kate and I sat together in the living room, lit only by the tiny white lights of the Christmas tree.

"I was thinking we should bury her in the periwinkle jacket," I said, staring into the lights. "And the new blouse and pin." My voice faltered as I cleared my throat and continued softly. "She would definitely want the pin, because it has the stones of all her grandchildren in it."

I laughed, wiping the tears from my face.

"She'd never let me hear the end of it if I didn't bury her with the pin that represented all her grandbabies."

Kate rested her head on the back of the sofa, wiping the tears with both hands from her face.

"I'm going to ask Dalton to say something at the funeral," I said. "I can't imagine anyone else doing it."

"I can't either," Kate reassured.

I glanced at my watch.

"Hugh's flight is at ten. They'll all get in at five-thirty tomorrow morning. We can plan the rest of the service with the pastor when he gets here." I leaned forward on the sofa and buried my face in my hands, rubbing tired, bloodshot eyes with the heels of my palms.

Kate scooted over, grabbed my hand, and set it on her lap, holding onto it as she fell asleep. I gently draped a throw over Kate and sat quietly in the stillness, staring at the Christmas tree, the way my mother had always loved to do. I recalled the day Hannah and Lily had decorated the tree, small hands digging anxiously through the boxes of decorations, each child clamoring to find the next prettiest bulb to hang on its branches. The tree was more than just a decoration to Mom. It was a daily reminder of the time she'd spent with her children and grandchildren. I wiped another tear from my face.

"What a lousy time of year to lose your mother," I said, rubbing my temples.

When my head started to bob, and I felt myself nodding off in the early-morning hours, I stood to retrieve a blanket from the hall closet for myself. I straightened Kate's legs on the sofa and started to empty my pants pockets when I felt the letter Dalton had given me earlier in the day. Amid all of the commotion, I had forgotten all about it.

I turned the letter toward the lights of the tree and began to read.

"Dear Robert," it began. "I know the hard part is just beginning, but one day you'll understand that it is worth it. . . . All of it."

I wept as I read the rest of the unfinished letter.

## EIGHT

Death's power is limited—
It cannot eradicate memories
Or slay love
It cannot destroy even a threadbare faith
Or permanently hobble the smallest hope in God
It cannot permeate the soul
And it cannot cripple the spirit
It merely separates us for a while
That is the only power death can claim
—No more
—Donna VanLiere

It was late when the phone rang. Kate and I both leaped for it at once. Kate got there first. I watched her face as the expression changed from tense concern to utter happiness.

"It's a boy!" she shrieked. *I'm a grandfather—we're grandparents*, I thought, my heart brimming. "She wants to speak with you," Kate said, handing me the receiver.

"Hello, sweetie," I said, "Congratulations. How's my little girl?"

"I'm fine, Daddy. I'm perfect," Hannah replied. Her voice sounded strong, full.

"Well, how's our grandson?" I could hardly contain my joy.

"He's gorgeous, Daddy, but he's got Uncle Hugh's feet," she exclaimed.

"Oh my, bunions already?" I joked.

"No, but he is pigeon-toed. . . . Somehow they're pretty adorable on him, though," she laughed.

"Well, does the little fellow have a name?" I asked. There was a brief pause on the other end of the line.

"His name is Evan Robert," she said softly. "After you, Daddy."

Evan Robert had arrived! He weighed six pounds eleven ounces and was twenty-one inches long. He's a beautiful pink baby with soft tufts of hair on each side of his head, causing him to look very much like a little old man with a terribly receding hairline. Hannah and her husband, Steven, live four hours away in a small town where she teaches the fifth grade and he works as a state trooper. Hannah is most definitely her mother's daughter, from her shiny black hair to her melodious laugh and compassionate heart. It makes me smile to see the mirror image of the Kate I first met so many years ago. Lily is finishing her last year of college and since interning at my firm this past summer, has been threatening to pursue a career in law. She loves to goad her father. She says I could use a little competition. I'd started my own firm a number of years back, and we'd won a couple of fairly high-profile class-action suits. Lily is as blond as her sister is dark and a true beauty, a fact that she seems to be entirely oblivious to—even if, to my chagrin, the boys on campus are not. Now, Hannah was bringing the baby home for his first Christmas.

Kate has been sent into a tailspin, readying the house for her girls and her new grandson.

"Move that over there, Robert," she says, only to change her mind a few seconds later, "No, move it back. It takes up too much room over there." I can scarcely keep up with her as she drags me along, baking and cooking in the kitchen, running to the attic for decorations, and shopping for Christmas presents for the baby.

"Our first Christmas with our grandchild," she squeals into my ear.

It seems what I'd always heard is true: You become a crazy person when you turn into a grandparent. Our refrigerator was already covered with pictures of Evan, smiling up at the camera from the tub, from the floor, from the crib, and from the car seat. Basically, it's the same picture—just a different location each time.

When the car pulled up in the driveway this afternoon, Kate shoved me out of the way and rushed out the door, her arms waving high above her head. "Merry Christmas!" she shouted, making a beeline for the car. After a quick round of hugging and kissing Hannah and Steven, Kate gingerly scooped up the baby and lifted him high into the air.

"There he is!" she exclaimed. "There's Grandma's

boy!" Hannah ran to me and planted a big kiss on my cheek before grabbing the baby's bag off the backseat. Together, she and Kate made their way into the house, oohing and ahhing over the baby, closing the door firmly behind them. Steven and I just looked at each other and laughed.

"Well, Merry Christmas to you too!" I yelled toward the door. Glancing at my watch, I said, "Steven, since we'll never be missed in there," motioning toward the house, "how about riding with me to pick up Lily at the airport?"

When we returned, the house was aglow with the Christmas lights and decorations I had put up the weekend following Thanksgiving. Kate oversaw the whole production, yelling up to me on the ladder "Those lights are sagging too much" or "Robert, move the wreath over toward the center of the window a hair." By the end of the day, the house was something Mother would have been proud of, complete with her yard sale Nativity lighting the front lawn. Lily burst through the front door, sweeping her nephew into her arms, gently tapping his small nose, exclaiming, "Look at you! Look at you!"

I pulled out the Dunhill Billiard and packed the cylinder bowl with tobacco that smelled like a forest of pine trees. I puffed on the plastic bit till the tobacco caught, flicking my right hand to put out the match. "Dad!" Lily whined. "Do you have to light that thing?" But Kate didn't say a word. She never knew why I sporadically smoked the pipe, but she never asked either. All she knew was it had something to do with bringing me back to her. And that's all she needed to know.

Evan giggled as Kate raised him high in the air, then brought him down toward her, sticking her nose in his round belly.

"Who's Grandma's angel?" she asked in a voice that, I imagine, alerted every dog in the neighborhood. "Who's Grandma's angel?" The baby laughed and gurgled, his tiny arms and legs wiggling in the air. Lily offered her finger for Evan to grab and proceeded to bounce his hand around like that of a tiny orchestra conductor, while Kate lifted him repeatedly up and down, up and down.

I sat back, puffing on the pipe, and smiled at what we'd become, a family, and wondered again what had happened to the small boy with the Christmas shoes who'd changed my life forever.

*Christmas, 2000*

The wind whipped at my face as I knelt down and carefully wiped the clumps of frozen leaves from the base of the tombstone. "Ellen Katherine Layton," it read. "August 15, 1917–December 26, 1985. Beloved Mother." I cleared the area in front of the stone as well and made the short trek back to the base of the hill. I opened the trunk of my car to retrieve some of my mother's favorite Christmas decorations: poinsettias, holly, and an evergreen wreath. Slipping the wreath up my arm and over my shoulder, I caught a glimpse of someone else in the cemetery. It occurred to me that it was an odd day to visit a cemetery. As a matter of fact, in all my years of visiting my mother's grave, I couldn't remember ever seeing anyone else here on Christmas Day. I shrugged, hoping the poor soul was warmer than I was, and closed the trunk.

Trudging back to the grave, the wind shrieked in my bare ears. I put my head down to avoid the icy lashing, shrinking my neck into the warmth of the coat collar. As I passed, I could see that the other man was holding a brown paper sack. I briefly caught the nice-looking young man's eyes. He was slender and tall, wearing a thick, navy down parka and a wool hat with a university logo on it.

"Morning," I said, waving my arm full of decorations toward the man.

"Good morning," the young man waved. "Merry Christmas!"

"Merry Christmas to you," I cheerily replied.

"You're the first person I've seen here on Christmas Day in years!" the young man yelled above the winds.

"I was just thinking the same thing!" I shouted.

The wind died down a bit, and the sun beamed, lighting the ice-covered boughs and tombstones until the whole cemetery shone.

"Did you go to the university?" I asked, gesturing toward his hat.

"Yes, still do," he responded with a smile.

"Class of seventy!" I replied, patting my chest. "We were still using inkwells back then, of course. What are you studying?"

"Oncology," he said somewhat shyly. "If I can stick it out, that is."

"Terrific. Pretty tough program, though. These roads are something, aren't they? I couldn't get up the hill here at all," I exclaimed.

"Yes, sir. I was just down Route Ten from the hospital. They've sanded, but it's not doing much. Maybe this sun will help."

"They've got you on call already?" I chuckled. The wind began to pick up again. I wrapped my coat tighter.

"Oh no, not yet," he laughed. The young man had warm, blue eyes; his cheeks were red from the cold. "I just do a little volunteer work there when I'm home from school."

"That's great. The hospital's no place to be on Christmas. I'm sure the patients appreciate you, though. Well, nice speaking to you. You have a Merry Christmas," I said, quickening my pace back to my mother's grave.

"Thank you, you too, Merry Christmas," he said.

I draped the holly over the top of the tombstone. I positioned the evergreen wreath to the left of the lettering and placed a poinsettia directly in front of it, with a matching poinsettia positioned to the right. Scratching at the stone, I dug out the frost that was wedged into the lettering. "There," I said, whisking any remnants away as I leaned back to admire my work. "She'd like that," I assured myself.

I know that most people decorated grave sites on Memorial Day, but my mother loved Christmas, not Memorial Day, so regardless of whether it was thirty-five degrees or thirty-five below zero, I made my way to the cemetery each year and decorated her stone, always placing an extra poinsettia on my father's stone beside her.

"It's awfully cold this Christmas, Mom," I said, banging my hands together. "I know someone who must have been extremely grateful for not having to decorate your house this year," I laughed, picturing the retired Dalton teetering on one of Mother's rickety ladders while she barked out the precise placement of each decoration.

"Hannah brought Evan home, and I'm not too proud to say he takes after his granddad in many ways: good-looking, suave . . . has a certain charm with the ladies. Oh, and did I mention modest? You'll meet him one day and see the similarities for yourself." I paused, looking again at the year of death.

"I still miss you, Mom," I shivered. "I miss you every day."

I stood to go and noticed that the other man had already left. Probably couldn't take the cold, I thought. Bracing myself against the wind, I started back down the hill when something caught my eye at the grave where the man had been standing. Approaching the car, I strained to see what had been placed on the tombstone. As I moved closer, my heart began to pound. I quickened my pace and saw that at the base of the stone lay a brand-new pair of glittery, beaded shoes. I quickly read the name on the marker and the date of death: "Margaret Elizabeth Andrews. March 17, 1951–December 25, 1985. Beloved Wife-Mother-Daughter."

I spun around in the direction of where the young man's car had been parked, but the cemetery was empty. His car was gone. So I placed one of Mother's poinsettias alongside the shoes on the tombstone, and drove home.

Smiling.

*Today*

If we're open to it, God can use even the smallest thing to change our lives . . . to change us. It might be a laughing child, car brakes that need fixing, a sale on pot roast, a cloudless sky, a trip to the woods to cut down a Christmas tree, a schoolteacher, a Dunhill Billiard pipe . . . or even a pair of shoes.

Some people will never believe. They may feel that such things are too trivial, too simple, or too insignificant to forever change a life. But I believe.

And I always will.

## "THE CHRISTMAS SHOES"

### by *Eddie Carswell and Leonard Ahlstrom*

It was almost Christmas time
And there I stood in another line
Trying to buy that last gift or two
Not really in the Christmas mood
Standing right in front of me
Was a little boy waiting anxiously
Pacing round like little boys do
And in his hands, he held a pair of shoes

And his clothes were worn and old
He was dirty from head to toe
And when it came his time to pay
I couldn't believe what I heard him say

CHORUS

Sir, I want to buy these shoes
For my momma, please
It's Christmas Eve and these shoes are just her size
Could you hurry, sir
Daddy says there's not much time
You see she's been sick for quite a while
And I know these shoes will make her smile
And I want her to look beautiful
If momma meets Jesus tonight

They counted pennies for what seemed like years
Then the cashier said, son, there's not enough here
He searched his pockets frantically
And then he turned and he looked at me
He said, momma made Christmas good at our house
Though, most years, she just did without
Tell me, sir, what am I going to do
Somehow I've got to buy her these Christmas shoes

So I laid the money down
I just had to help him out
And I'll never forget the look on his face
When he said momma's gonna look so great

REPEAT CHORUS

I knew I caught a glimpse of heaven's love
As he thanked me and ran out
I knew that God had sent that little boy
To remind me what Christmas is all about

REPEAT CHORUS

# The Christmas Blessing

For Gracie,
who proves the most priceless gifts come in small packages

ACKNOWLEDGMENTS

As always, my husband, Troy, was the first to read this manuscript and offer honest, sometimes painful, feedback. Thank you, Troy, for constant encouragement. Your enthusiasm is contagious.

We loved our daughter, Gracie, in our hearts long before they put her in my arms when she was ten months old. Thank you, Gracie, for your joy, happiness, imagination, laughter, smile, "Elmo–Pooh Bear–blankie," dances, "big hug," and kisses.

I made many eight-and-a-half-hour trips to northeast Ohio so my parents could baby-sit while I worked. It was a long way to drive for child care, but I always knew Gracie was loved and cared for. Mother and Pop, thank you for all the good food and the many days you gave us.

My agent, Jennifer Gates, always believes in my work and makes the journey of writing enjoyable. Thank you, Jennifer, for being able to see past rough outlines or fragmented chapters to catch my vision, however dim it may be at the time, and make it stronger. Thanks also to Esmond Harmsworth for his time and feedback, and to everyone at Zachary Shuster Harmsworth.

Jennifer Enderlin, my editor, encouraged me to write a sequel to *The Christmas Shoes* and provided invaluable guidance. I appreciate your work and the belief you have in this book, Jennifer. Many thanks also to John Karle and to the St. Martin's sales staff for making calls and pounding the pavement on behalf of this book.

Beth Grossbard is petite in stature but big on vision and belief! Thanks, Beth, and thank you, Craig Anderson, for making dreams and ideas reality.

Great thanks to Byron Williamson, Rob Birkhead, Derek Bell, and the staff of Integrity Publishers for all your work and effort in the CBA marketplace.

Three physicians helped me get this manuscript into shape. I couldn't have done it without their help. If there are medical mistakes in the book, the fault is mine, not theirs.

We met Dr. Skip Hagan in China while he and Melissa were adopting Janie. Although he was busy with three children and Emergency Department duties, Skip always had time for my medical questions. Thank you, Skip, but most of all, thanks for the friendship with you and Melissa.

Jackie Russell put me in contact with Dr. Ann Kavanaugh-McHugh with Vanderbilt Children's Hospital Division of Pediatric Cardiology. Thanks, Ann, for generously sharing your knowledge with me and helping with everything from a heart patient's diagnosis to treatment. Thank you, Jackie!

My cousin, Paula Ross, introduced me to Dr. Anne Wilkerson, who provided rich insight into her years of medical school and rotations. She was a tremendous help in making each medical scenario in the book realistic and believable. Your help was invaluable, Anne. Thank you, Paula!

Sandy Ivey guided us through our first adoption and is gently leading us again. Thank you, Sandy, for helping us bring our babies home! We couldn't do it without you.

I wrote much of this book at the Medina County District Library in Ohio. The staff was always kind, helpful, and, of course, quiet. Thank you all.

I'm blessed to know people, many of them teachers, who have consistently aimed for excellence in their work. They have inspired, motivated, or challenged me throughout my life. Thank you to Tim Cook, Wes and Rebecca Baker, Paul Dixon, Dorothy Elrick, David Foster, Jim Leightenheimer, Diane Merchant, Jim Phipps, Rick Powers, David Robey, and Jon Skillman.

Thanks to Eve Annunziato, Jenny Baumgartner, Jeff Brock, Eddie and Terri Carswell, Debbie Cook, Rebecca Dorris, Dave and Judy Luitweiler, Will Marling, Barbara McGee, Cheryl Reese, Tammy Rich, Peggy Rixson, Peggy Starr, Laurie Whaley, and Vince and Sharon Wilcox for your encouraging spirits, kindness, and for taking the time to be friends.

And, again, thank you to Bailey, who never left my side when I worked and was the first to remind me when it was time to lighten up and take a walk.

We are built for the valley, for the ordinary stuff we are in, and that is where we have to prove our mettle.

—Oswald Chambers

December 24, Present Day

It's Christmas Eve, and the lake in front of me is frozen hard. Snow surrounds the edge, crunching beneath my feet. The sun is beginning to sink, and the trees, heavy with snow, cast long shadows over the paved path that runs along the shore. Several runners make their way around the perimeter, careful not to bump into the occasional walker on the inside of the path. I stand for a few moments in that familiar spot, beneath the giant oak tree, looking out over the smooth surface. As I'd driven through the icy streets on my way to the park, past familiar shops and sights, I'd noticed few changes in the three years since I'd been gone. I take a deep breath and exhale, leaving faint clouds in the winter air. I have work to do. I open the tailgate of my truck and grab the legs of the heavy wooden bench that I'd loaded earlier.

When I was a boy, my father would wake me early on Saturday mornings, and we'd drive to a lake, much larger than this one, on the outskirts of my hometown, and push our tiny rowboat into the water. We'd always start before dawn. At the lake, we'd row out to our favorite spot and prepare our rods for a morning of fishing. Together we'd sit in silence and wait for the slightest tug on our lines. Often, we'd speak in whispers. My father was convinced that even the smallest noise spooked the fish, but when my father did speak, he'd say, "Be patient, Nathan. One will come," or "Be still, Nathan. Be still."

At the end of the day, we'd row back with our catch— we threw back more than we ever kept—and then, as we approached the shore, my father would sometimes tell me about his hopes and dreams and ask me about mine. "Even God's smallest plan for us is bigger than any dream we could ever hope for," my father said one morning, pulling the boat onto dry land.

I don't know why I have always remembered that moment; maybe I recall it because there was a time when I was a boy that I'd prayed for a miracle that never came, one that would have kept our family intact and saved my mother's life. I was eight years old when she died of cancer during the first morning hours of Christmas Day. Earlier in the evening I had run to Wilson's Department Store and bought her a pair of shiny beaded shoes. Looking back, I know they were gaudy and awful, but in my child's mind I thought she'd look beautiful as she walked into Heaven wearing them. I didn't know my mother would die that night, and as I climbed into bed and pulled the blankets high around my neck, I prayed again for a miracle.

As I helped my father pull our boat onto shore years later, I wondered how he could believe that God's plan for us was greater than anything we could have ever imagined if God wouldn't send a miracle when we needed it most?

A year earlier, I went with my mother one winter morning to visit my grandparents, who lived high on a hillside. We drove up the winding road that led to their home, and because the trees were naked, as I looked over the bluff at the top, I could see into the valley below. It looked so different from above, not as immense as I'd thought. We got out of the car, and my mother took my hand on that cold, windy day and looked down into the valley with me. "I liked it better looking up," I said to her. "Everything's too little from here." She knelt beside me and drew me close to her side.

"Time in the valley will teach you to be a man, Nathan. It's where your character will form." I looked down the slope and back to my mother. I didn't understand how roaming around in the valley below would help me to become a man. She laughed when she saw my puzzled face and stood up, taking my hand again. "You can only see small things when you're on top of a mountain. Do you know what I mean, Little Man?" I shook my head. *No, I didn't.*

She knelt in front of me and held my face in her

hands. "One day you will, I promise. But I hope you don't go straight to the top of the mountain, Nathan. I hope you go through the valley first so that you'll learn how to love and feel and understand. And when life wounds you, I hope it's because you loved people, not because you mistreated them." I didn't understand anything my mother was saying. She smiled and kissed me. "Always remember that regardless of what happens, Nathan, in the end there will be joy. I promise." As odd as it sounded, I've come to realize that it was her heart's cry for my life, spoken not necessarily to me, but for me.

People talk about a defining moment in life. I've come to realize that there is no one defining moment, but instead a series of events and circumstances that define who we are. They change us little by little, leading us to something bigger or unexpected or maybe to a closed door, and that is when we experience a grand moment of realization that drives us closer to our destiny. The times with my father on the lake and with my mother overlooking the valley are two such moments.

Today, I know that each of us is destined for something, a purpose that often seems muddy, or vague at best. We want nothing more than to know what our purpose is, to know that we haven't just been plopped down to fumble our way through to the end, but that there's a reason for our being here. We may not discover that purpose in the way that we'd want, as time in the valley will be longer and darker than we imagined, but if we are patient or still long enough, we will catch it in fleeting glimpses. We will see tiny sparks of revelation that push us closer and closer to our destiny. There will be pain; sometimes more than we bargained for, but as my mother promised so many years ago, in the end there will be joy.

# ONE

Late October 2000

All change is a miracle to contemplate;
but it is a miracle which is taking place every instant.
—Henry David Thoreau

I gunned the engine, pulled the truck out of my parking space, and flew over the speed bumps on my way out of the apartment complex. A young mother grabbed her toddler and gave me a dirty look. I thumped the face of my watch, and the second hand seemed to groan before deciding to move. *Too late now, I'll never make it*, I thought, glancing at the clock in my dashboard.

I couldn't believe it; I was never late. I'd noticed that my watch was having problems a couple days earlier and had been relying on an extra clock in my bathroom to make sure I was showered and out the door on time. As I was shaving I must have accidentally pulled out the cord just enough to stop the clock from running. The tires squealed as I pulled out onto the main road, and the gardener working at the entrance to the complex gave me my second nasty look of the morning, even shaking his head for effect.

If I made all the stoplights through town, I could get to the hospital in fifteen minutes. Turning into the hospital lot, I glanced at the clock—fourteen minutes—a new personal record. There was no time to circle for a spot, so I parked at the far end of the lot and ran for the main entrance. *Maybe he hasn't started yet.* Who was I kidding? Dr. Goetz never failed to start on time. I ran faster between the rows of cars.

As part of my third-year medical rotations, the university had placed me under the tutelage of Dr. Crawford Goetz—the best cardiologist in the hospital. Cardiology wasn't part of a normal rotation block, but the university felt that a rotation in cardiology would only enhance a student's studies. So, I was stuck for the next four weeks with Dr. Goetz. He was a Harvard and Vanderbilt man, the chief of cardiology, father of four, grandfather of two, and a thorn in my flesh. He specialized in pediatric cardiology, but since the hospital had only a small number of child patients a year, as department head, Dr. Goetz would also oversee the treatment of adult patients.

In each of our rotations, a medical student was part of a team that consisted of an attending physician, three to four students, and an upper-level resident. Peter Vashti was the upper-level resident on Dr. Goetz's team. My clipboard with the day's rounds was hanging at the nurses' station, the last to be picked up. The other students and Peter were already following Dr. Goetz from room to room. I checked the room number for the first patient to be seen and ran to catch up, sneaking in behind William Radcliff, an old friend and fellow student who, to my good fortune, stood six-five. Dr. Goetz was sitting on the patient's bed, a forty-seven-year-old man recovering from open-heart surgery.

"She's working like a thirty-year-old's heart," Dr. Goetz said.

"Does that translate to the rest of his body?" the man's wife asked, cracking a wad of gum. Dr. Goetz laughed. He had a carefree, easy way with his patients and their families; too bad that didn't translate to his students.

"So everything feels normal?" Dr. Goetz asked, resting his hand on the patient's shoulder.

"He's cranky again," the wife said, her gum exploding like a firecracker.

"Is that good or bad?"

"I don't know if it's good or bad, but for him it's normal," his wife continued.

The patient looked sheepish. Poor guy, no wonder he had heart surgery. She was relentless.

"All right, Jason," Dr. Goetz said, smiling. "You're ready to go home." The man shook Dr. Goetz's hand and I could see his eyes fill with tears; he started to speak, then stopped. He didn't want to get emotional in front of a handful of medical students. He pumped Dr. Goetz's hand again, nodded, and looked down at the sheet resting on his lap. Dr. Goetz squeezed his shoulder and turned to leave, nodding for us to follow.

Filing back into the hallway, we could hear Jason's wife get an early start on what could be heart attack number two. "What do you mean you're not going to wear the piece? Just because your heart's working again doesn't mean your hair's going to grow back. Put this on. Put this on, or I'm not walking out these doors with you. I mean it. I will not walk out these doors." For the sake of his heart, I hoped his head would shine like the new dawn as he left the hospital.

"Who's our next patient," Dr. Goetz asked, scribbling something onto Jason's chart. "Andrews?"

I looked down at the chart in my hands. "The patient in room 2201."

"Mr. Andrews," he said, as if giving a speech to a room of five hundred. "Just as you were not given a number at birth, but a name, you will find that your patients came into the world in the exact same manner. Learn *who* they are, not *where* they're located."

I could feel sweat break out on my upper lip. I never intended to seem demeaning toward the patient. "I didn't mean it that . . ." I began, but it was too late. Dr. Goetz had already learned the name of the patient and was leading the students through the halls.

"And Mr. Andrews, as a reminder, your rotation begins at six A.M. Not six eighteen." I felt my chest tighten. I should have known that Dr. Goetz would pick up on my tardiness.

During a break in rounds, I retreated to the lounge and sank into the sofa. I leaned my head against the wall and rubbed my temples. If I'd known there was going to be someone like Dr. Goetz in my future, I never would have signed up for medical school in the first place. I glanced at my watch and noticed it had stopped running again. I tapped the face, but the second hand wouldn't budge. I took the watch off and flipped it over to thump the battery casing. I ran my finger over the inscription: *With all the love in the world, Mom.*

My mother died about a year after she stood with me on the hill overlooking the valley. Maybe she knew she'd never see me grow up; perhaps she was preparing me for the long valley I would go through without her, or maybe preparing her family and herself for death was the final step of faith she would take.

I remember my father coming into my room during the early morning hours of that Christmas. He said that my mother had stepped into Heaven. He let my sister Rachel sleep; she was much too young to understand what was happening anyway. I ran to the living room, where my mother lay still on the hospital bed; my grandmother was holding her hand, weeping. I watched my mother for the longest time, praying she'd move again, that she'd reach for me and say, *You need to get back into bed, Little Man,* but she couldn't reach for me, and I knew it. She was thirty-four years old.

Wilson's Department Store was about to close on that Christmas Eve as I ran from one department to the next looking for the perfect gift until the shoes caught my eye on a sales rack. I ran them to the front register and pulled a crumpled wad of bills and loose change out of my jeans pocket. When the clerk told me I didn't have enough money, I was heartbroken. I just had to buy those shoes for my mother. I turned to a man behind me, and, before I knew what was happening, he paid for the shoes, and I ran out the door for home. When I helped my mother unwrap the shoes, she held them to her chest and made me feel as if I'd just handed her Heaven itself. We buried her in them. I started leaving shoes on her tombstone again when I was sixteen. The owner of Wilson's somehow found a similar pair every year and ordered them for me.

During the last weeks of her life, my mother wrote a series of letters to my sister Rachel and me. In one addressed to me she wrote,

Dear Nathan,

I have had many joys in my life but none that have compared to you and Rachel. I always want you to know that I fell more in love with you every day. Please don't ever dread Christmas, Nathan, but remember to look for the miracles instead. It may be hard to see them at times but they will always be there because Christmas is the season for miracles.

She finished the letter and signed it, *With all the love in the world, Mom.*

I was helping my mother string lights on the shrubs outside our home the winter before she got sick when she first told me about the miracles of Christmas. "Jesus was born at Christmas," she said, wrapping a long strand around a juniper yew. "He left Heaven to live here." She bent over the back of the yew and tugged at the lights, stuck on a low branch. I pulled along with her, and together we continued wrapping the bush. "That's kind of like us becoming a worm and living in the dirt," she said, wiping her nose. "Love came down on Christmas, Nathan. That's the greatest miracle of all. That's the true blessing of Christmas and why it will *always* be the season for miracles." She stood back and admired her work, frowning at the tangled mess. "It'll look better when the lights are on." She dug into the box and pulled out another jumbled string, talking as she worked. "If you get too busy, you won't see the miracles that are taking place right in front of you," she said, replacing a blown light.

Before she died, my mother bought special gifts for Rachel and me; she wanted my father to give them to us on our sixteenth birthdays. Rachel got a gold locket and I got this watch—a flat, gold-faced Timex with a simple black band. The inscription was a reminder of something I'd always asked her.

"Is your love for me as big as Texas?"

"Bigger," she'd say.

"As big as the United States?"

"Bigger."

"As big as the *world*?"

"It's even bigger than the world! But if you combined *all* the love in the world, it might come close to how much I love you," my mother told me.

I'd worn the watch every day since my father gave it to me, as promised, on my sixteenth birthday.

Soon after my mother's death I told my father and grandmother that I wanted to be a doctor. When people asked what I wanted to be when I grew up I responded the same. I wanted to be a doctor so I could help people just like my mother.

Before I knew it, I was through college and into medical school. *What a tribute to your mother's memory*, an aunt would say or, *What a tremendous way to honor your mother*, an old family friend would comment. I felt the pressure mounting—people were counting on me to become a physician—my mother's memory depended on it. But after three months of rotations and watching people suffer and die, and now a week with Dr. Goetz, I questioned whether I'd made the right decision. In all honesty, when someone died it left me emotionally drained, and I was taken back to the morning my mother passed away. I felt as if I didn't measure up, that I wasn't cut out for it. I opened my eyes and realized I needed to get back to rounds.

Our team gathered outside the patient's room, and Micah, another third-year med student on our team, stepped forward and began to give the patient's blood pressure, pulse, heart rate, and the results of a heart test administered the previous afternoon. Micah was the "gunner" of our group—a med student's term to describe a fellow student who was always the first to answer, the first to volunteer for a procedure, the first to give stats on someone *else's* patient, and the first to get on other students' nerves. The term had been around long before we ever applied to medical school. William and I shot each other glances as Micah handed out Xeroxed copies of an article on angioplasty from one of our textbooks, one of at least twelve articles so far, all of them filed after our rounds in the nearest garbage can. William and I suffered in silence; it was all we could do, there was a gunner on every rotation.

Helen Weyman was the next patient on our rounds. She was a fifty-two-year-old woman complaining of chest pain who had a history of cervical disc disease. I had done Helen's workup when she was admitted to the hospital the previous afternoon. I went over her progress notes with the team before entering her room. It was customary that the attending physician took over once the group entered the patient's room; it was our time to stand back and learn, but I felt it was important to greet my patients first.

"Good morning, Helen," I said, standing at her side.

"I see your daughter was able to bring your knitting to you. Now you're not so bored, I hope." Dr. Goetz glanced at me. "What are you making?" I asked.

"A baby blanket for my next grandchild . . . number three. I've made a blanket for all of them. She's due in the next week or two."

I picked up the blanket and turned it over in my hands. "You've even got her name in here!" I sensed Dr. Goetz waiting for me to finish. "Let's go ahead and take a listen to your heart again this morning." I listened to her heart and felt for her pulse. I was taking up too much time. "Dr. Goetz would like to listen to your heart today as well." I moved away from the bed. Dr. Goetz took my place and examined her. As he did, he asked her about all her grandchildren, where they lived, how long she'd been married, and if she'd make him a pair of slippers. She laughed, and I watched as Dr. Goetz won over yet another patient. Before leaving the room I squeezed Helen's shoulder and told her I'd be by later to check on her.


I walked with William toward the cafeteria for lunch when my pager went off. I walked to Helen's room. The baby blanket was still sitting on her lap. Her daughter Mary, looking very pregnant and uncomfortable, was sitting in the chair next to the bed. "Is everything all right, Helen?" I asked.

She leaned forward and rubbed her hand over her lower back. "My back has been hurting."

I helped Helen into a more comfortable position. "You've been immobile longer than usual, and that may be putting pressure on those discs in your back. Does that feel better?"

She paused for a moment. "Yes, thank you, I think it helped."

"So you don't think it's anything serious?" Mary asked.

"No, it may be just some inflammation around those discs. But we should rule out any other possibilities," I said, handing the knitting back to Helen. "How much longer before this is done?"

"Just a couple more days, I think," she said, taking the needles in her hand.

I left her room and went to the nurses' station to discuss follow-up with the nurse on duty and to page one of the residents when Mary came rushing from her mother's room.

"My mother needs help!"

A nurse ran past me and headed to Helen's room. I followed close behind. I had just stepped inside when the nurse called in a loud, firm voice.

"Page, Dr. Vashti."

I stood in the hallway, right outside Helen's door, feeling helpless as Peter wheeled Helen to the OR. I was ordered to stay behind and attend to the other patients on the floor.

I finished my duties and ran up the two flights of stairs to the OR. As I threw open the door, I saw Peter waiting for the elevator.

"What happened? How's Helen Weyman?" I asked.

"She died a few minutes ago," Peter said.

It couldn't be possible. Helen was knitting a few minutes ago.

"What happened?"

"She died from ascending aortic dissection," Peter said.

The elevator doors opened in front of us, but I couldn't step forward; my legs were too weak to carry me. Peter stepped inside the elevator and held the door open for me. "Nathan?" I looked at him but couldn't respond. My mind was racing. If Helen died of ascending aortic dissection, it meant the pain she felt in her back was caused from a tear in the aorta, not her cervical disc problem.

"She told me her back was aching. I thought that the pain was attributed to cervical disc disease. I had just gone to the nurses' station to—" Peter nodded, cutting me off.

"Given her history, I would have thought the same," he said. I stepped inside the elevator and watched the doors close. The elevator stopped, and I followed Peter into the halls of the cardiology department. "Helen was a woman with a long history of back problems, Nathan. She was much sicker than any of us knew, and sometimes there's just nothing we can do. This is one of those times."

I walked past the room where Helen had stayed, and a nurse was clearing away Helen's personal items. I leaned against the wall outside the door. It felt hard to catch my breath. I bent over, resting my hands on my knees. My mind drifted to my very first rotation. During that two-week surgery rotation, a twenty-seven-year-old was brought in after a car accident. His arm had been lacerated in the crash, nearly severing it. In an effort to save the arm and avoid any further nerve damage, the patient was rushed to surgery.

The surgery was proceeding well, until twenty-two minutes into it, the patient's heart went into failure and he died. It was the first death I had encountered, and it hit me harder than I'd imagined; intellectually I knew it came with the territory, but my heart wasn't prepared. My heart was with the family when they received the unexpected news; it was there as the phone call was made to the funeral home for final arrangements.

I stood in the operating room after the monitors were turned off and stared at the man's face, his hands, and his clothing. When he woke up that morning he had no idea that the jeans and pullover shirt he wore would be the last clothes he'd ever pick out; he had no idea it would be the last car ride he would ever take. I wondered what his last words were to his wife or what he had said to his mother or to his children. Did he have children? Even after the curtain was pulled around his body, I went back in and looked at him. It was hard to sleep for days. To make matters worse, I didn't see any of the other students suffering in the ways I did.

After Helen died, I confided my doubts to William during a game of one-on-one basketball.

"It's because our hours are so long," William said. "We've been thrown into the deep end, and we're going to sink or swim now. You'd see things differently if you just weren't so tired." He sank a shot over my head. I grabbed the ball and held him off with one arm. "You're taking Goetz too personally. He comes down hard on everybody." I ran around him and jumped in the air, aiming for the basket. The ball dropped through the hoop and William grabbed it, dribbling it close to the floor.

"It's not Goetz," I said, lunging for the ball. "A patient died under my care."

"She wasn't under your care. You were the med student on the team that was treating her," William said. He rested the ball on his hip, wiping his face with the back of his arm. "There was nothing anyone could have done. You need to stop blaming yourself." He was moving again. I charged for the ball and snatched it away from him, throwing in a sweet two-pointer. He caught the ball when it fell through the net and darted past me, up the middle.

"She trusted me, William." I wanted to tell him that

somehow I felt responsible for Helen's death, but I didn't know how to say it.

"Did you go into medicine thinking you could save everyone? If you did, you're going to burn out faster than any of us. What's important is that your patients feel safe with you. You're good with them. You know how to talk to them. Helen Weyman never thought for a second that she shouldn't trust you."

I wanted to jump in, and say, "Exactly! She felt she should trust me—that somehow I was going to help her but I couldn't."

"I don't think my patients like me," William said, moving past me, dunking another ball. I grabbed it and held him at arm's length.

"They're just afraid of you," I said, spinning on my heels. "You walk into their room, and they've never seen anybody as big as you. They're not sure if you're there to work 'em up or rough 'em up. You're an imposing black figure when you walk into a patient's room." I darted past him and jumped in the air. The ball swiped the bottom of the net and I groaned. William was ahead. He laughed and snatched the ball, dribbling it close to his body.

"You mean I'm like Shaft," he said, holding me away.

"You're badder than Shaft. You can insert a catheter." He laughed and tried to run around me. "Do you ever have doubts?" I asked, waving my arms in his face.

"Sure I do." He sank another shot over my head. I didn't believe him. But he was right about one thing: our hours were brutal, the work was intense, and together they left me physically and emotionally exhausted. Now Dr. Goetz seemed determined to turn my rotation into the most miserable experience of my education. If I was going to start swimming, I had to get out of the deep end of the pool with Dr. Goetz before he drowned me.

Sleep never came that night. I looked at the clock at 10:30, 11:45, 1:20, 3:00, and then again at 4:45 A.M., when I finally decided to get out of bed. I stood in the shower for thirty minutes, hoping that the water would wash away Helen's memory, but every time I saw her face, I saw my mother's, and I just didn't think I could go through that over and over again.

Meghan Sullivan poked her head inside the hospital room of twelve-year-old Charlie Bennett. When the college freshman saw that the boy was awake, she ran to his bed and plopped down on top of it. "I looked all over for you after the meet. Your dad found me and said you were here. What's going on?"

"Ask Mom," Charlie said, eyeballing his mother. "She's the one who made me come." Leslie Bennett smiled as she stood to leave the room.

"He had trouble catching his breath, Meghan."

"It didn't even last that long," Charlie said, rolling his eyes.

"Only long enough to cut a few years off my life, that's

all," Leslie said, smiling. She grabbed her empty coffee cup off the table by Charlie's bed and left the room.

"How do you feel?" Meghan asked.

"I feel great. I didn't need to come in."

When Charlie was born, only one ventricle of his heart worked. He had three surgeries during the first three years of his life so the blood flow into his heart could be rerouted, flowing to the lungs without the aid of the other ventricle. The surgeries worked, meaning that the one strong ventricle supplied blood flow to his body and allowed Charlie to live a life like other little boys his age. He rested when he got tired, but nothing slowed Charlie down for long. He looked like every other child on the playground and preferred it that way.

It was only in the last five months that he'd begun to have any sort of trouble. "How'd you do today?" Charlie asked, sitting up in the bed.

"I came in first," Meghan said.

Charlie pumped his arm up and down with the enthusiasm of a coach standing on the sidelines of the Olympics. "What'd you run it in?"

Meghan looked down and smiled. "Fifteen-thirty."

The boy's eyes lit up, and he cracked his knuckles. "Man, I wish I could have been there! When's your next race?"

"Friday."

"Good," he said, giving her a serious look. "Cut two seconds off."

"What? Two seconds? Are you crazy? I already cut my old time. I ran the fastest I ever have today."

Charlie brought his hands up under his chin and smiled. "Run faster."

Meghan sighed. Charlie cracked his knuckles again and pointed his finger. "Don't ever take your eyes off the finish line. If you take your eyes off the goal, you'll never make it to the end."

Meghan said the words along with him. "Never take your eyes off the goal! I know," she said, shaking her head. "You tell me the exact same thing every time."

Charlie turned into the stern taskmaster again. "Remember: two seconds." Meghan stood and kissed Charlie's face. He quickly wiped it off.

"Are you going to be there," she asked, "or will you still be in here?"

"I'll be there," he said. "There's no way I'm staying in here."

Meghan had met Charlie her sophomore year in high school. Fascinated with runners he watched on TV in the Olympics, Charlie begged his mom to take him to the local cross-country and track meets. To Leslie's embarrassment, the little boy would run alongside the runners, barking at them to run faster or keep their eyes on the finish line. He was quick to notice Meghan's ability. "You're the fastest girl I've ever seen," he said after one meet. At each race, Meghan started looking for the little boy in the stands. She introduced Charlie and Leslie to her family, and the two families had been sitting together ever since.

Meghan slung her bag over her shoulder and headed to the nurses' station, setting a clipboard on top of it. "Denise, would you mind if I left my sponsor sheet here so you could ask any of the doctors and nurses that I normally don't see if they'd like to sign up?"

Denise smiled and took the paper from her. She was well aware of what Meghan was doing; her name was already one of the first on the sheet. Meghan was organizing a run that would raise money for a pediatric heart patient fund. The money would go into a trust and be awarded each year to a pediatric heart patient as part of a college scholarship once the patient had been accepted to a college. "If they don't sign up, I'll inject them with some sort of sponsor-sheet injection drug we must have around here someplace," Denise said, looking in the drawers.

I walked toward the nurses' station and was looking over the notes on my clipboard when a young woman ran into me, knocking it out of my hands.

"I'm so sorry," she said, swooping the clipboard up before I could get to it. She laughed, and her blue eyes sparkled. Her light brown hair fell just on top of her shoulders, and when she smiled, her face lit up. She was lovely.

"No, no. It's my fault," I said. "I shouldn't have been walking on the side of the hall that's clearly designated for running." She laughed harder, handing me the clipboard.

"Just keep that in mind from now on," she said, smiling, jogging toward the elevator.

I set my clipboard down on the nurses' station and rubbed my eyes. I could feel the pressure building in my forehead.

"Another rough morning with Dr. Goetz?" Denise asked. I groaned and peeked at her through my fingers. "He's the best there is. Really."

I folded my hands on top of the counter. "You know, everybody keeps telling me that. But those people have never actually worked under Dr. Goetz."

Denise shrugged her shoulders. "Just telling you what I've seen for years around here. People love him."

"Med students don't love him."

"Med students aren't people," she said, straight-faced. I looked at her and she broke out laughing. I noticed the sponsor sheet next to my clipboard.

"What's this?"

"It's for a scholarship run for the pediatric heart patients." She started typing into the computer. "Each year there's going to be a run to raise some scholarship money for college. The money will go into a trust, and when the patient is old enough and accepted into college, they'll receive a portion of the money as a scholarship and hopefully it will help pay some of the bills." She pushed the sheet toward me. "Do something good in the world. Sign up."

"Is this your idea of peer pressure?" She put the pen in my hand.

"You bet. Now sign up and help the kids."

"Who's the sponsoring organization for the run?" I asked, signing my name.

"It's not an organization. It's Meghan Sullivan. She's one of the fastest runners in the state."

"Is she on staff here?"

"No, she's one of our heart patients."

## TWO

All happy families resemble one another,
each unhappy family is unhappy in its own way.
—Leo Tolstoy

Meghan was startled when the phone rang. She bolted upright in bed and stumbled through the dark hallway into the living room, where she picked up the receiver. It was Denise from the pediatric unit. Meghan's mother, Allison, crept up behind her and was able to make out bits and pieces of the conversation.

"What time," she heard Meghan ask. "How is she?" Allison watched as Meghan nodded and said, "Don't worry about it. We were up anyway," and hung up the phone. Meghan looked at Allison. "A heart is available for Hope." Hope Reed was a five-year-old who had been waiting for a heart transplant for six months. She had dilated cardiomyopathy, which meant her heart was enlarging, causing its ability to squeeze to deteriorate over time. An early-morning car accident five hundred miles away claimed the life of a five-year-old boy.

Meghan was quiet as she put on her running shorts and shoes and pulled her hair into a ponytail.

"I won't be gone long," she said as she closed the door behind her. The early-morning air was cold, and the sun was just beginning to break through the orange-and-red leaves of the trees. Fall was her favorite time of year to run. She went to a nearby park and started to stretch, looking for the runner with the neon ball cap. When she saw her, Meghan took off, speeding behind her.

Meghan pushed herself to keep up as the runner in the neon cap made one lap after another around the lake.

"She's like a gazelle," Meghan told her father one day. "I clunk around like a goat compared to her."

"It's because she's taller," her father said.

"No, it's not, Dad. It's more than that. There's a beauty when she runs."

Jim Sullivan held his daughter's face in his hands. "There's a beauty when you run, Meghan, and everybody around you can see it." Meghan dismissed what her father said. Of course, he had to say that, that's what fathers do. He put his arm around her and pulled her down next to him on the sofa.

"Why do you wait around for her every day?"

"Because she's the best runner I've ever seen. If I'm going to run, I'm going to run after somebody better than me."

The fall air was stinging Meghan's lungs, but she

pushed harder to keep up. When the runner finally slowed down and walked over the crest of the hill toward her car, Meghan stopped, breathing hard, and stretched her arms high over her head. "One of these days I'll catch up to you," she said toward the empty hill. "And then I'm going to *pass* you!" She sat down on the wet grass beside the lake and pulled her knees up to her chin. "Help Hope through the operation," she whispered. "Please let this new heart work." She paused, looking out over the lake. She rested there for several minutes, tossing tiny pebbles and acorns into the lake, and watched as small ripples spread out over the water's surface. She got up, brushed herself off, and ran home to help her mother get Luke and Olivia ready for school. Although most students lived in the dorms or nearby apartments, Meghan wanted to live at home for her first year in college.


At first I thought it was too cold for a run. I hadn't been a diehard since my college days, but today I decided it was okay and drove to the park. I stood by my truck and stretched my legs. In the distance I saw two other runners on the path, a young woman wearing tight black spandex and a neon ball cap who blazed around the lake, and another woman wearing a knit cap. I watched Neon Lady as she ran the perimeter of the lake; she was serious and focused. *No doubt a gunner,* I thought. *A gunner runner.* But she was a great runner, all fluid motion when she breezed around the path, but then I noticed the young woman running behind her; she was pacing herself against Neon Lady. *That's what it looks like when you're doing what you're supposed to do,* I thought, watching them. They finished their run before I started mine. I walked toward the lake to begin my run when the young woman with the knit cap sat beneath the giant oak tree by the lake. *Probably routine for her,* I thought. *Runs her body hard, then clears her mind for the rest of the day.* It was something I should have done, but instead I finished my run, then jumped back into my truck and drove to my apartment. I had to get to the hospital.

I arrived at the hospital thirty minutes early to speak with Peter; he was the only one who carried enough weight to help me.

"I was wondering if I could possibly be part of another rotation." My voice sounded weak inside my own head, but I hoped it sounded convincing to Peter. He seemed a bit distracted, and I couldn't help but feel that things were already off to a poor start. He looked me over for a moment.

"But Dr. Goetz is a fine physician. I would say he's the finest at the hospital." I rubbed my temples. I couldn't take the "fine physician, one-of-the-best" speech again.

Peter took off his glasses. "Is this because of Helen Weyman? Because if it is, there will be other patients who will die unexpectedly. The hospital's not in the habit of accommodating the wants of medical students, anyway. You know that." I sensed that the bomb was about to drop—there was no way Peter was going to pull me from this rotation.

"It's not necessarily a want, Peter. I need to change to another rotation," I said.

"Why?"

"Because I'm thinking of dropping out of med school, and if I stay under Dr. Goetz, I'm sure I will." There was a long pause. I hated putting Peter in the middle of my problem. He was supposed to be responsible for the med students on his team; coddling a student's emotional dilemma wasn't part of that responsibility.

"I'll see what I can do." I felt the weight of the world lift from my chest.

I looked at my watch; I had to get going. The other med students and I had to scrub in to observe a heart transplant for a five-year-old patient.


Meghan opened the door and saw Luke and Olivia eating breakfast at the kitchen table. "Was Neon Lady there?" Luke asked, as she stepped into the kitchen.

"She was there."

"Did you beat the pants off her?" Olivia asked, mashing the eggs on her plate into a fine, yellow mess. Meghan slid in next to her sister at the table.

"Nah, I let her win. I feel so bad for her. She's fast, athletic, attractive. How's she ever going to get ahead in this world with those kinds of attributes? If I didn't let her beat me every morning, she wouldn't have anything going for her."

After breakfast Meghan helped dress Olivia for school. "I can do it myself, you know," Olivia said. Meghan pulled a fuzzy sweater over her sister's head.

"I know you can, but I like to do it." Olivia sighed as Meghan tucked and pulled and straightened and buttoned her into her clothes for the day. Truth was, Olivia loved all the attention her older sister gave her. Meghan was more than generous with the time she gave both her sister and brother. Outside the bedroom door, Allison listened as Meghan and Olivia talked. To think that for so long, she and Jim never believed they'd have a family of their own. After seven childless years, Meghan was born in 1981.

Every night when Meghan was a little girl, Jim would carry her to the back deck and lift her head toward the stars. "That's the Big Dipper," he'd say, pointing, "not to be confused with the big dope . . . that's your daddy." He'd show her one constellation after another, then, pointing to a bright light, say, "That's what you are, Meg. You're a star. You're daddy's little star."

As he lifted her from the crib one morning, Jim noticed something was wrong: Meghan was lethargic and nonresponsive. He was in the car with Meghan and backed halfway out of the driveway before Allison knew what was happening. She jumped in the car beside them and rode to the hospital without taking the time to put on her shoes.

The doctors took X rays and Meghan screamed; they drew blood, and she screamed louder. "You need to get her to a heart specialist," the emergency room doctor said. Jim and Allison were terrified. How could this be? The baby they'd tried so long to have was sick.

Dr. Crawford Goetz held the squirming child close to him and cooed in her ear. When Meghan looked into his eyes, a small smile broke over her face. "There's a hole in her heart," he said, gently running his pinky over Meghan's cheek.

"Oh my God," Allison gasped.

"However, it's an odd size. Normally, if the hole is too big, we go in and repair it. When they're small, we just leave them, knowing they'll eventually close on their own." Jim and Allison waited for him to continue. Dr. Goetz cradled Meghan in one arm, pulling her close to him. "I don't think this hole is big enough to repair."

"So it will close on its own," Jim asked.

"It may not close all the way."

"What if it doesn't? What will that mean?" Jim said.

"You'll need to monitor her activities, make sure she doesn't do anything too strenuous."

"But she can live a normal life," Allison said, taking Meghan from the doctor's arms.

"With restrictions she can. She might not be able to ride her bike as fast as the other kids in the neighborhood or jump in the pool twenty times in a row or run up and down the street playing tag, but it's too early to tell. We'll need to examine her throughout the years to monitor any changes."

Jim and Allison took their child home determined to treat her as a fragile gift, but Meghan rejected any acts of delicacy from the beginning. She loved to stand, balanced on top of her daddy's feet, and he would dance her around the living room, making her giggle and laugh with every spin. "Be careful, Jim," Allison would caution.

"She loves it!" Jim said.

"She might get too worked up."

But Jim would pick Meghan up and spin her till she kicked and bounced in his arms. If Meghan was sick, she didn't know it.

On her fifth birthday Jim and Allison took her back to Crawford Goetz, who took more X rays of her heart. For the last several years, the hole hadn't closed at all, but Dr. Goetz always beamed when he saw Meghan; she was proving him wrong, and he couldn't be happier. The child wasn't fragile and frail; she was a ball of fire. He listened to her heart through his stethoscope and smiled. "It sounds strong."

After school, Meghan would hop on her bike or run up and down the street with the neighborhood children. Allison would watch through the window from inside, rocking from one foot to the other, and chewing the inside of her mouth.

"Let her be," Jim would always say.

"What if something happens to her, and we don't see her fall," Allison snapped back, craning her neck to see Meghan through the window.

"She has to play, Allison. We have to let her play."

"The doctor said we'd need to monitor her."

"He didn't say to obsess over her." Allison moved from the window, pretending to busy herself around the house, but she always kept an ear tuned for Meghan's voice.

In second grade, after her parents had given up hope of having more children, Meghan became an older sister when Luke was born. Four years later, Olivia was born. When Meghan was in the third grade, the Sullivans moved to a larger house to accommodate their growing family. Their new home was situated on the other side of the city, in a different school district. Meghan was distraught over the move. She was moving away from her friends and beloved teacher. "Meghan," Allison said, tucking her in bed one night, "just think about all the new friends you're going to make."

Tears filled Meghan's eyes. "I don't want new friends."

"But you don't know who you're going to meet

there," Allison said, stroking her daughter's hair. "This could be the best thing to happen to you. This one little move will change all our lives. You just wait and see." The little girl nodded, telling her mother she understood. But when Allison left, Meghan cried herself to sleep, thinking of the friends she would be leaving behind.

Instead of riding the bus like she used to, Meghan became a "walker." Allison walked with her those first several weeks, pushing Luke in the stroller. "You can't walk her every day," Jim said. "We have to let her walk with the other kids."

So the next day, Allison helped Meghan with her backpack and sent her out the door for her first solo walk to school. But Meghan didn't make friends on her walk that morning and found none at school, so when the final bell of the day rang, she ran down the stairs and all the way home. Meghan ran to and from school every day for the next three years. Of course, Meghan's running made Allison a nervous wreck, but Jim would say, "Maybe she was born to run."

"Not with that defective heart, she wasn't."

"Dr. Goetz said her heart is strong, Allison. Let her run if she wants to."

Allison couldn't deny that Meghan's heart was strong. It was stronger than any of them had ever expected: their sick little baby was an athlete.

• • •

After Meghan finished getting Olivia ready that morning, Meghan showered and dressed, pulling her hair into a ponytail.

"The meet starts at three, Mom," Meghan said, putting her books in her backpack.

"Look for us, right side, fourth row up," Luke said.

"By the foghorn man," Olivia added. So that Meghan could spot them with ease, the Sullivans sat in the same place every time for her races: fourth row up, right side, by the coach with the bullhorn.

I washed every inch of my hands and arms, then a nurse slipped the surgical scrubs up over my shoulders and slid gloves onto my hands. Dr. Kenneth Jonan, one of the transplant surgeons, would perform the surgery, with Dr. Barry Mann assisting. Dr. Goetz filed our team into the operating room, and we waited for the transplant to begin. When Dr. Goetz entered, he bent low to the girl's ear and whispered something, squeezing her leg. As third-year students, theoretically, we were prepared to participate on some level in the operation, but Dr. Goetz kept us from it, with the exception of handing the surgeon an instrument if he chose to ask us for it.

From time to time, Dr. Jonan would speak to us without taking his eyes off his work. I noticed that on several occasions, Dr. Goetz leaned down and whispered in the girl's ear. "Doing great, Hope. Everything's looking good." Hope's new heart was inside a plastic bag filled with a sterile solution, sitting in a pail of slushy ice water. I was drawn into the surgery in a way I hadn't expected. I saw the heart beating inside the girl's tiny chest and was so moved by the sight that my throat tightened. Dr. Jonan stopped her heart and removed it; it was swollen and dark red. He passed the heart to a nurse, and she set it on a towel, where we watched it pump several times before stopping altogether. *Unbelievable*, I thought. The new heart was pale pink and glossy. Dr. Jonan rolled the heart into Hope's empty chest cavity, and we watched as he connected the back of the heart first. After thirty minutes of stitching, the heart was in place. Dr. Jonan removed the cross clamp and we waited for the blood to flow into the coronary arteries that fed the heart and watched as it began to pump. I felt like throwing my hands in the air and cheering. It was the most remarkable thing I'd ever seen.

"Amazing," Dr. Goetz, said under his breath, watching the heart. "It just never ceases to amaze me." He clapped Dr. Jonan on the back, and I could see him smile through his mask. Dr. Jonan bent over toward the heart again and continued his work.

"Clamp." There was silence in the room. I glanced up and saw Dr. Jonan looking at me. He held out his hand. "Clamp." I looked at the instruments and was afraid I'd hand him the wrong one. "Clamp," Dr. Jonan said, looking at William. William stepped forward and handed him the instrument, securing a better spot for the remainder of the surgery.

Dr. Jonan and Dr. Goetz had a focused, professional rapport throughout the surgery and it was obvious that the medical team also respected Dr. Goetz in a way I didn't. *Maybe he is the best*, I thought.

After scrubbing up, Dr. Goetz met with us to recap the operation and to answer any questions we might have. For a brief moment I looked down at my watch and realized it had stopped running again. As I gave it a couple of quick taps, I noticed that Dr. Goetz was no longer speaking.

"Am I boring you, Mr. Andrews?" I could feel the weight that had been released earlier with Peter fall heavy on my chest again.

"No, sir."

"I would only hope that your patients will have your undivided attention and you won't be so easily distracted when talking with them." He reached for a pair of glasses in his pocket and began cleaning them with the sleeve of his white coat. "May I ask if you feel this is your calling, Mr. Andrews?" I could feel the eyes of my peers on me.

"Sir?"

"Is medicine a calling or a responsibility for you?" I was stunned. I don't know if I was more taken aback because Dr. Goetz was embarrassing me in front of my classmates or because he sensed my apprehension. "If it's not a question you've addressed yet, I would suggest that you do." Whatever positive feelings I'd had about Dr. Goetz during the surgery vanished in an instant.

At the end of the day I made my way to the parking lot. My truck was on the far end, and I didn't think I had the energy to crawl, let alone walk to it. "Why don't you make life easier on yourself and get a new watch?" William said.

"The watch isn't the problem."

"It was today!" he said, chuckling. I was glad someone could get a laugh from my misery.

"Is medicine a calling or a responsibility for you?" I asked.

He zipped his coat and smiled. "Hey, you're the one who's supposed to answer that. Not me."

I put my hands under my arms and walked faster to keep up. "What's that 'calling or responsibility' stuff supposed to mean, anyway?"

William shrugged. "I don't know," he said. "I think he just means that sometimes you act like you're becoming a physician because you owe it to the world." William stood outside his car. "Listen, when a doctor asks for a clamp, hand the man a clamp! You're not going to kill the patient, you know." He got into his car and started to drive out of the parking lot.

"So it's wrong to care?" I yelled after him. "Is that what you're saying? Doctors shouldn't care?" He waved and squealed his tires as he pulled onto the road.

When Friday came, I couldn't wait to get to my apartment and crash. On my way home, I drove past the university and noticed buses and cars lined along the street. The sign in front read, ROSS ROUNTRY MEET TODAY. In spite of my throbbing head, I laughed when I read it, wondering what the kid was like who made off with the missing "c's." On a whim I pulled into the drive. I parked the truck and made my way across the grass to the bleacher seats just as a pack of lean male runners grouped together at the starting line. At the sound of the gun, parents and classmates were on their feet, screaming and cheering. It was a large crowd for a cross-country meet, much larger than the spattering of parents who came out when I was running. As I looked at the crowd, I had to smile. My father, grandmother, and sister sat in seats just like these many years ago to watch me run against the best in the district, cheering till their voices were hoarse.

The race ended minutes later when a fine athlete from a competing school crossed the finish line in first place. A group of female runners walked toward the starting line, preparing for the sound that would send them bolting toward the woods and meadow beyond. As they gathered, a small girl in the middle of the crowd broke the silence. She cupped her hands around her mouth and screamed something, but I couldn't hear what she said. Embarrassed, the girl's mother covered her mouth as the runners shot off their marks. A girl, tall and lean, her light brown ponytail tossing in the wind, blew past the other runners and took the lead. The crowd was on their feet shouting her name. I couldn't make out what they were saying, but it was obvious she was the hometown favorite, if not the competing universities' favorite as well. I got up and screamed along with everyone else. "Go, go, go!" I said with every step she took. I could see her wend her way through the woods, her strides long and fast. The other runners were pushing as hard as they could to catch up.

The crowd was so loud that I missed much of what the announcer said. All I heard as the winner crossed the finish line was, ". . . shaved three seconds off her previous five-K record. She ran it today in fifteen minutes and twenty-seven seconds." I'd never seen a girl run that fast—3.1 miles in just over fifteen minutes. No wonder the crowd was so big; the university had a star on its hands. I sat down and watched the crowd. I recalled that same frenzied energy from when I ran in high school and college. At the meets, I'd look up into the stands and scan the faces until I found my father, grandmother, and sister waving at me from the bleachers, my grandmother clasping her hands above her head and pumping them back and forth like a boxer taking the ring. I laughed at her and waved back, always wishing that my mother could be sitting with them. My head was pounding, so I decided against watching another race and headed home.

Michele Norris, one of the coaches for the women's team, caught Meghan and her family before they left the field. She was clutching a large brown envelope, smiling. "I didn't want to blow your concentration before the race," she said to Meghan. "But Stanford called me today. They've got a full scholarship with your name on it." Jim threw his arms over his head in victory. Meghan was too astonished to speak.

"That's the second school," Allison said. Georgetown had called a week earlier.

"I think there'll be others," Michele said. "I wouldn't be surprised if Colorado Boulder called. They all seek out the best and know that you slipped under their radar last year in high school. They know they're missing out on one of the best runners in the country." She put her arm around Meghan. "Now comes the hard part. Choosing." Meghan stared down at the envelope. Jim picked his daughter up, whooping as he bounced her up and down.

"They wouldn't even know who I am if it wasn't for you," Meghan said, between bounces.

"You do the hard part," Michele said. "All I did was create a little buzz."

Jim threw his hands into the air and whooped again,

this time picking Michele up and shaking her like a rag doll. "This is my problem," Michele said, grunting as Jim bounced her from side to side. "No single guys are ever interested in me, because married men keep picking me up."

Leslie Bennett drove Charlie to the hospital before Meghan's race. He begged his mother to take him to the meet, but his breathing was labored again so the race was out of the question as far as Leslie was concerned. Dr. Goetz admitted him for an overnight stay, and, once his medications were adjusted, Charlie fell asleep. Leslie stayed at his side. In recent weeks, she and Rich had noticed that Charlie had less energy and was sleeping more than usual. When Rich arrived at the hospital after work that evening, Charlie opened his eyes. "You can go home, Dad," he said. "I'm just going to go to sleep." Rich sat down and squeezed Charlie's hand.

"That's okay. I'll wait," his father told him.

Rich watched as his son fell back to sleep. He and Leslie had been overjoyed when their first son was born, at a healthy nine pounds. Even years after Charlie's surgeries he was still the picture of the active, normal child.

When Rich was dating Leslie, and in the early days of their marriage, he was in the Air Force, and like many service families they moved from base to base. When he left the service, Rich and Leslie moved back to where they'd both grown up. That transition had been one of the most difficult of their lives. Unemployment was high, and Rich struggled to find work. He'd eventually found a job driving a truck for a local package delivery company.

Leslie resigned from her part-time day-care position within the last few months, when Charlie's visits to the hospital became more frequent, often leaving Matthew, Charlie's ten-year-old brother, with her parents.

Rich's job didn't provide the insurance coverage needed for all of the medical expenses, but it covered some, and anything helped at that point. Rich was taking any overtime hours he could get, hoping the extra income would help ease the burden of their mounting hospital bills, but there was only so much one man could do. The months of stress and worry were showing on both their faces. Leslie looked older than her thirty-five years. She had once enjoyed making herself up in the morning before heading out the door, but after sleeping on a bed no bigger than a cot by her son's side, makeup was the last thing on her mind.


Meghan walked to the nurses' station on the fourth floor. Claudia looked up from her files. "Charlie's doing great," she said.

"What happened?"

"He needed his medications adjusted. He's fine now. Hope did great, too. She's up in ICU."

Meghan tiptoed into Charlie's room. Rich and Leslie smiled, motioning her to come closer to his bedside. Meghan sat on a chair, leaning on the bed, careful not to disturb the maze of wires that were monitoring everything from Charlie's heart, blood pressure, pulse, and oxygen level. She squeezed and patted his hand.

"I didn't take two seconds off, Charlie," she whispered. "I took three." Rich and Leslie smiled as Meghan kissed his forehead. "I missed you, though. I couldn't have done it without you."

"Congratulations," Rich said.

"When's your next race?" Leslie asked.

"Thursday."

"He'll want to see you before then."

"That's what I'm afraid of!"

An hour later, Charlie strained to open his eyes. Rich and Leslie jumped to their feet and bent toward him, touching his face. "You're still waiting," Charlie whispered to his dad.

"I'll wait forever if I have to." It was something he and Charlie had been saying to each other for years now. When Charlie heard it, he smiled and fell back to sleep.

## THREE

Most people run a race to see who is fastest.
I run a race to see who has the most guts.
—Steve Prefontaine

I was walking toward the lounge when I passed Hope's
room. Since her transplant, our team had made sporadic
visits to see her, but only long enough to check on her
progress. Her mother, Beth, a part-time social worker,
was always with her. Her room looked like a florist shop
filled with flowers, balloons, and stuffed animals. Hope's
father, Gabe, was a loan officer at a nearby bank, and many
of his customers had sent gifts. I peeked through the window in her door to see how she was doing. She caught
my eye and waved me in, her little body dwarfed by the
tangle of tubes and wires and machinery surrounding
her. Her eyes crinkled up when she smiled at me.

"In the middle of a so-so day, I know there's always
Hope," I said, as if reciting poetry. Hope smiled and
looked at her mother. "When people demand more of
my time and I think I just can't give any more, I know
there's always Hope." She giggled and looked again to

her mother. "When I need a pick-me-up but just don't know where to turn, I look for Hope." I stood at the side of her bed. "I don't know what I'd do without Hope in my day." Hope giggled, and her mother laughed, squeezing Hope's hand.

"Dr. Andrews," Hope said, "you're one of my favorite doctors."

"I'm not a doctor," I said, leaning toward her. "I'm a med student. It's this jacket. See," I said, taking it off. "When I take it off I look like an accountant." I put the jacket back on. "It's amazing, because people think they have to go through years of medical school and training to become a doctor when all they really need is a white jacket." Hope shook her head.

"No, you're a doctor," she said. "And you're my favorite."

"And I thought I was your best guy!" I turned to see Dr. Goetz standing in the doorway.

"You're both my favorites," she said, holding on to each of our hands. "But don't tell anybody else. They won't like it." Dr. Goetz put his finger to his lips as if he would keep her secret. I slipped from the room and walked toward the lounge.

"Are you on your way to see a patient?" I stopped when I heard Dr. Goetz behind me and turned to look at him.

"Uh, no," I said, unable to think fast enough. I regretted the words as they fell from my mouth.

"Good," he said. "Walk with me as I check on Charlie Bennett."

*Great*, I thought. I never wanted to be with Dr. Goetz as part of a group, let alone soak up some one-on-one time with him.

When we entered Charlie's room, he was propped up in his bed, watching television. Two small blue ribbons were hanging from his hospital gown. Leslie sat at his side. Dr. Goetz stopped in the center of the room, opened his arms wide, and waited for a word from his young patient.

"It's still beating away in there," Charlie said.

Dr. Goetz walked to his bed and sat down. "Pain?"

"No."

Dr. Goetz pretended to make a larger-than-life check mark on Charlie's chart, which made Charlie laugh. "Breathing problems?"

"No," Charlie said.

Two big check marks. Leslie chuckled at Dr. Goetz. "Sleeping?"

"Yes."

Dr. Goetz pretended to make enormous exclamation points on the chart, circling his arm in the air at the end for a grand finale. I couldn't help but be impressed by the banter between doctor and patient. Dr. Goetz listened to Charlie's heart and took his pulse and blood pressure before placing an ankle on his knee, balancing the chart on his leg.

"Are they treating you okay," Dr. Goetz asked him. "Leaving a mint on your pillow every night?"

"They won't give me ice cream," Charlie said, annoyed.

Leslie laughed and rose to her feet. "I told them not to bring it. I didn't know if that should be part of his diet or not."

Dr. Goetz leaned in close to Charlie. "If I can get Mom to okay the ice cream, will you spend one more night with us so we can monitor how the meds are doing?" Charlie nodded yes, but everyone in the room knew that the boy would have given anything to go home.

A large, bearlike roar caught my attention on the television. I turned toward the set to see a wrestler body-slamming another wrestler to the mat. "Who's your favorite?" I asked, pointing to the screen.

"Ice Man," Charlie answered without hesitation.

I threw my hands in the air. "No way! Ice Man's all water. The Rock crushes him every time."

Charlie straightened up in his bed and stared at me, wide-eyed, cracking his knuckles. "Water turns to ice and freezes over rocks."

I shrugged my shoulders as if that were no big deal. "But then the ice melts and turns to water and guess who's still standing . . . The Rock!"

Leslie laughed. "Please don't encourage him."

Dr. Goetz rubbed Charlie's head and turned to leave. "Ice cream's on its way." Charlie waved, and I smiled, following Dr. Goetz into the hallway. "I didn't know you watched wrestling," Dr. Goetz said to me.

"I don't. The only guy I've ever heard of is The Rock."

Dr. Goetz led me through the hall as he made his way to the next room. "I've watched you with patients, Nathan; especially the children. You have a way with them, a natural ability that we can't teach." I could be wrong, but it seemed as though Dr. Goetz had just complimented me.

"We can teach you the clinical side of medicine," he continued. "But we can't teach personal care. Either a student has it, or he or she doesn't. Sometimes you tend to take that care a little too personally on yourself, but again, that's something we can work on." He crossed his arms and looked at me. "But I've watched how kids respond to you, and they already have a trust in you." He looked at me and paused. "Have you ever considered pediatrics or even pediatric cardiology?"

"No," I answered honestly.

"You might consider one of them, perhaps training with me in cardiology."

After those words, I didn't hear anything else. Dr. Goetz's mouth kept moving, but my mind couldn't process what he was saying. Long-term training with him was not even a consideration at that point.

"I'm being switched to Dr. Hazelman's rotation," I said, spitting out the words.

Dr. Goetz didn't falter. "Very good then." He tucked Charlie's file beneath his arm. "Let me know if I can help." He disappeared around the corner, leaving me standing in the hallway. I leaned my head against the wall and closed my eyes. Was there even the slightest possibility that I was making a mistake? Maybe I should tell Peter I was wrong and complete my rotation with Dr. Goetz. I shook off the idea and walked toward the nurses' station.

The transition to Dr. Hazelman's rotation happened the next day, much quicker than I'd anticipated. He was part of the surgery block, which I had already completed, but his specialty lay in emergency medicine. I started with his team the last week of October and would spend the next eight weeks in the emergency room. I jumped into the work with both feet, anxious to prove to Peter and, maybe to myself, that I'd made the right decision in changing rotations.

On my first morning in the ER, we watched Dr. Hazelman perform an emergency gallbladder surgery. "Many women her age experience gallbladder problems," Dr. Hazelman said. "Why is that?"

"The four f's," Melanie, the "gunner" of my new group, said. "Female, fat, fertile, and forty. So, pregnant women are more likely to develop gallstones. Although this patient is not pregnant, she still meets the criteria." Dr. Hazelman nodded. Melanie clutched the clipboard tight to her chest and sighed, dazzled by her own brilliance.

Days later, a nurse directed me to a room where a sixty-six-year-old man was complaining of lower back pain. I was assigned to do his evaluation before a doctor saw him. I walked into the room, and the man was clutching his back, groaning.

"My name's Nathan, Mr. Slavick," I said, holding his chart. "I'm here to do your evaluation." He leaned forward to ease his back and groaned.

"Are you a doctor?"

"No, sir. I'm a med student."

"Get me a doctor now. I can't take this pain." I moved toward him to begin my examination but stopped. We had been taught during our first two years in med school that we were the main advocates for our patients. Sometimes the attending physician or the residents would be too busy to take much time with them, and that's where we came in, giving quality time and attention to the patient. We were told to be completely thorough in each of the evaluations we performed, but something was wrong here.

"I've never seen him like this," his wife said, wringing her hands beside me. I tried to listen to Mr. Slavick's abdomen but he grabbed my wrists, pushing me away, making it hard to hear through the stethoscope.

"I'll get a doctor," I said. I found Dr. Rory Lee, the fourth-year resident on our team, by the nurses' station. He followed me to the room where the Slavicks were waiting. "He's complaining of lower back pain," I said.

Rory put his stethoscope on Mr. Slavick's belly and felt his stomach with his free hand. Rory was pushing the gurney into the hallway and barking orders before I knew what was happening. I ran behind him.

"Call the OR. Tell them I have an abdominal aortic aneurysm about to rupture," he yelled to a nurse.

"Where are you taking him?" Mrs. Slavick asked, following us to the elevator.

"Your husband needs surgery," Rory said, pushing the gurney through the rush of people exiting the elevator.

"What's happening?" she cried as the doors closed.

A nurse approached me and stuck another chart in my face; I ignored her. I walked outside, stumbling over the curb. I sat against a wall and ran my hands through my hair. What a horrible day. I knew that someone would start looking for me, wondering where I was, but my legs couldn't lift me. Time passed slowly: twenty minutes, maybe forty. I'm not sure how long I had been crouched against the wall when Rory found me.

"Did he die?" I asked.

"No."

"I didn't hear blood rushing through the aorta."

"Because you don't have enough clinical experience," Rory said. "You can't read something in a textbook, then expect to pick up on it the very first time a patient walks through the door."

"Mr. Slavick was in pain," I said. "If I can't figure out why a patient is in pain, then I'm not doing my job. He could have died. He *would* have died if you hadn't saved him."

"If someone's in pain, and we can't figure it out, or if a patient dies, it doesn't mean we're not doing our job, Nathan. During my ICU rotation in med school, I had four patients die in one night! I had two die last night in the ER. Sometimes bad things happen even when we do everything right. You have to let go of this idea that everyone is going to live because the fact is, people die. We apply everything we know to help our patients, but after that we have to let go." He looked to the end of the drive and watched cars pull in and out of the hospital. After a long pause, he said, "Have you ever considered taking a break from your studies, Nathan? Perhaps finishing your rotations at another time?"

It was one thing for me to admit to Rory that I didn't think I was measuring up. It was another for him to agree. "Maybe you should take a break and clear your head," he said. I sat speechless, my shirt wet with perspiration. "You won't be the first to do this. It happens more often than you know." I didn't know how to respond to him.

"What do you think, Rory?" I asked, but he just shook his head and looked down at the ground.

"I think you'd make an excellent physician, Nathan. You're smart, but you worry too much about getting an answer wrong. You're great with the patients, better than any of the students on this rotation, but you don't trust yourself, and as a result you don't handle the pressure very well, and there is a lot of pressure when a patient is dying. But they do die, Nathan, and there's nothing even the world's best doctor can do about that."

I could hear myself breathing. "There's nothing wrong with what you're going through," Rory continued. "It might just be an indication that you need to step back. If you chose to break away right now, you would still have plenty of time to decide if this is right for you—to decide if this is really what you want to be doing—but I hope you don't do that." He stood to his feet. "I hope you're able to sort through whatever is clouding your thinking right now so you can move on to what I think you're meant to do."

He clapped my shoulder and walked back into the hospital, leaving me alone to wonder what I would do with my life.

That night, after flipping through seventy-plus channels on T.V., I knocked on William's door. I figured that even if he'd already eaten dinner, a man his size wouldn't object to another meal. I was right. William was always up for food. We decided to walk to Macbeth's Pizza up the street.

"How'd it go in the ER?" he asked, pulling a knit cap over his head.

"Don't ask."

"Somebody vomit?"

"I wish that had been it, but you left out the urine."
William pretended to stumble from laughing. Macbeth's
was packed with university students, but I saw Melanie,
the new "gunner," waving to me from across the room.
Melanie was the classic type A personality, always dialed
up to ten; everything was much bigger than it needed to
be. She was ambitious, gregarious, and obnoxious all
rolled into one, and there was no way I wanted to have
dinner with her.

"Pretend you don't see her," I said, looking in the
opposite direction. But it was too late. We ordered our
pizza and had a few moments of small talk before
Melanie brought up procedures, patients, exams, and Dr.
Hazelman. I wasn't in the mood to talk about the hospital and was hoping William wasn't either.

"Can you believe everything we're doing?" Melanie
asked. "Some days it's staggering, but always accompa-
nied by this adrenaline rush. Do you find that to be
true?"

"It's an adrenaline rush times ten," William said,
throwing all ten fingers in the air for exaggeration. I shot
him a glance, and he smiled.

"I'm just amazed at what we're learning and how I'm
processing all of it, aren't you?" I nodded again.

"I'm amazed at how smart I really am," William said. I
shot him another look, hoping to shut him down, but
there was no way; he was having too much fun.

"Can I ask you something, Nathan?" Melanie asked.

"Sure."

"Do you think you'll ever make it through a procedure without breaking down in some way?" She laughed so hard I could see a dull silver filling in the back of her mouth. I felt the hairs stand up on the back of my neck. Our pizzas arrived and to my relief, William jumped in and changed the subject. He led the rest of the dinner conversation with a story about his grandmother, who served as a nurse during World War II, and how she amputated a soldier's leg when no doctors could be found. The amputation lasted till we got our check.

"Thanks for saving me back there with Melanie," I said, on our walk home.

"She's harmless. Bags of wind usually are." I started laughing, recalling William's story about his grandmother.

"I didn't know your grandmother was a nurse during World War II," I said.

"That's because she was a laundry woman in Philadelphia." I stopped and looked at him. "Melanie's not the only bag of wind you know. You need a good lie . . . I'm your man." I walked into my apartment and lay down on the sofa, replaying what Melanie had said in my mind.

When my father and I would fish together on Saturday mornings he would sometimes get aggravated with me. I'd lean over the boat and play in the water, slapping the surface till it made a cracking sound. Dad, still speaking in whispers, although I'd been noisy enough to scare any fish within a ten-mile radius, would say, "Nathan, you either need to fish or cut bait." I knew I had to do that now. I either had to stay and finish what I'd started or get out of medical school and move on.

## FOUR

No trumpets sound when the important decisions of our life are
made. Destiny is made known silently.
—Agnes de Mille

I picked a cake up at the supermarket after work the next
day. I'd ordered it that morning, a white cake with white
frosting, yellow lilies, and *Happy Birthday Gramma* written
across the top. Before my mother died, my grandmother
had moved in to help with her care. She had been saving
up for a cruise ever since my grandfather passed away
and was planning to go with her sister when my mother
became ill. She gave her ticket to another sister in
Phoenix instead. "I don't want strangers taking care of
Maggie," she told my father. "She's my daughter. When
you're not home, I'll take care of her." She had taken care
of my family ever since.

Lorraine, Gramma's best friend who lived up the
street, met me at the door. She was wearing a bright
multicolored nylon sweat suit, sequined with toucans
and other tropical birds, and pink sneakers. She had
struck up a friendship with Gramma when she'd moved

in with us. They had soon become the best of friends, although they had only one thing in common: baseball.

Lorraine's team was the Atlanta Braves, although no one could understand why when there were teams that played much farther north and closer to home. Gramma's favorite was always the underdog—that, or any team opposing the Braves. Being in a room with Gramma and Lorraine while baseball was on was like watching a sitcom. If Rachel or I was there, Gramma would warn Lorraine not to swear in front of us. Lorraine would oblige until one of her men was called out, then she couldn't help herself. She'd start spewing words that would make Gramma explode.

"Don't swear in front of my grandchildren, Lorraine!" But Lorraine would be oblivious, letting loose on the umpires.

"Lorraine! The kids are in the room!" Gramma would shout.

At that, Lorraine would snap to attention and look at us, giving a sheepish grin. "Sorry, dolls," she'd say. We'd laugh and leave the room. And as soon as we did, we'd hear Lorraine screaming at the set again.

Lorraine kissed my cheek and eyed the big white box I was carrying in my arms.

"Why did you spend good money on a cake, Nathan?" Gramma asked, when I came into her kitchen. My sister Rachel was already home from college.

"Gramma, this is number seventy-seven. I think I can afford the fifteen dollars for a cake. It breaks down to just pennies per year." A familiar smell wafted from the kitchen. "Is that lasagna?" My grandmother jumped to her feet, remembering something.

"Yes it is, and I better put a pan under it before the cheese melts over the side and sticks to the bottom of the oven." She made her way to the kitchen, her hip still stiff from a recent replacement.

"But lasagna's Nathan's favorite," Rachel said, "not yours. Shouldn't we be having something you like for your birthday?"

"I've been eating all my life," she said, sliding a flat pan beneath the heaping pan of lasagna. "I've had lots of opportunities to eat my favorites, but I doubt either of you have had a decent meal in weeks." She was right about that. I'd usually just grab something on the run. I began to set the table for dinner.

"Don't bother with that now. You two sit down," Gramma said to Rachel and me. "I want to tell you something." There was a glimmer in her eyes, a sparkle that told me she was up to something. She and Lorraine sat on the opposite side of the table, smiling.

"I'm setting your father up." Gramma slapped the table and laughed. "But the best part is he doesn't have any idea what I'm up to." Grandma slapped the table again, proud of her covert operation.

"Who is she?" I asked, curious.

She leaned toward us, whispering, as if the room were bugged. "Her name is Lydia, and I met her at church. She has three grown children and a grandchild. Her husband died five years ago. Well, one Sunday Lydia came in and sat beside me and we started talking and she's been sitting beside me every week. She's on one side and your dad is on the other. The only thing separating them is me. But not for long!"

"What's she like?" Rachel asked.

"She's a gem. So nice." Gramma faded for a moment, thinking. "Sometimes people aren't so kind after they lose a spouse; it's too easy to get bitter, but she's a kind person, and so is your father. I don't know, but it just seems to me that two people like that should at least know that someone else like them is out there somewhere."

"Is she pretty?" I asked.

"She is, but not as pretty as your mother." No one was ever as pretty as my mother. "So here's my plan," Gramma continued. "Lydia is in the habit of sitting in the same seat every week. Your father's in the habit of sitting in the same seat every week. I'm always taking up that middle seat between them, so I'm not going to show up one week! Then Lydia will ask where I'm at, your father will say I'm under the weather, and before we know it, wedding bells will finally ring around here." The timer on the oven buzzed, and she jumped to her feet.

"I'll get it," I said, opening the oven door.

"Don't either of you dare tell your father what I'm up to," she said, squawking like a nervous bird behind me. "For once I'd like to keep something to myself around here."

I knew I should have told Gramma about the doubts I was having about med school, but I didn't want to worry her. If I told her I was thinking of dropping out, she would have conjured up the worst-case scenarios. She'd seen one too many television news shows. "You know, Nathan," I imagined her saying. "A young woman dropped out of med school and was gunned down in a strip mall parking lot. If she hadn't dropped out of school, she wouldn't have gotten shot," or maybe, "A man was found living with the winos down on the docks. Turns out he dropped out of med school." It was better to wait and tell my family when they were together.

When my father walked through the front door, I could smell the familiar scent of the garage; the scents of fuel and grease always clung to his hair and skin until he showered. He'd been working at the same garage, City Auto Service, and for the same men, the Shaver brothers, since before I was born. Carl, Mike, and Ted Shaver had been faithful to my father during my mother's illness and death, even paying him for days he couldn't work. Over the years he had been as loyal to them. Just as he never considered dating a woman, I don't think he ever considered finding another place to work.

I did my best to keep the dinner conversation focused on Rachel and off my rotation. I teased her about not bringing home a boyfriend to meet the family.

"And where are all those women who aren't standing

in line to go out with you," she asked. "That's right. They're out with other men."

"It'd be nice if somebody around here dated," Gramma said, eyeballing my father, who wasn't paying attention to her.

After dinner, we sang "Happy Birthday" to my grandmother. It was a pitiful rendition, two baritones and an alto in desperate need of melody. Gramma blew out the candle, and I placed my present in front of her. "Nathan, you shouldn't have spent your money on me." I rolled my eyes and cut her a piece of cake. Truth was I didn't buy it; I'd made it with my father's tools. Gramma ripped the paper and removed a small wooden box with lilies painted on the side.

When Mom died, Gramma encouraged us to write letters to her on special occasions: her birthday, Christmas, Mother's Day, but sometimes even the most insignificant details of our lives inspired them. Over the years, she used one shoe box after another to store them in, scribbling *Letters to Maggie* on the side of each new box.

When I was nine I wrote:

*Dear Mom,*
*I've decided that my favorite snack is cheese. I loved E.T. and wish you could have seen it with me.*

*I love you*
*Nathan*

One letter after another filled the shoe boxes. So often over the years, I'd observed the special care my grandmother took with the letters, even reading them in the quiet of her room. The wooden box brought tears to her eyes as she ran her fingers over the words on top, *Letters to Maggie*. She raised the cover and pulled a single letter from the bottom of the box.

I had written it earlier in the day:

*Dear Mom,*
*Today is Gramma's 77th birthday. She cried when I gave her the present I made for her and then she cried again when she read this letter.*
*She loves you very much and so do I,*

*Nathan*

Gramma laughed, wiping her tears with a napkin, then swatted me for making her cry.

When Gramma started to clean up the table my father stopped her. "Nathan and I will get these," he told her. "You and Rachel go in the living room." Gramma picked up another plate.

"You always get them," she said. "I'll get them to-night. Go visit with the kids." But Dad took the plate from her hand and led her to the living room, sitting her down in a chair.

"You cook. I clean. That's been the deal for years now," he reminded her. I smiled, watching them. It was a scene that had played out hundreds of times in this house. I scraped the plates into the disposal and handed them to Dad to load in the dishwasher. "How's everything at the hospital?" he asked.

"Everything's great." He rearranged the plates to make more room in the rack.

"Now that that's out of the way," he said, taking the glasses from me, "how are things really going at the hospital?" He leaned against the counter, looked me in the eyes, and waited for my answer, an honest one.

"Did you ever think you should have done something else besides being a mechanic?" I asked.

He laughed and closed the dishwasher. "Every man thinks he should have done something else. Some days I'd have my head under the hood of a car and think of a hundred other things."

"Why didn't you do anything else, then?" He shrugged and started filling the sink with water and dish detergent.

"I don't know. There were times I wished I could have had enough business sense to own my own place, but I wouldn't have been good at that." He rinsed a pot and set it in the drainer before taking a scrubber to a pan burnt with sauce. "For whatever reason, I can take apart a car engine. I don't know why, except it's provided a way for me to take care of my family, it's given me steady customers for the last hundred or so years, and I like to think that maybe the elderly folks or single mothers that come into the shop know I'm not going to take advantage of them. Maybe I was put there for no other reason than to watch out for people like that."

As I was growing up, the phone rang often at our house for my father: an elderly woman's car wouldn't start or a single woman was broken down at the side of the road. Dad would load his tools in the back of his truck and let me ride alongside him as he went to fix the problem. Many times he bought parts out of his own pocket. He'd shut the hood, wipe his hands, and watch as the stranded motorist drove off before we headed back home. I'd climb in the truck and look at him, wondering what in the world those people would have done without him.

"And if I hadn't been a mechanic, I never would have met your mother, so I guess there's a reason for everything." He wrung out the dishcloth before wiping down the counters. "Do you want to be a mechanic?" he asked, smiling. I shook my head.

"I'm not so sure what I want to be anymore," I said. I waited for the lecture. I waited for the you've-got-to-be-kidding-me speech, followed by arms thrown in the air. But it never came. If he was displeased, or worse yet, disappointed, Dad never showed it. He kept any advice or words of frustration to himself.

"Everybody's meant to do something," he said, assuring me. "You'll know what you're supposed to do; a moment will come, and you'll know."

"I think that moment has come," I said, dreading what I was about to tell him. Dad turned off the lights in the kitchen and sat in his recliner. I sat on the sofa next to Rachel, hoping I'd gain some level of support from her. "I need to get going," I started.

My grandmother jumped up and headed for the kitchen. "I've got Tupperware full of food from this week." She exited through the dining room and brought back four Tupperware containers, stacking them on my lap. "This way I know you're eating something good."

"Um," I said. Any conversation that begins with "um" is always off to a roaring start. I cleared my throat and started again. "Um, one of the residents talked to me yesterday." All three of them looked at me; they could tell by my tone that what I was relaying wasn't good news. "He suggested it might be a good idea for me to shelve medical school—to take a break for a while."

"What sort of crazy is he?" my grandmother snapped.

"He's not crazy. He's the resident for my current rotation."

"Why did he say that?" my father asked. I shuffled on the sofa; the Tupperware began to topple at the movement.

"Because something's not clicking with me, Dad. I don't know what it is." The room was quiet, with the exception of the television news playing in the background. My grandmother looked at my father, who, much to my discomfort, had never taken his eyes off me.

"But you still want to pursue medicine, right," he asked.

"I don't think so." I sat holding the Tupperware, hoping I didn't sound as dumb as I looked.

"You need to tell that horrible doctor that he's making you think awful thoughts about yourself and making you all crazy in the head," my grandmother said. She nodded toward my father, as if he was supposed to take over from there.

"He said he thought I'd make a good physician, Gramma."

"So what's the problem?" My grandmother was beside herself and threw her hands in the air. "People go through life wondering what they're supposed to do when it's always right in front of them. They should do what they're good at."

"But I'm not good at this."

"Nonsense! You're good at it all," my grandmother said, throwing her hands up in the air again.

"So this doctor is suggesting that you get out of medicine and do what?" my father asked.

"I could do anything: research, work in a hospital lab, maybe some sort of administrative position." My father nodded but didn't say anything.

My grandmother slapped the armrests and rocked

back and forth in her recliner. Dad wasn't handling this the way she wanted. "You were meant to be a doctor," she said. "From the time you were a boy you were meant for this." They didn't say it, but I knew my family was disappointed—I'd gotten this far only to drop out. We all stared at the floor, wondering what to say.

"This is what I think," my father finally said. "I think you need to fulfill your duties through the holidays. With Thanksgiving and Christmas coming up it seems much of the staff would be on vacation, and they would appreciate any help they can get around the hospital. Hopefully, during that time, you'll be able to think and figure out what you want to do." I'd have till December 23 to figure things out, that's when the rotation ended and med students went on Christmas break.

On the drive home I felt relieved. At least everything was out in the open, and my father was right; I needed to finish the rotation. It was the right thing to do. But looking back, I know that if I had walked away at that time, if I had made the decision to move on to something else, that my life wouldn't have been shaken up and turned upside down and inside out. Like Dad said, there's a reason for everything.

## FIVE

We meet no ordinary people in our lives.
—C. S. Lewis

Meghan was up and out of bed before anyone else. She ran to the park and hovered around the massive oak tree, waiting. *She should be along soon,* Meghan thought. *Here she comes.* Meghan pretended to check her laces as the woman in the neon cap pushed a button on her stopwatch and took off. Meghan bolted upright and ran after her. The young woman's legs were longer than Meghan's, and her strides were fluid and graceful. But Meghan pushed hard, her pace gradually quickening.

The woman slowed to a jog and began walking up the hill on her way out of the park. Meghan shook out her arms and legs and walked along the lake before she finally fell to the ground, and rolled around in the grass, laughing. *I did it. I finally did it.*

. . .

Charlie snapped the television off when Meghan walked into the room dressed like a burly football player. It was the Halloween party at the hospital, and she was going to push Charlie in the parade of costumes. Charlie got down to business right away. "Did you run this morning?" Meghan nodded. "Was she there?" Meghan nodded again. "Did you beat her?" Meghan lowered her head. "Oh come on," Charlie said, disappointed. "You gotta beat her someday."

Meghan raised her head and smiled. "I did."

Charlie let out a whoop and pumped his arm in the air, as though Meghan had just scored a winning run. "I knew it'd happen someday. Next stop: the Olympics."

"How about, next stop: Halloween Party? Come on; get your costume on. Besides, I can't train for the Olympics while you're in this hospital bed. If you're going to coach me, you've got to be out in the field with me."

"I'm getting out of here just as fast as I can," he said, cracking his knuckles.

"Stop doing that," she said, leaving Leslie to help him with his costume. "Or you're going to have ape hands like all those wrestling freaks."

Meghan's family arrived early to help with the party; Luke was dressed like a fireman, and Olivia ran around the unit wearing red tights and leotard and a black hat with a piece of white rope bobbing from the top. Meghan found a wheelchair and pushed it back to Charlie's room, where she found him dressed as Charlie Chaplin, waiting for her. Leslie stood nearby, smiling, proud of her creation.

Leslie helped Charlie into the wheelchair, and Meghan pushed him to the pediatric unit, through the parade of costumes that filled the hallway. The staff clapped and cheered as the children, dressed like Disney characters, horror monsters, and superheroes, filed by. Med students had been volunteered to man the empty patient rooms as the children went from door to door yelling, "Trick or treat."

I was standing behind a door when I heard a loud knock. I opened it to find a small boy dressed as a fireman and a little girl with a rope sticking out of her hat. I tried to make out her costume.

"What are you today?"

"A firecracker," she said, beaming. Her mother sighed and nodded.

"I always thought firecrackers were loud and annoying, but now I know different because you're quiet and very pretty." She opened her mouth, embarrassed, and hugged her mother's waist. "What's your name?"

"Olivia." I put candy in her bag.

"Olivia sounds like the name of a princess. Are you a princess?"

Olivia shook her head and buried her face in her

mother's side. Her mother thanked me for the candy and pulled her daughter toward the next room. Olivia peeked up at me, smiling. "Hey, what's your name?" she yelled from down the hall.

"Nathan."

" 'Bye, Nathan," she said, reeling from her first crush.

How could I have known then that that little girl would remember my name? That simple act would confirm again that sometimes God uses the smallest of messengers to help get our attention.


The next morning I pulled a hooded sweatshirt over my head and slipped on a pair of sweatpants. I called William and asked if he wanted to go for a run. He didn't. William hated to run. I persisted, and he walked into my apartment wearing a pair of orange shorts over his sweatpants. I looked at him, wondering if it was a joke or not.

"What?" he asked. "Don't runners always wear shorts over their jogging pants?"

"I don't think so."

He looked down at himself. "I swear I saw this in a magazine on some big-name runner. Name some big-name runners, and I'll tell you if it was that guy or not."

I laughed and grabbed my keys. "No big-name runner would wear an outfit that looked like that."

William checked himself out before following me out the door. "Am I still like Shaft," he yelled down at me on the stairs.

"Even Shaft couldn't be cool in that outfit," I said, sliding behind the wheel of the truck.

We drove to the park and started our run. "Hold on, man," William said, pulling me back. "Don't go so fast. What's the point of running, anyway?" I looked at him and shook my head. He crouched to the ground and untied his shoe. "I need to fix my shoe. You go ahead and I'll catch up." I left him there, knowing William's run was over for the day.

I ran a few laps around the lake. I pushed myself hard until the sweat rolled down my back. Running had always been a good stress reliever for me, although recently it seemed as if nothing was relieving the stress anymore. I ran faster, wondering why I couldn't be more like my father. I'd been asking myself the same question ever since I was a child.

I remember writing a letter to my mom. I must have been about ten at the time:

Dear Mom,
When I grow up I hope I can be like Dad and even work in the garage with him. Sometimes he lets me play with the jacks and the lifts and I'm really good with them.

I love you,
Nathan

I laughed at the thought. Working in a garage would have been so much easier than going into medicine. People always said that I was like my father because I was quiet, but Dad's qualities ran much deeper than his silence.

Many times, I'd awaken in the night and see light coming from the living room. I'd creep there and find my father sitting alone, flipping through the family album, looking at pictures of my mother. From time to time, he would lean his head back against the sofa, his eyes closed. Watching him, I always imagined that he was entering a secret passageway, one that brought the moments captured in those pictures to life—those times with Mom that were so sweet, yet so painful to think about. Sometimes, I would tiptoe into the room and sit next to him on the sofa, but usually I would just go back to my bed without letting him know I was there. Somehow, even as a small boy, I recognized that those moments were sacred for him, special times he had carved out to be alone with my mother.

"God didn't take your mother," he'd always tell me, echoing what Mom had told me weeks before her death. "He received her. There's a difference." He had promised my mother that he would explain that to me until I finally understood.

One Saturday, Dad was working on Lorraine's car in our driveway when she made a comment about how God had taken my mother to Heaven. "He didn't take her," I said, protesting. "He received her." My father slid out from underneath the car and looked at me. On that day, he realized that I understood. And he was right. I knew that God wasn't striking people with disease; I knew He was loving. My mother had shown me that love before she died. And after her death, though my father wasn't as comfortable with words as she had been, he gave that love hands and feet and wings every day; but I never understood why she *had* to die.

"God loved your mother very much," he'd tell me, trying to comfort me after I'd awoken from a nightmare and gone into his room. As a boy, I had a recurring dream that he'd died, too. "He loved her so much that he stopped the pain she was in," my father explained. He'd lift the covers on his bed and let me crawl in next to him. "Go back to sleep," he'd say, kissing my head. I'd try, but often I'd lie awake, thinking about my mother: *If God knew she was going to be sick, why didn't He make her better? Why pray at all if people are just going to die anyway? Why do so many good people have to die?* And as many times as I'd ask those questions, I never found any answers. All I knew was that I would never be as strong as my father.

William stepped onto the path and broke my concentration. "Unless somebody's chasing you, there's no reason to run that fast," he said, stretching.

"Are you ready to break a sweat?" I asked.

"As long as it doesn't drip down into my shoes."

A female runner slowed down to pass us, turning back

to look at me. She stopped and walked up to us. "Is this official doctor stuff?" she said. I looked at her, and she smiled the prettiest smile I've ever seen. "We met a few days ago when you were walking in the clearly designated running side of the hallway." I remembered who she was; I just wasn't used to women coming up and starting a conversation with me. William picked up his legs and ran in place.

"I gotta keep moving," he said. "I'm losing my stride." He leaned toward me, and whispered, "Keep it together this time." William knew I was notorious for blowing it with women. It wasn't in my genes to be suave and cool. I watched him run off and nearly laughed. For somebody who was so agile on the basketball court, William was a lousy runner. I walked with my new friend around the lake.

"I'm Meghan Sullivan, by the way," she said, extending her hand.

"Nathan," I said.

Megan noticed William, who was no longer running but talking with two women on the other side of the lake. He met women everywhere he went, and they always loved him. "I think your friend has lost his stride," she said, watching William.

"No, I think he's definitely found it." She laughed, and I noticed how pretty she was, even early in the morning, without makeup. I put my hands in my pockets and thought about her name; it was so familiar. "Are you the Sullivan who's organizing the scholarship run at the hospital?" She turned toward me and her eyes lit up.

"Did you hear about it?"

"I signed up as a sponsor." I looked at her, remembering something. "Denise said you're one of the fastest runners in the state." She was embarrassed and didn't say anything. "She also said you were one of the heart patients."

"I like to think of myself as a close, personal friend of Dr. Goetz, not as a heart patient."

I smiled, wondering why anyone would want to be friends with Dr. Goetz. "Why are you such close friends with him?" I said, playing along.

"A ventricular septal defect that never closed." Hole in the heart. I looked at her, and she read my mind. "I don't know why I can run. Ever since I was a little girl, doctors said I'd live a normal life, but I'd just never be able to overexert myself."

"Doesn't running qualify as 'overexerting' yourself?" I asked, knowing the answer.

"Yes. Dr. Goetz said running would be out of the question."

"How about a dart? Would they have let you dart somewhere?" She grinned and suppressed a laugh.

"If it was a slow dart."

"Same with a dash?"

"A slow dash would be fine, but I could never make a mad dash anywhere." I laughed out loud, and Meghan joined me. She was attractive, athletic, and funny.

"Have you ever been concerned when you run?" I asked. She shook her head.

"My mind knows there's something wrong with my heart—I've seen the X rays; I know it's defective. But when I run, it's like my heart doesn't know it. It's as if I was created to do it. Do you know what I mean?"

"Yes," I said, unsure whether I believed that or not, because I couldn't imagine what I was created to do.

"If something happened, it'd just be part of the race. Like your job. You have great days when people are healed, but there are days when they're not, where nothing you do will make them better. You take the bad with the good but in the end, the good will always outweigh the bad." Again, I wasn't sure if I believed that or not. "What kind of doctor are you?" she asked.

"I'm not a doctor. I'm a third-year med student."

"Are you studying to be a cardiologist?" I told her I wasn't. "Why not? The heart's where all the action is. Without the heart nothing happens."

"That's exactly what they teach us in med school. They say, 'without the heart, everything goes splat.'" I made a nice wet sound for dramatic effect, and she laughed. I was on a roll.

"So what's it like being a med student?"

"Oh, it's as many cups of weak coffee you can stomach a day and so much more."

"So what you're saying is that with the urine samples, catheters, bedpans, and weak coffee . . . it's all glamour, right?"

"And all of it could be yours if you want to go to school for the rest of your life." Meghan was easy to talk to; for once I wasn't stumbling over my tongue. "What year are you?" I assumed she must be in her fourth year of college.

"I'm a freshman." I snapped my head and looked at her. I couldn't believe it. She seemed so much older than the other freshmen I knew from the university.

"I thought you were older," I said.

"I'm nineteen. I missed the cutoff day for kindergarten by one day." Still, I thought she was in her twenties.

"What are you studying?" I asked.

"Just the basics now because I'm not sure, but I think I'd like to teach."

"You want to be a gym teacher?" She bent over, laughing. "What? Is that not politically correct? Is it a recess facilitator?"

"People haven't called them gym teachers in years. I should have known it'd be some guy trapped inside a hospital drinking weak coffee."

"Now you see what all my loans are paying for."

"I want to teach high school and coach. Maybe teach social studies and health—" I stopped her there.

"I had health in eighth grade. Our textbook was called *Healthy Living and You*." She looked at me and stared. I held up my hands. "I'm telling you the truth . . . as best I can remember it. Mrs. Pringle taught the class and she stood about five-foot-five and weighed 180 on a thin day." Meghan put her face in her hands and shook her head back and forth. "We were taught healthy living by a woman named after a potato chip and shaped like a cookie."

"That was not her name!"

I held up a hand and crossed my heart with the other.

"I swear it was. And her husband's name was Lemmy. Lemmy Pringle. Do you think he got beat up as a kid?"

"Maybe Pringles' chips weren't around when he was a kid."

"It wouldn't matter. With a name like that you were just begging bullies for a beating." We both laughed, and I found myself not wanting the conversation to end. William bounded back down the hill toward me. I shook my head at the sight. I couldn't understand how someone dressed like that could attract not just one, but two women so early in the morning.

"I've got to get to the hospital," he said, breathing hard as if he'd been exercising all morning.

"Headed back into the world of glamour?" Meghan asked. I nodded and walked toward William.

"Yep. I hope we run into each other again, Miss Pringle." I walked up the hill and could hear her laughing. I couldn't remember having a better day at the park.

That afternoon Meghan stretched alongside her teammates on the track. Every day, she looked forward to practice, first because she loved it, but also because she loved her coach, Michele Norris. Michele had a way of coaching that brought the best out in her. Michele was thirtysomething and single, and the team loved teasing her about dating. It seemed they were always trying to set her up with an eligible uncle, cousin, brother, or even handyman. Michele knelt beside Meghan on the track. "Has Charlie told you to shave off another second?" she asked.

Meghan pulled her foot toward her, stretching her upper thigh. "No."

"What?" Michele said, feigning disbelief. "We've got a big meet here. He should have been demanding things days ago!" She gave Meghan's arm a playful squeeze and rallied her runners, instructing them to run warm-up laps for the day's meet.

When Meghan stood up, it felt as though her legs would buckle. She had been dragging ever since her morning run in the park, which was odd, because the run usually left her energized. She shook out her legs and rolled her neck from side to side. Once Meghan started running, the laps came easier. Running always made her feel better.

Meghan paced back and forth on the field, waiting for her race to be called. She looked up into the stands and waved at her family. Luke and Olivia were already on their feet waving with both hands.

Coach Norris put her hand on Meghan's back. "Ready?" Meghan nodded, keeping her head down. "Run it like you did on Friday and you'll pin another ribbon on Charlie." When her race was called, Meghan blended in with all of the other runners standing thirty-to-forty deep at the line, but when the gun fired she bolted to the front position. Jim Sullivan jumped to his feet, cheering her on. Luke and Olivia screamed, "Go, go, go, go," in rapid-fire succession. They watched her wend her way through the woods and disappear.

"Ten minutes in," Jim said, staring at his watch. "Ten-and-a-half minutes in," he said, thirty seconds later. "Eleven-oh-two now. Eleven-ten."

"Would you stop that babbling, Jim?" Allison said. "You're making me a nervous wreck over here." Jim tried to be more discreet but couldn't keep his eyes off the second hand.

"Eleven-forty-five," he said, whispering into Luke's ear. Allison shook her head. This was why she never watched sports with him at home; her nerves were always frazzled by the time the event was over. Jim spotted a head or two at the end of the meadow. He stood to

his feet and scanned the figures looking for Meghan—
*here she comes*—and then he looked down at his watch.
"Thirteen minutes," he said, excited.

"She's running faster than Friday, Allison." He realized
what he was doing and sat down in silence. Allison stood
and watched Meghan run toward the finish line, now
glancing at Jim for an update, but he remained quiet.

"Well, come on, Jim! What's her time?" Allison
shouted. Jim jumped to his feet and held his arm up so
that Allison could see his watch.

"Thirteen-forty," he said, his excitement building.
"She's never run this fast!" The stands began to shake as
people realized what was happening. Cheers erupted for
Meghan as she stretched across the finish line in first place.

"Fifteen-twenty!" Jim yelled, loud enough for everyone around him to hear. Allison shushed him, embarrassed that she was the only member of her family with
any civility. Meghan walked to the side of the track and
bent over, trying to catch her breath. Allison stood taller
to get a better look. *Stand up, baby,* she thought. *Straighten up.*
Meghan shook it off, straightened up, and walked toward
Coach Norris. "That's the way to run a race!" Michele
said, hugging her tight.

"Charlie better be happy with my time," Meghan said,
gasping. She was walking with Coach Norris toward the
rest of the team when she collapsed.

• • •

"I'm fine," Meghan said for the hundredth time. Dr. Goetz stuck a thermometer in her mouth and listened to her heart.

"Any chest pain or breathing problems?" She shook her head. "At your checkup six months ago you were nauseous and achy. Any of that now?"

"Just a little tired and my muscles hurt," she said, balancing the thermometer in her mouth. "I've had a headache, but it's no big deal."

Dr. Goetz took the thermometer out of her mouth, looking at it. "No fever," he said. He washed his hands and leaned against the sink, drying them. "If you had a fever, it would have made sense as to why you collapsed. Since there is no fever, I'm concerned you might have an arrhythmia." Meghan sighed. She was familiar with the term; it was an abnormal heartbeat pattern. "That would decrease how well your heart performs, causing you to faint."

"If I had an arrhythmia, I wouldn't have been able to race today," Meghan said.

"I'd like to put you on telemetry overnight so I can monitor the heart for any irregularities."

"Overnight," Meghan said, frustrated. "Why?"

"Well, given your history and the fact that you're my favorite girl, I'd feel a whole lot better if you were here so we could enjoy your company."

"What's telemetry?" Allison asked.

"We'll put several patches on her chest with wires—kind of like an EKG—and we'll be able to monitor the heartbeat day and night at a workstation where computers will warn us of any problems. I also want to do some blood work to rule out anything else," Dr. Goetz said.

Meghan groaned and flopped back on the examining table. "Not more blood! Every time I come here you people squeeze me for more blood."

When the X rays came back Dr. Goetz walked to Meghan's room and sat down. "No physical change in the heart," he said, holding the X rays to the light. "But we'll still keep you overnight to make sure there's no change in the heart pattern." Meghan shook her head; she was not happy.

"If I have to stay here, can I at least be in Charlie's room?"

"In pediatrics?" Dr. Goetz asked.

"If it's just one night, who cares," Meghan said. Dr. Goetz threw his arms up in the air, surrendering.

"All right! I'll do anything to get on your good side again." He walked into the hall, and Jim and Allison followed. "I honestly suspect she'll go home tomorrow," he said.

"I was so afraid it was going to be something serious," Jim said.

Dr. Goetz smiled. That's exactly what he'd been afraid of, too.

When I got to the hospital that afternoon I went to the lounge to hang my coat in my locker. It was jammed. I was used to this. While I jiggled the handle I banged on the bottom left side. It opened every time. A nurse stopped me on my way out. "Claudia in pediatrics has been buzzing for you." I walked back into the lounge and picked up the phone.

"You've got a little girlfriend up here in 1216 who's been asking about you," Claudia said. Besides Charlie, I didn't know any of the other patients in that unit.

"Who is it?"

"Obviously an admirer of yours. She's been asking about you since she got here an hour ago. If you have the time, you might want to swing by and say hello." I hung up the phone, grabbed a soda, and drank it on my way to pediatrics. I walked toward 1216 and recognized it as Charlie's room, but I knew he didn't have a sister. I stood outside the door and listened to the chatter of little voices.

"What's your favorite word," a small voice asked.

"Love," a woman said.

"What's your least favorite word?"

"Yuck." The little voice laughed.

"*I* always say yuck, Mommy."

"I know."

I peeked my head inside the room and saw Charlie and his mother and another woman I didn't know. "You came," the owner of the voice I'd been listening to shrieked, making me turn on my heels. It was Olivia.

"Well, of course I would come see Olivia." She was surprised I had remembered her name, and her mouth dropped open; she covered it with both hands. She pointed a small finger in my face.

"What's your favorite word?"

"Rhinoceros. I like how it rolls off the tongue." She giggled and shook her head.

"What's your least favorite word?"

"Egg," I said with a straight face. "Listen how ugly that sounds . . . egg. Blah. What an awful word, and when some people mispronounce it and say 'aygg,' it sounds even worse." Everyone laughed at my odd choice of words. "Is it your birthday, Charlie?"

"No. They're all with Meghan." I spun to look, and saw Meghan sitting on the bed, wearing a hospital gown. I was shocked.

"What's going on? What happened?" I attempted to read Meghan's chart, but Olivia was separating the fingers on my hand, swinging it from side to side.

"I'm actually in here because I don't have a fever, if you can believe that. Dr. Goetz is blowing it out of proportion and making me stay overnight in the hospital!" Olivia let go of my hand, and I was able to scan Meghan's chart. Dr. Goetz was observing her for a possible heart arrhythmia. "I'm being held against my will," Meghan said, watching my face.

"You collapsed?" I asked. She shrugged it off.

"I've been tired, that's all. I'll guarantee you I don't have what Dr. Goetz is checking me for."

"It's good that he's keeping you," I said. She rolled her eyes.

"You medical people are always so serious."

My beeper sounded, and I pressed the button to turn it off. There is a brief time in a med student's life when he feels important to have a beeper; but months into wearing it, he begins to dread the sound. I wanted to stay longer and talk with Meghan about what happened, but I couldn't. I walked toward the door.

"Will you come back later?" Charlie asked.

"Please," Olivia begged, holding my hand.

"Please," Meghan said, smiling. I walked out the door, realizing that smile was going to occupy my mind for the rest of the day.


Early in the evening I remembered I had promised Olivia I'd come back to see her, which meant I'd also see Meghan again. I stuck my head inside the door but could see that Charlie was sleeping. Meghan saw me and propped herself up, smiling. I pulled the divider curtain to keep the noise down for Charlie.

"So where is everybody?"

"They'll be back soon, but Olivia said she was going to die if she didn't eat. She's the drama queen of the family." She motioned for me to sit. "Could you stay till everybody gets back?" I looked at my watch to see what time it was and discovered it had stopped again. I shook my wrist and tapped the face till the second hand moved. I knew my pager would beep soon enough, but in the meantime I was more than happy to stay with Meghan.

"How are you feeling now?"

"I'm fine," she said. "I've been fine since I got here. Honestly, there's nothing wrong."

"Maybe so, but it's still good that Dr. Goetz . . ." She held up her hand, stopping me.

"I'm going to scream if one more of you people in white tells me that it's good that Dr. Goetz kept me overnight." I smiled and kept quiet.

"Meghan Sullivan sounds like a nice Irish name," I said, changing the subject.

"It used to be O'Sullivan, but a hundred years ago it wasn't good to be different, so they dropped the O. Of course there was barely any Irish left by the time my dad was born. We're mostly a Heinz 57 bunch now."

"None of the pure Irish left?"

"My great-grandfather was the last of the full breeds. He died before my father was born—cirrhosis of the liver. Same with my grandpa—he died before I was born of alcohol poisoning. My dad dried out before he married my mom. He always says that alcohol took him down, but a little five-foot-four-inch woman picked him up. He's helped out at AA for years."

Meghan and I talked about music—she loved Ella Fitzgerald. "What about all the hip acts that college kids love? Do you like any of them?"

"Like who?"

"I don't know all their names. Snoop Diggity Do and all those hip cats." Meghan shook her head and laughed. We talked about movies—she loved anything made before 1964. No wonder I thought she was older; she was an old soul in a young body.

"So what's your favorite movie?" I asked.

"*To Kill a Mockingbird*." My mother would have liked Meghan. She made my father and me watch *To Kill a Mockingbird* with her when I was in first grade. It must have been the twentieth time she'd seen it, but she still cried at the parts that made her weepy-eyed the first nineteen times.

"Does your family live here?" she asked.

"They're about an hour away. Well, my dad and grandmother are. My sister's in college."

"And your mom?" Meghan said, sitting up in the bed.

"She died when I was eight."

"Of what?"

"Cancer."

"So that's why you want to be a doctor."

"I think that's how it started."

"So I bet you're studying oncology." I smiled and she looked me over. "You don't look like an oncologist to me." I looked down at myself.

"What do I look like?"

"You remind me of Dr. Goetz." A gust of air rushed through my mouth, and I grabbed my head. "You do!" In my mind it wasn't a compliment to be compared with Dr. Goetz. "You must be studying pediatrics or something with kids, right?" I groaned inside, but knew I should just tell her the truth and be done with it.

"I'm actually finishing up this rotation and getting out of medical school."

"Why would you do that when you're so good at it?" I shook my head and smiled.

"I just don't think it's right for me."

"Well, I do," she said, surprising me. "Trust me, I know how doctors are around kids, and you're amazing. You've got my little sister right here." She held her pinky in my face. "Maybe it's not right for you now, but what about all those patients who are going to need a doctor like you? You need to finish up for them." She smiled and folded her hands. "I'm going to get off my soapbox now."

"Phew," I said, pretending to wipe sweat from my forehead.

"So what about you?" I asked. "What about all these scholarships people are buzzing about?" She smirked as if what she did wasn't all that remarkable. "So, what makes you so good?"

"I found someone to pace myself with," she said, sharing her secret. "You always have to run with someone better than you." For a brief moment I felt ashamed.

I had been pacing myself with Dr. Goetz, someone better than me, someone who could have made me better at what I do, but instead of choosing to run alongside him, I chose to take the easy way out and run away. In annoyance I tapped my watch again. "What's wrong with your watch?"

"It stops every now and then. All I have to do is tap it or snap the back where the battery is and it starts working again."

"Why don't you get a new one?"

"My mother wanted me to have this one. It works okay, I just need to coax it along every once in a while." Meghan watched me flip the watch over and thump the back of it.

"The watch isn't your mother, you know. It's just a reminder." Dr. Goetz entered the room, and I stood to leave.

"Are you moving in on another one of my best girls?" I backed away toward the door.

"Hey, I don't want no trouble. I didn't know she was your girl."

"Oh please," Meghan said. I smiled at her, anxious to leave the room now that Dr. Goetz had arrived. "Will you come by again?"

"There was a day when she used to ask me the same thing," Dr. Goetz said, lowering his head. I left the room, smiling. It was going to be a good day at the hospital, after all.

I couldn't make it to Charlie and Meghan's room until later in the evening. I wasn't sure if either one of them would be awake, but wanted to say good night if they were. I stuck my head inside, but both of them looked asleep. I started to close the door when I heard crying inside the room. I followed the sound to Meghan's bedside and sat down. "Are you in pain?" I said, whispering. She wiped her eyes and shook her head back and forth on the pillow. "What's wrong?"

"I'm just feeling sorry for myself." I sat down and she looked at me. "No offense, but I'm really sick of hospitals."

"I guess that's why it never makes any of the favorite vacation destination lists." She tried to smile, but wasn't in the mood. "You'll be out of here tomorrow."

"Tomorrow's too late." She was frustrated.

"For what?"

"There's an all-night charity dance at the university, and all my friends are there. Not that I'm some great dancer, but I'd rather be there than in here." I handed her a tissue and headed for the door.

I ran to the nurses' station and grabbed the boom box and set it on a table in the waiting room. I whispered my plan to the nurses, and one of them disconnected the wires from Meghan's chest. I pushed a wheelchair to Meghan's side. The nurse winked at me as she left the room; she would keep this a secret.

"What's that?" Meghan asked, looking at the wheelchair.

"What does it look like? It's a limo." I slipped a lab coat over her arms. "And this is the finest Italian silk dress that I could find in the storage closet." She smiled and sat in the chair. I grabbed her Ella Fitzgerald CD out of the portable CD player by her bedside and wheeled her to the waiting room, where I had moved all the chairs up against the wall. The nurses watched from the desk as I popped the CD into the boom box and pushed play. I offered her my hand. "Could I have this dance?" She was embarrassed but offered me her hand. I danced her around the room, dipping and spinning her till laughter replaced the tears. She twirled under my arm, and the nurses behind the desk laughed, watching us. At the end of "Mack the Knife" I dipped her so far that she reached back and touched the floor for dramatic effect.

In one of the letters she wrote during her last week, my mother said:

Dear Nathan,

I know you think it's gross now, but one day you'll see a young girl and your heart will skip a beat when she smiles at you. That was how I felt about your father the first time I saw him. Then the moment will come when you know you love her and if it's true love, the day will come when you realize that you can't live without her. People may try to tell you that love doesn't last these days but don't believe them. Love can and still does last, and I know the love you'll have will be the lasting kind.

I pulled Meghan up and she lost her footing. I held tighter to keep her from falling and looked in her eyes; at that moment my heart skipped a beat. She caught my gaze and grew still, looking at me. Embarrassed, she took her hands from my shoulders. I pushed the wheelchair toward her and knelt on one knee, placing each of her feet on a footrest. "Let's get you back to your room," I said. She sat down, looking up at me.

"Do I have to? Unless it's for medical reasons I'd like to stay here a while longer." I cleared my throat and sat down in one of the waiting room chairs.

"I don't think Dr. Goetz would have a problem with that." I fumbled for something to say.

"Olivia's never going to forgive me," she said. "I just danced with the man she loves." I smiled. "That was better than dancing with a bunch of college guys any day. Thank you."

"It was my pleasure." I smiled, and she looked at me. "Really." She looked down and fidgeted with the hospital gown on her lap. Now she was fumbling for something to say.

"You're a good doctor."

"I'm not a doctor," I said. "I told you, I'm barely a student anymore. How would you know anyway? I've never treated you."

"Because I've been around doctors all my life. I know the good ones from the bad ones. You're gifted at it." I shook my head. "You are! My dad says a gift is something that comes so naturally that you don't even realize you're good at it until somebody points it out." I cocked my head, and she laughed. "It's true. You're a natural at this, but you don't know it." I didn't say anything. She sighed and gave up. "Will you run in the scholarship race?"

"I'll run it with bells on," I said, meaning it.

I looked down and tapped the face of my watch. Meghan shook her head. "Life's zooming past you while you stand around tapping that watch." I wheeled her back to the room and helped her into bed. "Thank you, Nathan." I smiled and turned to look at Charlie, but he was asleep, so I slipped out the door, nodding for the nurse to attach the wires again. I'd be leaving for home soon, and I knew that I'd think of Meghan for the rest of the night.

Charlie stirred shortly after midnight. Rich was lying on a cot, but he sat up when he heard Charlie move. He stood and walked to his side.

"You okay?" Rich asked.

Charlie nodded. "Just tired."

"You get some sleep and when you wake up, we'll be here waiting," Rich told his son.

"Dad, I'm tired, but I'm not sleepy," Charlie said. "Tell me about Alaska."

Rich's first year in the Air Force was spent in Alaska,

and Charlie loved to hear his dad talk of hiking through the mountains and seeing moose and caribou and bears and of fishing for halibut and watching sea otters or walrus play near the boat. "I'll take you someday," Rich said, "and we'll fish and hike and watch the beluga whales come in every day to eat."

Five years into his marriage to Leslie, Rich had left the Air Force. He later claimed that leaving was the worst decision he ever made. He went from one failed job interview to another as Charlie's medical bills mounted. "All I do is go to an interview, then go home and wait," he said time and again in frustration. "While I'm waiting someone else is getting my job!" Charlie knew his parents weren't getting along, and their arguments scared him.

"Daddy, tell me about Alaska," Charlie said to his father during a particularly heated battle. Maybe, Charlie hoped, he'd get his father's mind off of money and bills.

"Charlie, we're never going to Alaska. We'll never be able to afford it, so stop asking about it." Rich regretted the words the moment he said them. He wanted to tell Charlie that he would take him to Alaska, but he knew it would be a lie. There was no way they could afford it; they'd never be able to afford it. Leslie's part-time job wasn't enough to live on, and the stress of wondering how they would pay their bills each month only worsened.

When the bill collectors started sending notices in the mail, Rich spiraled deeper into depression. He left when Charlie was five and Matthew was three. "But we'll be all right," Leslie pleaded as he packed his bags. Rich didn't believe her. It seemed clear to him that it would be better for his boys if he left. He'd send whatever he could, still do whatever it took to support them, but he had to go. He wasn't the father or the husband his family needed.

Five months into the separation he called Leslie. "I need to come home." She listened. "It's better to be poor with you and the boys than to be crazy without you." Rich finally found a steady job driving a truck for the package delivery service. But they were told they'd have to wait to get into a house since Rich didn't show a solid income for over a year.

"I'm sick of waiting! I can't stand this apartment," Rich said. He and Leslie were sitting on their bed with Matthew between them. Charlie listened at the doorway. "We're decent people, Leslie. We work hard. That should count for something."

"I'll do it with you, Daddy." Charlie jumped up on the bed and edged between his parents, bouncing Matthew up and down on the mattress. His mom and dad had separated before; Charlie would do anything to prevent it from happening again.

"Do what?" his father asked.

"I'll wait with you. I'd wait forever if we have to."

When Charlie was a baby, Rich and Leslie waited in agony as doctors diagnosed his condition, then they suffered the agonizing wait as Charlie went from one surgery to another. He had been healthy, with few problems for the last several years. Five months ago, Dr. Goetz admitted him to the hospital for tests when it was apparent his heart was malfunctioning.

Dr. Goetz sat in a chair opposite the couple, leaning toward them. "Charlie's heart has developed an irregular beat."

Leslie held tight to Rich's hand. "What does that mean?" Rich asked.

"It might just mean that we need to put him on medications."

"Or," Leslie asked, knowing there was more.

"Or it could mean that his heart is weakening," Dr. Goetz said.

Tears streamed down Leslie's face. When Rich and Leslie were ready, Dr. Goetz led Charlie into the room and told him a portion, but not all of what he'd told his parents. Charlie looked at his mother and could tell that she'd been crying.

He looked up at Dr. Goetz. "Have you treated a bunch of patients who have the same thing I have?"

"A whole bunch."

Charlie looked up at his parents and back at Dr. Goetz.

"What's the worst thing about the medications?"

"Waiting to see if they work," the doctor told him.

A broad smile crossed Charlie's face. "No problem! We're great waiters!"

Charlie had fallen asleep as Rich told him story after story of Alaska. He opened his eyes and saw Rich sitting at his side, reading. "Still waiting, Dad?" Charlie asked.

Rich looked up from his book and smiled. "I'd wait forever if I have to, Charlie."

As promised, Dr. Goetz released Meghan in the morning. "No arrhythmia," he said, examining her. "But I want you to go home and rest for a few days till these flulike symptoms you have work themselves out." Meghan opened her mouth to protest but Dr. Goetz grabbed each side of her face. "No running. None."

"For how long?"

"A week."

"What! I'm better. You said so yourself."

"No, I said you don't have an arrhythmia, but you still collapsed from something, so no running. I hope this is the last I see of both of you for a while."

"Am I getting out, too?" Charlie asked.

Dr. Goetz pointed to the door. "Get out! Leave! Begone." Charlie threw the blankets off and swung his feet to the floor. "It's a good thing I don't take your excitement to get away from me personally, Charlie." Leslie laughed and helped Charlie gather his clothes. Allison wrapped the cord around Meghan's CD player and stuck it in a canvas bag.

Meghan hugged Dr. Goetz. "Don't take it personally, Dr. Goetz." He stood at the door to leave.

"I won't. But I will take it personally if I don't get a moonlight dance."

Meghan looked at him, shocked. "Who told you?"

Dr. Goetz smiled and slipped out the door. "I've got eyes and ears all over this place."

Meghan ran to the door and yelled down the hall toward him. "Big-mouth nurses."

## SIX

The supreme happiness in life is the conviction that we are loved.

—Victor Hugo

Early that morning, before most people had even eaten breakfast, I had already been vomited on in the ER. I changed into dry slacks (opting to throw away my soggy khakis) and made my way back to the ER for another full day of stress when I saw both Meghan and Charlie at the ER desk. Charlie saw me first. "We're getting out today," he said, excited to be going home. Meghan smiled.

"We wanted to let you know," she said. "I mean, we wanted to let you know that we wouldn't be upstairs in case . . ." She tried to find the right words. I let her squirm and smiled as she groped for a way to tell me she was leaving and that she'd like to see me again. "You know . . . in case anything medically comes up, and you need to reach us." Charlie gave her a confused look that nearly made me laugh. He had no idea what she was doing.

"Okay," I said. "If there are any charts or graphs or

X rays that I need to discuss with either one of you, I'll be sure to contact you at your respective homes." Charlie looked at me and scrunched up his face.

"I'm sure medical records has each of our home numbers," Meghan said, grinning. I watched as she walked with Charlie down the hall and realized I didn't care what happened for the rest of the day.

Meghan lay propped up on her living room sofa, resting. Two days of practice had come and gone, and she was unable to run in the meet scheduled for that night. She was getting restless. She hadn't gotten any more sponsors for the scholarship run, and that made her even more frustrated. "For the last time, you're not going," Allison said.

"Mom, it won't even take any energy. All I have to do is drive from place to place and ask people if they want to sponsor me in the run." Allison folded the basket of towels and shook her head.

"Dr. Goetz said rest, Meghan."

"I've missed two days of practice. All I've been doing is lying here. Who's going to sponsor a runner who doesn't run?"

Allison slipped into the kitchen and retrieved the phone book from a drawer. She picked up the telephone and plopped the phone and the book in Meghan's lap. "Let your fingers do the running for you."

Meghan stared at the phone book, then up at her mother. "You're no help at all." But she flipped to the yellow pages anyway and started with the A's. *Accountants and Attorneys*, she thought. *Maybe this won't be so hard.* She picked up the phone and made her first pitch.

"Hello, I'm organizing a scholarship run for heart patients. Would your company be interested in sponsoring me?" They weren't. Meghan hung up the phone, disappointed. *The least they could have done was listen to my pitch.* But come to think of it, she didn't have a pitch. She thought for a moment before dialing the next number. "Hello, I'm running to raise money for heart patients and am looking for people to sponsor me." The person on the other end of the line hurried her off the phone. Meghan hung up in frustration. This wasn't easy; it was annoying.

She made several more calls without sparking even a hint of interest. On her tenth try to an attorney's office, she got a nibble. "Layton and Associates," the woman said, answering the phone. "This is Jodie." Meghan threw her pitch again. Jodie Gavin had been working for Robert Layton for five years. She started in college, working afternoons and through summer vacations, before going full-time after graduation three years ago. Jodie never bothered Robert with unsolicited calls, but this one was different; the young woman on the other end of the line sounded so sincere. There was something in her voice that made Jodie want to help.

Meghan heard the phone click.

"Robert Layton," a man on the other end said. Meghan was startled at the sound of his voice. She'd never actually gotten past the secretary before. She stumbled as she made her appeal. "Who's running?" Robert asked. After so many rejections, Meghan hadn't expected questions.

"Uh, I am, and some of the staff and doctors from the hospital." Robert asked a few other questions, which, to Meghan's surprise, she answered with confidence. Her nerves were gone.

"Can you put me down for five hundred dollars?" Jodie smiled and closed Robert's door. Meghan's jaw dropped. She scribbled down Robert's information and gave him her name and phone number should he have any other questions. She hung up the phone and kicked the blanket off her legs. "Mom! You're never going to believe this!"

I called Meghan the next day and we made plans to get together Saturday after my rounds. When Saturday came I had no idea what Meghan and I would do that evening.

On my lunch break I decided to make a quick trip to Hope's room. When I saw her, I knew she wasn't herself that day: her face was drawn, and her upbeat disposition was gone. I sat down on the side of her bed and smiled. When she saw me a small tear ran down her cheek. She reached her arms for me, and I leaned down and hugged her.

"Is something wrong, Hope?" I whispered, wiping the tears from her face. "Do you need Dr. Goetz?"

She shook her head, resting it against my chest. "I'm sad, Dr. Andrews," she said. I smiled; no matter what I did or said, nothing would convince Hope that I wasn't a doctor. I pulled her from me so I could see her face.

"Why are you sad?"

"Because a little boy died for me." A stream of tears covered her face, and I grabbed a tissue next to her bed. "A little kid died, and that makes me so sad." I wiped her tears and hugged her again. "I can't ever say thank you," she managed to squeak between sobs.

"You say thank you every day," I said, stroking the back of her hair. She looked up at me.

"How?"

"You open your eyes and you breathe."

"But that's not saying thank you," she said.

"It's the greatest thanks you could ever give, Hope, because every day when you open your eyes, it means you're still here."

"But I don't know why I'm here and he isn't." I helped her lie back on her pillow and held on to her hand.

"He knows," I said, patting her hand. "He knows everything now, and I just know that he's so happy he could help you." She was quiet for a moment.

"Are his mommy and daddy still sad?"

"Yes," I said. "There will always be a part of them that will be sad because when someone we love dies, it's like a wound that will never fully heal. It gets better as time passes, but the wound just never heals up completely. Do you know what I mean?" Hope nodded, drawing a Pooh bear close to her. "But even though his parents are sad, they're so happy to know that there's a child somewhere in a hospital who is hugging a little Pooh bear today." Hope hugged Pooh tighter and kissed the end of his soft, black nose.

"How did they know to help me?" she whispered.

"Because they're people with a lot of love in their hearts. They didn't know who you were; they just knew that somewhere there was a child who was sick, and they wanted to help."

"Even though they were sad?"

"Right in the middle of their sadness, they knew that somebody needed help."

"And that was me."

"That was you," I said, pulling the sheets around her and Pooh. She motioned for me to come closer, as if she was going to tell me a secret. I leaned down and she wrapped her little arms around my neck, kissing my cheek.

"I love you, Dr. Andrews," she said, giggling. For a moment, I couldn't imagine the possibility of not working with children like Hope again. I patted her arm as her mother returned to the room, holding a cup of coffee and a stack of children's books and toys, anything she could find to help bring a smile to Hope's face. She saw that Hope was laughing again, and she looked at me, wondering what I had done to her child.

I wandered down to the cafeteria for a large cup of coffee and a sandwich for lunch, but maintenance had closed it off—a pipe had burst, flooding much of the kitchen floor. I walked across the street to Macbeth's, and for the first time ever I saw Dr. Goetz outside of the hospital. I didn't realize the chief of cardiology would set foot in a place like Macbeth's. I avoided eye contact, hoping he wouldn't see me, but I heard him say hello. I waved, acting as if I hadn't seen him there, and made my way to his table. "Have a seat," he said. I slid into a chair, uncomfortable to be sitting with him.

"How's the rotation going?" *He obviously hasn't heard*, I thought. I assumed that all the doctors knew which medical students were crashing and burning.

"I love meeting new patients," I said, avoiding the question.

"I can see that. Hope is impressed. That's not easy to do." I took a sip of coffee and shook my head.

"I don't know how you can keep yourself from not getting attached to kids like her and Charlie and Meghan."

"Who said I'm not attached?" He wiped his hands on a napkin. "I held Meghan when she was just a few days old. I can't tell you how old that makes me feel. Her parents would take her to their family doctor, but they'd always bring her to me afterward, concerned about a diagnosis, or the use of certain medications. It got to the point where they were bringing her to me first whenever something was wrong." I couldn't imagine any other chief of cardiology seeing a patient on those terms.

"Why didn't you just tell them that you weren't their family physician?" He took the lid off a black coffee and swirled it round in the cup before taking a long drink.

"I don't know, but for whatever reason, when Meghan looked up at me with those huge blue eyes . . . I just knew that I needed to be her doctor. There's something about children who have a heart condition. They perceive life differently than the rest of us. They listen with the heart. They see things through the eyes of the heart. When a child sits in my office and looks at me, I know he or she sees right past the degrees and awards on the wall. They see me, and that's a terrifying thought." I never knew Dr. Goetz had a sense of humor.

"Do you remember all your patients from over the years?"

"I don't think I could place all the adults, but I remember the children." He was quiet. "I remember all of them." I knew he was talking about the ones he couldn't help. "I can see the picture of so many children in my mind, but they all have a big question mark stamped on them. Why did that child have heart disease? Why didn't he have a strong heart like other children? I lost a four-year-old two weeks after a transplant last year and her face will pop into my mind and I just can't explain why she's not running across a playground today." For the first time since I met him I realized that I liked Dr. Goetz. He didn't think he was superior in any way; he was more in touch with the fact that he was human than I was at the time.

"Did you ever want out?"

He leaned back and smiled. "I got out."

"When?"

"Eighteen years ago. I was out for six years." I couldn't believe that Dr. Crawford Goetz would ever walk away from medicine—from day one I just knew he had to have been a gunner in med school.

"Why did you leave?"

"I couldn't take the sadness anymore. Couldn't deal with the sickness. I was going home to my family depressed every day. I had taken my limit of people dying, so I took a job in landscaping. It had nothing to do with medicine. I could go out each day and break my back but never worry about another patient dying under my care."

"What brought you back?"

"The very thing that drove me away."

I don't know if Dr. Goetz said the things he did because he knew I was leaving med school or if he was just showing a student that even doctors walk through dark days, sometimes walking through years of darkness before finding their way back.

I left the restaurant and walked back to the hospital, thinking about my conversation with Dr. Goetz and about Hope and Charlie and so many of the kids in the pediatric unit. How could I live my life running from what scared me, when children were facing their fears head-on every day? I decided to take the coward's way out and think about that tomorrow.

I left the hospital at five that afternoon. I was picking Meghan up at six. I called earlier in the day to make sure she was feeling up to it, and she assured me she was, saying she was tired of resting when there was no reason to rest in the first place.

"When's the last time you went out on a date?" William asked, amused.

"I don't remember. All I know is none of the last ones went all that well, so I don't want to do what I did with them."

"What'd you do with them?"

"I took the last two girls to a museum."

William looked at me and shook his head. "You mean fossils?"

"I don't remember."

"Take her someplace nice to eat and try to charm her,"

he said, entering a patient's room. Then he stuck his head out the door. "If you can do that without fossils," he yelled after me.

I drove home, wondering how I would charm Meghan. I wasn't very good in that department, not at all like William. A thought occurred to me, and I opened the phone book. I had heard about a small theater in the next town over that played independent and classic films. I called them, and they were showing *The Philadelphia Story* with Katharine Hepburn. Perfect.

Olivia opened the door and smiled. "Are you and Meghan going out?" she asked. I nodded. Meghan put her hands on Olivia's shoulders, pulling her away from the door. To this day, I remember what Meghan was wearing that night: jeans and a dark brown pullover cable-knit sweater that looked stunning on her. Olivia dragged her father to the door.

"So you're the man who's stolen my little girl's heart," he said, swaying Olivia back and forth on top of his feet.

"Daddy, don't embarrass me," Olivia said.

"You can expect something a hundred times worse than this about ten years from now," Jim said. I liked Jim Sullivan. He reminded me of my father: No one was getting to his daughters without going through him first. I talked with him and Allison for a few minutes, long enough for them to discover my age, family background, future plans, and social security number, before I helped Meghan into my truck.

"Sorry about that," she said, as I climbed in. "It's easier to break into the Pentagon than it is to date one of Jim Sullivan's daughters."

I wanted to take Meghan to the Italian restaurant in town, one that made each course a meal in itself, but she wasn't interested.

"Oh, why don't we go to Macbeth's or some place where it's not so stuffy?" I knew then that my grandmother would love Meghan. I drove to Chuck's. "What's this?" Meghan asked.

"This is the best cheeseburger and shake in America," I said, pointing to the half-blown neon sign above the entrance. Meghan read the sign and laughed: THE BEST CHEESEBURGER AND SHAKE IN AMERICA.

I can't remember all we talked about that night. All I know is that it was effortless with Meghan. She was lovely and bright, and I couldn't help but think she was perfect . . . for me.

Dear Nathan,
You won't find a perfect person to love, so please don't think you will. But you will find someone who is perfect for you. She won't be everything you ever dreamed of. She will be more. So give her only your best—your heart, and all the love in the world!

Mom

I refrained from holding Meghan's hand during the movie. I didn't even put my arm around her; it was, after all, our first date, and I've always been chicken, to say the least, so the decision not to do anything was easy for me. The temperature had dropped from the time I had picked Meghan up, colder than most Novembers in recent years, so after the movie I wrapped my jacket around her and helped her to the truck. I drove her home and scurried her to the front door, lowering my head to avoid the high wind. She got her key out and turned to look at me, shivering. "Keep my jacket," I said. "I'll get it some other time." I didn't know what to do, so I smiled and turned to leave. "I'll call you," I said.

"You can kiss me if you want." I turned back around, put my hands under my arms and looked at her. "I mean, it's okay, if that's what you were thinking. But if it's not what you were thinking, then I've just really embarrassed myself and . . ."

I grabbed her and kissed her and forgot about the cold and the wind and the fact that I had to get up at five o'clock in the morning.


Days later, I went to one of Meghan's cross-country meets and sat fourth bleacher up, by the "foghorn man," next to Olivia. Meghan looked up from the field and smiled at us. The air was crisp, and she was wearing spandex pants and a long-sleeved shirt with the university's name printed on the front. I zipped up my jacket and waited for her race to be called. Jim bolted out of his seat the second the gun went off for Meghan's first race. He pumped his hand in the air, screaming, "*Go, baby; go, baby; go, baby*," as Meghan blazed through the woods and across the countryside. Allison cowered in embarrassment, and I laughed. I had a feeling this was routine for them. Meghan was unbelievable; too fast for the competitors. She crossed the finish line in first place, and Jim pounded my back, shaking my shoulders.

I helped Meghan gather her things and walked her to my truck. We hadn't talked about her scholarship offers since her overnight stay in the hospital, but after I saw her run again I just had to bring it up. "When are you going to visit Stanford and Georgetown?" She sighed, leaning her head on the back of the seat.

"I have no idea. I don't know what to do anymore because I really love my coach here, I love the university." She grabbed my hand and smiled. "I love everything the city has to offer."

"But you can't stay here." She turned her head to look out the window. I pulled her shoulders around to face me. "When you run . . . it's one of the most unbelievable things I've ever seen. You're a star, Meghan. You were meant to shine. Those schools have the best running programs in the nation." She wasn't responding. "That has to be important for you. Running has got to be one of your dreams, right?"

"Sure, but I've got more dreams than that," she said.

"Like what?"

"I want the scholarship run to help put kids through college."

I nodded. "And you can work on that while you're at either school."

"I want to help change my small part of the world."

I nodded again and smiled. "You've already done that. What else?"

"I want to fall in love."

"I'm sure you will," I said. She looked at me and squeezed my hand.

"I'm sure I already have."

I should have told Meghan then and there that I loved her, but I didn't. I don't know why. I guess I just assumed there would be plenty of time left for me to do that.


Meghan and I were supposed to go out the next day, but she was tired and sore and had a headache that was keeping her in bed. I could tell by her voice that she didn't feel well.

"Whatever you do, don't tell Dr. Goetz," she said on the phone. "He'll throw me in a hospital bed and strap me down for a week." We rescheduled for the next day.

When I picked her up, she looked great. She didn't tell me that she felt lousy and that none of her symptoms had gone away.

I drove her out of the city and toward my hometown. I drove through town and up the road that led to the hillside where my grandparents once lived. I hadn't been on the road in years and had forgotten how windy it was. We made it to the top and I opened the door for Meghan. The November wind whipped through her hair, and she wrapped her coat around her; it was much colder on top. "What an incredible spot," she said.

I hadn't stood on top of this hill with another woman since my mother died. I watched as Meghan looked over the top of the ridge into the valley below. Her hair kept blowing in her eyes, and she tried in vain to keep it out of her face. She pulled it back and held it away with her hand; she had high cheekbones but the most delicate features. She was beautiful. The wind blew her coat open and she screamed, wrapping it around her again as she ran into me, burying her head in my chest. She wrapped her arms around me, and I smelled her perfume. Thanksgiving was just over three weeks away, then Christmas would be upon us before we knew it; and although I had no idea what I would do once my rotation was over, I knew that life didn't get much better than this.

## SEVEN

The best and most beautiful things in the world cannot be seen
or even touched. They must be felt with the heart.
—Helen Keller

Meghan grabbed two ibuprofen out of the bathroom
cupboard and poured herself a glass of water in the
kitchen. The two ibuprofen she'd taken earlier hadn't
touched her headache, and she didn't want to be sick on
Thanksgiving. She peeled potatoes and put them on the
stove to boil. "Are these the last things that need to be
done?"

"That's it," Allison said.

"Let me peel them," Michele said, sliding in next to
Meghan at the sink.

"You're our guest today," Allison said. "You're not
supposed to work." She opened a drawer and pulled out
a tablecloth with fat turkeys all over it. "Here you go,"
she said to Michele. "If you want, you can set the table."

Meghan caught a glimpse of the tablecloth. "No,
Mom. Please don't use that. The Pilgrims had better table-
cloths than that thing."

Michele snapped the tablecloth in the air. "Do you normally line the turkeys up across like this?" Michele asked.

"Just make sure the fat one rests right in the center," Allison said, pulling the cloth over the table with the finesse of a fine artist.

Jim sliced the turkey and set it in the middle of the table. "I already know what I'm thankful for," Olivia said. Every year the Sullivans went around the table and said what they were thankful for, it was a tradition Allison started when Meghan was a baby. Jim set a thick slice of breast meat on Olivia's plate.

"All right," he said. "Olivia's going to start us off this year."

"I'm thankful for this," she said, pointing to the turkey on her plate. Luke was thankful for the snow that would soon be on its way, which meant early school dismissals. Allison's eyes misted over when she said she was thankful that her husband and her children were all in good health.

"Mom, you cry every year," Luke said, embarrassed.

"What are you thankful for, Daddy?" Olivia asked.

"That you're all right here at this table," Jim said.

They turned to look at Michele, who was busy filling her plate. She set her napkin in her lap and realized that everyone was looking at her. "You don't have to participate," Jim said, giving her an out.

"That's okay. I know exactly what I'm grateful for. My

father said there wouldn't be any money in teaching, that the hours would be long, and in the end I wouldn't be fulfilled. Well, the way I see it, one out of three isn't bad! My job is fulfilling. I love to teach, I love to coach, and I love the girls. And as an extra bonus I get to meet great people who open their homes to me on Thanksgiving."

Allison's eyes were tearing up again. "I bet your father is proud," she said, blowing her nose. "I bet he's so, so proud."

"All right, Meg," Jim said. "We're ready to eat. What are you grateful for this year?"

"What we have together," Meghan said. "Not everybody has what we have and we have it year-round, not just one day a year."

Allison's eyes were streaming by then. "For heaven's sake, Allison," Jim roared. "Go get a towel and mop yourself up so we can eat." Allison snorted through her nose and cried harder.

I picked Meghan up after my rounds ended. My grandmother had called me twice at the hospital to confirm that Meghan was still coming to Thanksgiving dinner. I opened the door to my father's house and Gramma and Rachel were practically sitting on the doorknob, waiting for us. I sighed and gave them a look, hoping they'd get the hint and back off. They didn't. I tried to lead Meghan into the house, but Gramma stopped her, taking her coat.

"My! What a pretty coat," she said. "Is that wool?" Meghan nodded. "I love wool. It's so warm, isn't it?" I smiled at Gramma's attempt at small talk. Rachel led Meghan to the sofa. I don't know why I'm always amazed at the information women are able to pump out of someone in five minutes or less, but watching the process in action always left me in awe. Meghan smiled, but never managed to get out much more than uh-huh or hmm during the grueling interrogation. It didn't matter though. Gramma had gathered enough information to base her opinion.

"She's so sweet," she whispered on her way into the kitchen.

Whatever nerves I had about Meghan meeting my family disappeared at the dinner table. In William's words, she was charming, and her laugh was infectious, even causing Dad to laugh out loud. She somehow managed to choke down her second Thanksgiving meal of the day, mmming and ohhing after each new thing she tasted.

When I stood to take Meghan home, Gramma jumped up and hugged her, asking her to come back soon. I walked Meghan to the front door of her house and noticed she looked tired.

"It's probably all the food I've eaten today," she said, laughing. "I'll sleep it off and feel great in the morning. You are coming over tomorrow, right?"

"Yes."

"And the next day?"

"Yes."

"And the day after that?" She smiled and my heart skipped a beat again. "Happy Thanksgiving," she said, leaning in to kiss me.

Happy Thanksgiving indeed!

I walked back into my father's house, and Gramma was asleep in her chair. Dad was still watching football. I noticed that Rachel wasn't in the room and assumed she was getting ready for bed.

"Meghan's nice," Dad said. I sat down on the sofa, watching the game. I always loved talking to my dad but when it came to talking about girls and dating, I just froze, not knowing what to say anymore. "What's her family like?"

"They're great," I said. "Really nice people." Dad looked over at me and knew I was squirming.

"She's really pretty," he said. I nodded. "Did you kiss her good night?"

"I'm trying to watch the game here, Dad," I said. He grinned, and I knew he was trying to get at me. He stood and grabbed his coat out of the closet. "Did you need something?" I asked. "I could have gotten it when I was out."

"I'll just be out for a while," he said, keeping his voice down.

"I can go get something for you, Dad."

"I'm just going out for coffee." Gramma snapped to attention in her chair. Dad's shoulders fell, and he rolled his eyes. She still had ears like a bat.

"Where are you having coffee?" she asked, curious.

"Over at Lydia's house," Dad said, pulling on his gloves before escaping out the door. Gramma threw her arms over her head and kicked her feet in the air, whooping in celebration.

"And it only took fifteen years!"

I went to find Rachel to tell her one of Gramma's ploys had finally worked. I saw her in Gramma's room, looking through the letters we had written to our mother.

I had always thought that Mom's death was gentler on Rachel than it was on the rest of us. She had no clear memories of Mom; all she had was what we told her along with the photo albums, the locket, and letters. I sat beside her on the floor and filed through the notes written with colorful markers, crayons, pencils, or ballpoint pens. Pictures of stick people or animals were often scribbled on the pages to help illustrate the letter.

I wrote this letter on what would have been Mom's thirty-fifth birthday:

Dear Mom,
It's your birthday today and I hope they made you the biggest cake in Heaven. We planted impatunce with Gramma. She said

*they were your favrite flour and that they'd be real real pretty in a*
*few weeks. I hope you can see them.*

I smiled, reading the rest of the poorly spelled letter. I scanned several letters, my memory blurred about many of them.

I wrote this one the Christmas after she died, when I was nine:

*Dear Mom,*
*When I grow up I want to be a doctor so I can help peopel get*
*better. I thought you'd want to know that on Christmas.*
*Merry Christmas! I still love you,*

                                                                    Nathan

*Were it only that simple,* I thought.

"I always wonder what she'd look like now, don't you?" Rachel asked. I nodded. Each year as I noticed gray hair in my father's head I wondered if Mom would be graying or if she'd still have the rich, dark color I always remembered. "I always wonder what we would do together now," Rachel continued. For the rest of our lives we would wonder about so many things.

I picked up a letter written in pencil when I was ten without the added touches of badly drawn dogs or ducks to jazz it up:

Dear Mom

Today Gramma explained that you know why you died. She said
God made sure bad things didn't happen to you. She said sumday
I'll understud that better. I hope she's right.

> I love you,
> Nathan

When Rachel and I were still children I found a verse
from the Bible written on a crumpled piece of paper at
my father's bedside. "... For I know the plans I have for
you ... plans to prosper you and not to harm you, plans to give you
hope and a future." I studied the paper, but making no
sense of it I took it to my grandmother. She read it and
grew quiet.

"You need to put this back on your father's nightstand. These are words that are helping him." I took the
paper from her and headed back to my father's bedroom.
I stopped and turned to look at her.

"But I don't understand what they mean." She took
my hand and led me into Dad's room, setting the paper
back on the stack of books he kept on the table by his
bed. She sat on the bed and stood me in front of her.

"Your father has obviously put this on top of his
things so that he's reminded that there's a longer look of
our life that we can't see. All we see is what's right in
front of us." I looked down at the words again.

"I don't get it." She hugged me to her.

"I think that if your daddy didn't have a reason to hope, he'd have a hard time getting out of bed every day." I looked at her, confused. "He'll never understand why your mother had to leave us, none of us ever will; but she knows." I looked up at her. "As soon as she stepped into Heaven she could see the big picture of her life, and I bet when she saw it that her jaw dropped open and then I bet she started doing cartwheels and handstands and whatever else she used to do with you in the yard." I looked down at the words written in my father's handwriting on the paper.

"How does that help Dad?" She sighed and pulled me up on the bed beside her.

"Because if your daddy didn't believe it, he'd go absolutely crazy without your mother." I stared at the paper on the nightstand.

"My mother was a good person, wasn't she?"

"She was the best kind of person that ever was, Nathan."

"Then why did she get cancer and die?" Her lips tightened.

"Because she was human," she whispered. "There is no other reason." She ushered me out of my father's room. "Come on, go show me one of those cartwheel flip-flop things you do." She ran me outside and watched as I flipped from one side of the yard to the other, taking my mind off my mother's death for the moment.

Rachel picked up a letter and laughed, reading the letter written in crayon on a paper bag:

Dear Mommy

I don't like Nathan any mores so culd you send me anuther bruther from Heven? If you cant find one, a dog wuld be beter.

Love,
Rachel

I snatched the aged letter and looked at it.
"When did you write this?"
"Last year," she said, breaking into laughter.

Now that the holidays were in full swing, staff members took days off here or there, leaving the medical students to help out where necessary, seeing patients who weren't part of our normal rounds. Some of the medical students were even volunteered to help decorate certain floors of the hospital for Christmas. This was my assignment for the day, and I was grateful to get out of the emergency room for a while. Normally, Christmas would sneak up on me, leaving me in a lurch to find Christmas presents for everyone, but this year I couldn't wait. I hadn't been this excited about Christmas since before my mother died.

I filtered through the boxes of tinsel and bulbs and

helped Denise and Claudia spruce up the nurses' station on the pediatrics floor. I even hung tacky icicle lights from the ceiling so they'd dangle over the entire circumference of the desk.

"I'm going to leave those up till July," Denise said.

"So you're the neighbor in the apartment next to mine," I said, jumping off the ladder. I found a small tabletop tree in a box and pulled it onto the desk, straightening each limb. I was going to leave it at the nurses' station when a thought struck me. Digging through the boxes, I found a small string of lights and little bulbs that were perfect for the tree. I poked my head into Hope's room.

"Knock, knock." Hope looked up and motioned for me to come in. Her mother was sitting beside her on the bed. "Who'd like a little Christmas cheer in here?"

"Can I have that to myself?" she asked, looking at the small tree in my hands.

"You can have it, but you have to do the work." I put the tree on a cart and rolled it to Hope's bedside. Her mother helped her sit up and winked at me; Hope reached for the string of lights, sizing them up. I left to find a few other decorations.

"Playing favorites?" Denise asked. I stopped digging through a box by the nurses' station and looked up at her.

"Is this bad?" She pulled out a cheap, dancing Santa and handed it to me.

"If it is, I'm guilty, too. Take her whatever she'd like."

When I returned to Hope's room later in the day to check on her, I laughed out loud at the sight. There sat the tiny tree, drooping from the weight of ornaments; red ribbon hung from the lamps and tinsel surrounded the bed, window, door, and TV. A small wooden nativity sat on the bed stand next to Hope, and the Santa stood on the tabletop next to the tree, swinging his hips from side to side to "Rockin' Around the Christmas Tree."

"Denise kept coming back with things," her mother said.

"Couldn't she find any tacky plastic lawn ornaments?" I asked.

"She's still looking," Hope said, smiling.


The Sullivans dragged the large Douglas fir through the back door, and Jim grunted in satisfaction. "Now that's a man's tree. Isn't it, Luke?" Luke pulled off his coat and gloves and threw them on the floor.

"Yeahhh," Luke said, grunting like his father.

"Three whacks, and this baby was on the ground begging for mercy," Jim said, struggling to stand the tree up.

"Thirty whacks is more like it," Allison said. "The poor thing was saying, 'Please, just get it over with, already.'" Jim laughed although no one could see him through the tree's branches.

"When I stand it up, slip the tree stand under it." Meghan tried to help her father lift the tree, but she had no energy. A bout of early-morning vomiting had left her nauseous and tired throughout the day. She didn't tell her parents she was sick; her mother tended to blow even the most minor illnesses out of proportion.

"We'll be finding pine needles in August," Allison said, bending over to put the stand in place.

"Before Christmas, Allison," Jim yelled through the mass of needles. "These things are killing me!"

Allison tightened the bolts on the stand, which started a verbal volley of *lean it to the left, more to the right, it's leaning backward now, turn it toward the window, turn it away from the window, back it up, pull it forward, more, more, more, no, move it back again.*

When the tree was all but decorated, Jim hoisted Olivia into the air to place the angel on the top branch, which just missed the ceiling. Olivia stretched her small arms to the upper reaches of the tree. "She's beautiful," Olivia said, pulling her shirt back down to cover her belly. Jim turned off all the lights, and the family sat together on the sofa, admiring their work.

"We should sell tickets for people to come see it," Meghan said, exhausted from the effort.

Allison raised her cup of cider. "Here's to the official beginning of another Sullivan family Christmas. May it be the most beautiful one ever!"

· · ·

At one in the morning, Meghan woke her mother and father. When Jim turned on the light and saw her face, he swept her up in his arms and ran to the car.

The ER was quiet. Rory was on duty. He paused when he looked at Meghan; her skin and eyes were yellow in color. "I think I have food poisoning," Meghan said. "It's either that or the worst flu I've ever had." Rory took her temperature, and she was running a high fever. His physical exam revealed that her liver was enlarged and felt firm to the touch.

"We need to do some blood work," Rory said. Meghan groaned.

"Dr. Goetz just drew blood a few days ago. Can't you just read those results?" Rory shook his head.

"You probably weren't jaundiced a few days ago."

"I'm sorry you had to wait so long," Rory said, pulling open the curtain. Another doctor was with him. "But I wanted Dr. Lucas, one of our gastroenterologists, to read these results, as well as one of our infectious disease specialists."

Allison and Jim were quiet, staring at Rory and Dr. Lucas.

"I'm Dr. Lucas." Meghan shook the doctor's hand. "Your blood tests revealed that your hepatic enzymes are elevated." Meghan sat still, looking at her. "We'd like to do a needle biopsy of your liver to rule out hepatitis."

"When?" Meghan asked.

"Right away."

Dr. Lucas clutched Meghan's file to her chest and walked into the room where Jim, Allison, and Meghan had been waiting for the last few hours for the biopsy reports from pathology. "The biopsy is showing an undifferentiated hepatitis."

"What is that?" Meghan asked. Dr. Lucas paused and took a breath.

"You have something that is causing your liver to be inflamed. Normally we can identify that as hepatitis A, B, or C; but in your case we can't identify the cause." Meghan and her parents sat in silence, trying to grasp what Dr. Lucas was saying.

"She hasn't done anything to get hepatitis," Jim said. Her illness just didn't make sense.

"This is a viral hepatitis," Dr. Lucas said. "Meghan saw Dr. Goetz six months ago for her annual exam and told him she'd been feeling nauseous previous to that but that it eventually went away." Meghan nodded. "I would speculate that that is when the hepatitis was affecting your liver."

"But where did it come from?" Allison asked.

"We can't determine what the infectious agent was. It

could be a million things. It could have been anything airborne."

"What will you do?" Jim asked. Dr. Lucas hated this part of her job. She held tighter to the file and looked at Meghan.

"Judging by your biopsy, this is progressing at a rapid pace, and we need to get a transplant surgeon involved with your care immediately." Meghan felt her heart drop but never took her eyes off Dr. Lucas. "I've contacted a transplant surgeon to speak with you as soon as possible." Allison jumped to her feet.

"Oh God, no," she wailed. "There must be something else you can do."

"This is the only thing we can do," Dr. Lucas said.

My rotation started at six; I figured I'd call Meghan later in the morning, once I knew she was up. At ten, I reached for the phone on the nurses' station in the ER but stopped dialing when a folder in a stack of files caught my eye. Meghan's name was on it. I scanned it and snapped my head up, looking for Rory. He was in the lounge, getting his things together to go home. He was still answering my questions as I bounded up the stairs.

• • •

"Here I am," Meghan said. "Back at my favorite vacation destination." I glanced at Jim and Allison, who looked like they'd logged ten years in the last nine hours.

I snatched her chart at the end of her bed and glanced over it, feeling my heart beat faster as I read the notes Dr. Lucas had written: *vital signs stable, patient condition jaundiced and deteriorating. Biopsy report shows fulminant hepatitis.* I could hear myself breathing—full-blown hepatitis. Then I read, *Consult transplant team.* Meghan watched me read through the notes. "It's not as bad as they say," she said, trying to smile. It felt as if the wind had been knocked out of me and I couldn't speak. I kept staring at the chart—*fulminant hepatitis.* Meghan motioned for me to sit on the side of her bed.

"Dr. Lucas said there's the possibility of finding a living donor." I nodded. Since the liver regenerates itself, a portion is all that is necessary for a successful transplant. Jim and Allison's hopes would soon be dashed when they learned that neither of them, nor extended family members, were a close enough match. I immediately went through the tests and would learn later that even Dr. Goetz was tested. None of us came close enough to matching.

"You doctors are always so serious," Meghan said, comforting *me.* She grabbed my hand and held it tight. "You always forget that Christmas is full of miracles." I looked up at her. "There's always a miracle at Christmas," she said.

A thick, dry knot formed in my throat. I knew otherwise. How many times did I pray for a miracle? How many times did I beg God to heal my mother and make her well? I knew that miracles still happened, but I also knew that sometimes it was as if the heavens were silent.

## EIGHT

Hope, like faith, is nothing if it is not courageous;
it is nothing if it is not ridiculous.
—Thornton Wilder

Dr. Goetz pushed a wheelchair to Meghan's room.

"For m'lady," he said.

"I can walk, Dr. Goetz," she said. He pointed to the chair.

"Hospital policy. Sit."

"Don't you have orderlies who do this?" she asked.

"You want an orderly to take out my best girl," Dr. Goetz said, teasing her. "I don't think so!" He pushed her through the halls and into the elevator. Jim pulled the car around, and Dr. Goetz pushed Meghan to the curb, opening the car door for her. He helped her out of the chair and held on to her, afraid she might fall on the melted snow on the pavement.

"I can walk on my own, Dr. Goetz," she said.

"I know you can," he said. "But I might fall."

He smiled and helped her into the car. Then he did something he'd never done with any of his patients: he kissed her forehead. He closed the door, and Meghan waved at him through the window. He felt a catch in his throat and put his head down to avoid eye contact with anyone who might stop him to talk; then he pushed the chair back into the hospital.


I made it through my rounds but it felt as if I were walking through a long tunnel of a dream that wouldn't end, but I was confident that I'd awaken and learn that the doctors had made a mistake: Meghan wasn't sick after all. I can't remember how many times I told myself that when my mother was ill, but it should have been enough to learn by now that Meghan was sick. In a little while, if she didn't get a transplant, she would get very sick. After my rounds, I made my way to the lounge and tried to open my locker. It was jammed. I jiggled the handle and pulled it toward me, but the locker wouldn't budge. In frustration I tried several times. I leaned my head on the locker. *This isn't happening again.* I lifted the handle. Nothing. In anger I beat my fists into the locker and pounded it over and over and over. *Why did I meet her?* I couldn't go through it again. I couldn't watch someone I love get weaker every day until death finally snatched her away.

In one of her letters my mother wrote,

*Life never has and never will be fair, Nathan. I won't be the first person you lose; there will be others. You'll stand by their side as they lie dying or beside their grave in a cemetery and it's there that you'll have to make a decision. You can either lean into God or turn away. It will always be your choice, Nathan, not His.*

I closed my eyes. She never turned away. Even in death, my mother chose to go through the pain with God rather than without Him. I didn't know if I could make that same decision.

There are days when I can remember everything Meghan and I did together over the next three weeks, then there are days when I can't remember anything at all. She would turn off all the lights in her family's living room, leaving only the lights on the tree to light up the room, and we'd sit there for hours and talk about everything or we'd watch the lights on the tree and say nothing at all. Sometimes, we'd drive to the park and walk around the lake. Each time we were there Meghan would look for the runner she used to pace herself against, but we never saw her. "It's the wrong time of day," she would say, disappointed. "I hope I get to see her again." Neither of us knew if she would—her body was reminding us every day that time was short.

One day our walk around the lake was slower than usual. I held firm to Meghan's hand, afraid she would slip on the patches of ice on the path. She stopped beneath the giant oak tree and looked out over the frozen water. She loved it there. She looked from side to side, taking it all in as if it were the first time she'd seen it. We stood in silence as she watched the runners making their way around the perimeter of the lake, and I knew she'd give anything to be running with them.

My mother wrote in her last letter to me:

*Dear Nathan,*

*You have grown so fast. It was only yesterday your father and I brought you home from the hospital. As I watched you grow into the fine little man you are, I was reminded time and again that life is a mist. We're here for a while and then we just fade away, leaving little bits of ourselves behind for the people we love. You'll be a man like your daddy before you know it and I hope that when you're grown that you won't let life slip by. I hope that for every loop and drop this roller coaster takes you on, that you'll keep hanging on for the rest of the ride. Just know that the ride is over before you know it and if you close your eyes, you'll miss it.*

I didn't want to miss a second of the ride with Meghan.

Meghan woke to sounds of her mother in the kitchen. She tiptoed through the living room and stuck her head around the corner: Allison was making every effort to be quiet, closing cabinets and removing bowls and pans with care. "What are you doing, Mom?" Meghan asked. Allison jumped at her voice.

"Don't scare me, Meghan; I'm getting too old. Did I wake you?"

"No. What are you making?"

"Peanut butter fudge." It was Luke's favorite. Her mother made it every year for Christmas, along with date balls for Jim, cookies by the dozen for Olivia and her class, and homemade candy that took an hour to beat to perfection for Meghan. Meghan ran back toward her room.

"I'm going to change and come help you." Allison stopped her.

"I can do it, Meg. Just lie on the couch and rest." Meghan stopped in the hallway and turned back to her mother. For days her mom and dad had walked on eggshells around her. Meghan was tired of it.

"Would you stop treating me like a baby, Mom?"

"I wasn't. I was trying to treat you like normal." Allison wanted to treat her as she always did, but things were different now and she no longer knew how to act or what to do.

"Well, you're not, Mom. If you were, you'd talk about what's happening." Allison stuck her head in the refrigerator. "See, you're avoiding it right now!" Allison pulled out a pound of butter and set it on the counter. "Mom, look at me." Allison clutched the recipe box and looked at Meghan. "A transplant might never become available."

Tears pooled in Allison's eyes. "Don't say that, Meghan."

"Mom, you heard the doctors. I either get a transplant or . . ." Tears fell down Allison's face as she cut Meghan off.

"Please don't say that, Meghan," she whispered. "I can't think about . . ." She couldn't finish. She picked up a dishcloth and buried her face in it.

"Mom, if I die, you can't be sad forever." Allison didn't respond. "You're going to look out the window and life will still go on. That's just how it is." Allison wanted to say it was a whole lot more than that for the people who were left behind, but she remained quiet. "Do you know what I want more than anything, Mom?" Allison looked up.

"What?"

"I want to help you make peanut butter fudge." Allison tried to laugh and handed Meghan a bowl.

They spent the morning talking and laughing as one Christmas treat after another was prepared. When Meghan lay down to rest after lunch, Allison cleaned up the mess in the kitchen, turning the TV news up to drown out the sound of her crying.

Meghan pulled a folder containing information about the scholarship run out of her desk in the bedroom. She sat Jim and Allison down, going over every last detail from how she wanted the sponsorships organized to the day of the run itself. "We're doing this awfully early, aren't we," Jim said. "Isn't the race in June?"

"Dad, it has to be organized so we'll know what else needs to be done."

"Besides my bank account, where else is all the money going once you collect it?" Jim asked, hoping to make Meghan laugh. She was all business.

"That's where I need help. Once the money goes into a trust we're going to need a lawyer or somebody to help us make all this legal." Meghan wrote the word "lawyer" on her legal pad and circled it. She'd have to find a lawyer she could trust.

They finished the work an hour later, and Meghan put everything back into her folder. "I want Charlie to be the first recipient," she said. She looked at her mom and dad. "It's important to me that somebody know that."


I pulled into Meghan's drive after my rounds one day and saw Charlie sitting on the swing set in the backyard. It was so cold, the snow crunched beneath me as I walked toward him. I zipped my jacket and sat on the swing next to him.

"It's awfully cold out here," I said.

"I don't mind it," he said, watching his feet dig into the snow as he twisted the swing from side to side. I stuck my hands in my pockets.

"Did you visit with Meghan?" He nodded. "How was it?" He shrugged his shoulders.

"Will they find a transplant?" His voice was soft. I barely heard the question.

"As soon as a match is available, they'll get her to the hospital."

"But will they find one?" I paused, looking out over the white yard.

"I don't know." He nodded and leaned farther over the swing, staring at his feet.

"Why aren't more people organ donors?"

"I don't know. Afraid that if they actually say they are that something will happen to them; as if they're inviting death into their home."

"That's stupid," he said. "People are dying every day because they need a kidney or liver or a new heart." He stopped swaying back and forth and looked at me. "She says there are always miracles at Christmas. Do you believe that?" My heart sank. I didn't want to answer him, but I knew there was no way around it. Charlie was too smart for double-talk.

"If we can't believe that miracles happen, then we may as well stop believing anything at all." He looked down at the ground again.

"Do you love her?" he asked. He waited for me to answer.

"Man to man?" I asked.

"Man to man."

"Yes."

"Then you better tell her soon because I love her, too, and if you don't tell her, I will."

I smiled. Charlie was a rare gem. I reached over and squeezed the back of his neck, praying that the miracle Meghan believed in would happen soon.

## NINE

A miracle, my friend, is an event which creates faith.
—George Bernard Shaw

Meghan was lying on the sofa; nausea had hit her hard that morning, and she had vomited right before everyone came to visit. Charlie sat on a chair with two of Meghan's teammates, who were perched on each arm of the chair. Leslie grinned as he turned three shades of red when one of the girls would flirt with him, teasing him about being Meghan's secret coach.

"Does she rub your head before she runs?" one of them asked, rubbing Charlie's head and messing up his hair.

"Or does she kiss you?" another asked, turning and kissing Charlie on the cheek. His eyes widened, and Leslie stepped into the kitchen before he saw her laughing.

Before Meghan let the girls leave she grilled them about how much money they were raising for the race. "Trust me," Michele said. "They're all working hard.

You're going to raise more money for this run than you ever imagined."

Meghan's teammates filed out the door, rubbing Charlie's head for good luck. As soon as the winter break was over they'd all be at practice again and told Meghan they expected her there.

Meghan was quiet. Everyone was always so cheerful, taking great strides to step around any questions about her illness. With the exception of the first, *How do you feel?* nobody asked anything else. Nobody, that is, except Charlie. He walked to the sofa and sat down beside Meghan.

"Are you getting sicker every day?"

Meghan knew she'd have to tell him the truth. "Yes."

He was quiet. "When will you have to go back to the hospital?"

"I don't know," she said, but she knew it would be soon.


Allison and Leslie sat in the family room listening as Meghan laughed and visited with Charlie and her friends. "All these years I've been so worried about her heart," Allison said. "I never dreamed anything like this would happen." Tears fell down her face, and Leslie squeezed her hand. "I should have known her heart wouldn't give out. She's always had more heart than any of us." Leslie stayed quiet and listened; she knew there was nothing she could say. She could try saying something like, *A liver will be available soon*, but she didn't know that. "Sometimes I try to prepare myself," Allison whispered. She stopped. "I try to prepare for the day when . . ."

"There's nothing to prepare for, Allison. She's still here." A tear fell down Allison's cheek, and she brushed it away.

"Every day I look at her and say, 'Oh God, please! Please save my little girl's life.'" She covered her face and wept, letting her tears fall in her hands. Leslie touched her arm.

"She's still here, Allison. She's looking at you and Jim and loving you every day, and while she's doing that there's still hope. She's still here," Leslie said. Allison nodded and tears fell from her chin.

"But for how long," Allison whispered.


Leslie and Charlie pulled on their coats to leave. "You need to keep your eyes on the finish line," Charlie said, cracking his knuckles. "Don't ever take your eyes off the goal because your miracle's coming. I just know it." Meghan grabbed his hands.

"Stop doing that," she said. "Your fingers are going to look like breadsticks." Allison and Leslie watched at the door, smiling. Given their ages, Charlie and Meghan were the most unlikely of friends, but both women knew there was a deep bond between them. Meghan hugged Charlie. "Thanks for coming over today," she said in his ear.

"I'll come by every day," he said. He put his head down and wouldn't look at her. "You're my best friend, Meghan." He darted for the door before she could respond.

"I want to get tested to see if I can be a donor for Meghan," Charlie said, on the drive home. Leslie looked at him; she knew he was serious.

"I know you love Meghan, but you just can't do that, Charlie. Your heart would never make it through the surgery."

"I knew you'd say that," he said, snapping his head to stare out the passenger window.

"Dr. Goetz would never let you," Leslie said. "You know that." Charlie wasn't listening. "Meghan wouldn't let you, either." He turned to look at his mother. "You know that, too." Charlie remained quiet.

"Mom?" Leslie looked at him. "For weeks I haven't been able to pray for Meghan's miracle because I knew that somebody would have to die. I mean, if a living donor wasn't found." He looked at his mother. "But we have to pray for that now. Somebody has to die, or Meghan will."

• • •

I got to Meghan's late one day. I was doing the workup of a patient that took longer than expected, and I could hear time tick away in my ears as one thing after another kept me at the hospital for another hour. I walked into her house and found her on the sofa.

"Would you take me to the park?" she asked. I drove to the park and opened my door, but she stopped me. "I just want to look at it," she said, watching ice-skaters on the lake. She looked at the small gazebo on the other side of the lake. Someone had decorated it for Christmas with huge red bows, swags of spruce, and bright colored lights. Snow clung to colored bulbs that covered a huge evergreen in the middle of the park. "I can't believe it's almost Christmas," she said. She was quiet as she watched two runners make their way past my truck and around the lake. "Was your mother afraid when she died?"

The question took me off guard. "No."

She kept watching the runners.

"When you think about her now, do you remember the way she died or how she lived?"

"How she lived."

She nodded. She watched as runners made one loop after another around the lake. Tears filled her eyes and made their way down her face and over her chin, spilling onto her hands. "I'm never going to run again," she said, wiping her face. "It's funny how you draw up a plan for your life." Her voice was stronger now. "Then something happens that proves you wrong." She was crying harder, and I pulled her to me, wrapping my arms around her. "You're reminded that you only have a few years: eighty, maybe sixty-five . . . or nineteen." Her shoulders were shaking. "I don't want to leave my family," she said, sobbing. "I don't want to leave you, Nathan." She was grabbing my face, searching my eyes.

"We have to hold on for your miracle, Meg," I said, holding on to her. I opened my door and slid her off the seat, into my arms. I walked down the slope leading to the path around the lake and started to carry her around it.

"What are you doing?" she asked. I pulled her closer and picked up my pace, running. A few runners ran off to the side, staring as I ran with Meghan in my arms. She lifted an arm up toward the sky and squinted into the sun, feeling the wind on her face. She smiled; she was running around the lake she loved.

## TEN

Only a life lived for others is the life worthwhile.
—Albert Einstein

Meghan was admitted to the hospital on a Thursday. Her condition was declining, so physicians would no longer permit her to stay home. Doctors would keep her as comfortable as possible and do everything they could to keep her from catching even a common cold. They had to keep her as healthy as possible. Allison held on to Olivia's hand and walked with her and Luke down the hall, toward Meghan's room.

"Is Dr. Goetz keeping you here again?" Olivia asked, jumping onto Meghan's bed. Meghan shook her head and motioned for Luke to come closer, then, making things as clear as possible, she told them everything.

I had planned to stay at my dad's for Christmas break, but when Meghan got sick I decided to stay in my apartment, closer to the hospital. I finished up my rounds on the twenty-third and gathered my things to leave. Peter Vashti saw me in the cafeteria. I hadn't seen him since he helped get me out of the rotation with Dr. Goetz. We talked about Meghan, and I shared with him my decision to leave medical school. He had seen several of his own classmates drop out during their third year, so what I said didn't take him by surprise.

"I think it's going to be hard for you to walk away," Peter said. He leaned forward in his seat and looked me in the eye. "Don't make this decision because things got tough for a while. You'll go through rough times again. There were doctors that I hated during my third year."

I smiled at Peter. I knew what he was thinking. "I haven't made my decision because of Dr. Goetz or any other doctor. I just know that some of you are meant to be doctors, and some of us aren't."

"Or maybe some kept working through the tough times while some bowed out. I know that some of my classmates regret the decision they made. I just hope you won't."

I didn't have time to dwell on what Peter said. I pulled my things together, said good-bye to everyone, and walked out the doors leading to the parking lot. They closed behind me and I stopped. It felt so final, as if they were closing forever, but I couldn't take the time to think about that. Not now anyway.

. . .

I visited Meghan when Allison took Luke and Olivia home. I sat down on the side of her bed and could feel that something was wrong. She wasn't looking at me. I reached for her hand, but she moved it onto her chest. For the last two days it felt as if she was distancing herself from me. I started to speak. "Are you . . ." She turned toward me; tears were on her face.

"I can't do this to you," she said.

"Do what?" I asked, confused.

"I can't put you through this again." Tears streamed down her face now.

"Meghan . . ."

"You're not going to sit around and wait for me to die like you did your mother. Nobody deserves to go through that again." She turned her face away and I tried to turn it toward me but she resisted. "Please go, Nathan." I turned her face with my hands and looked at her.

"What are you talking about? Let me decide what I should or shouldn't do."

"I don't want you to come see me here. It's too hard!" She was sobbing. Jim ran into the room and looked at us. "Daddy, please make Nathan leave." Jim squeezed my shoulder as I walked out the door.

I drove the hour to my dad's. He and Gramma weren't expecting me. Gramma was already in bed for the night. Dad made a pot of coffee and sat across the table from me. I was so tired I could have put my head on the table and slept there for the night.

I avoided eye contact. I knew if I looked at my dad that my emotions would unravel, and I didn't want that to happen. I held the cup between my hands and swirled the black liquid up one side and down the other.

"How's Meghan?" Dad asked.

"Not good. She's getting weaker." I paused. Dad didn't ask a lot of questions or offer up what my grandmother called "bubbles of hope," a statement that is as solid as a bubble. We heard lots of them when my mother was sick: *Maggie's going to lick this*, someone would say to my father, or *Everything's going to be all right, Nathan.* Dad had lived long enough to know that Meghan might not be all right.

"How are you?" he asked.

I bit the inside of my mouth and nodded. I tried to hold back the tears. I tried to suck it up and hold it together. "She said she doesn't want to see me again." My voice was so small. "She said she can't put me through it again."

"Can you go through it again?" Dad asked. I didn't look up at him.

"Yes," I whispered.

"Then that's where you need to be." I kept my eyes on the table.

"Dad," I said, "do you think it's possible to fall in love after knowing someone for only a couple of months?"

"I fell in love with your mother the first day I met her," he said. "So a couple of months seems long to me."

"I just keep wondering why I met her," I said, squeezing the cup between my hands. "Why did I have to meet her?"

"Because you were supposed to love her," Dad said. His words struck me hard. Was I supposed to meet Meghan for no other reason than to love her as she died? I felt my shoulders shaking. Tears were on my face, but I was silent. Dad pulled my head into his chest and I grabbed on to him, sobbing.

"Love her while you can," he said, bending low to my ear. "Love her as long as you can."

I drove to my apartment and pulled out the letters from my mother. I glanced through them and found the one I was looking for.

Dear Nathan,

One day, maybe in a few months, or a few years, you'll start to look at women (maybe a friend's mother or someone you work with) and wonder why I couldn't have lived to be as old as she is. You'll wish that I could be there with you to meet a girlfriend or fix your tie on your wedding day or hold your children, but don't dwell on the pain. Focus on the happiness that you feel on those days and the happiness that I had as your mother. If I was given another five, ten, or forty years, I don't think I could be happier than I was during these 34 years because it's not about how long you live but how you live and who you love and I loved you. More than you'll ever know.

I felt tears run down my nose and across my cheeks. I had long since resigned myself to the fact that my mother's words would bring tears to my eyes for the rest of my life. She went on:

The pain you feel now will help you care for others, Nathan. It will help you love them through the hardest times. Always remember that Love wins. Remember when we looked at the valley together on top of the ridge last year? Regardless of the pain or sorrow you go through in the valley, there will always be love at the end. It may be hard to walk through, but God will use your time there for good. I know He will.

I folded the letter, slipping it back inside the envelope, and grabbed my keys.

The ICU was quiet. Meghan had been asleep for hours. I saw Jim sitting in a chair in the waiting room; he was half-asleep. I walked toward him, and he opened his eyes when he heard my footsteps. I sat down beside him. "She can say whatever she wants, but I'm not going anywhere," I said. Jim clapped my shoulder and rested his hand there. Sometime in the early-morning hours, we both drifted to sleep.

I stirred when I heard a nurse on the phone giving her husband a detailed list of what to buy at the grocery store. Jim was still asleep; his neck bent back in a tortuous position. I walked to Meghan's room and looked inside. Allison was asleep on a bed shoved against the wall. I crept inside and stood next to Meghan. She turned toward me and opened her eyes.

"Just so you know," I said, whispering. "I'm just as stubborn as you are, and I'm not going anywhere." She was too tired to argue. She smiled and fell back to sleep.

Someone was always with Meghan; sometimes two or three of us were in the room at the same time, the nurses disregarding hospital policy regarding the number of ICU visitors. "Are we driving you crazy," Allison asked, brushing Meghan's hair off her face. Megan smiled; she was getting too tired to sit up, let alone speak. She fell asleep and Allison and Jim slipped out of the room. They were never gone long. They would take just enough time to cry alone in the bathroom or wander the halls, hoping to find a miracle hidden in the cracks of the floor or behind a door.

I sat beside Meghan and held her hand. *Is this what it was like for my dad? Did he watch my mother sleep for hours during the last days of her life?* Meghan opened her eyes and smiled. "I dreamed we were dancing again," she said. "We were in the waiting room and it was decorated for Christmas and

I was wearing a gold, silk dress this time, not some cheap doctor's jacket." I laughed.

"Hey, it was all I could afford at the time." She smiled and closed her eyes; she was dreaming again.

Jim pulled the small, fake tree through the door and set it on a rolling cart in Meghan's room. Olivia followed, carrying two big bags that were bigger than her, and Luke had strings of lights hanging around his neck. Jim put up his hands when he saw the look on Allison's face.

"No pine needles with this one," he said. They decorated the tree while Meghan watched, and Jim hauled in a huge plastic bag filled with presents. Christmas was two days away.

Charlie and Leslie dropped by later in the morning. Meghan pointed out a gift under the tree, and Charlie picked it up. "Open it," she said. "It's for you."

"But I don't have anything for you," he said. "That's not fair."

"Don't argue on Christmas Eve. Just open it." Charlie tore the paper and pulled out several ribbons and trophies. "For my coach," she said, watching Charlie's eyes.

"Why are you giving me all your trophies and ribbons?"

"You were the one who annoyed me so much and

made all those impossible demands like 'take two more seconds off. No, I changed my mind, take ten.'" Charlie raised his eyebrows and smiled.

"I just try to do my job." He sat on the edge of her bed and grew quiet. "It's coming, isn't it?"

"What?" Meghan asked.

"Your Christmas miracle."

"I hope so," she said.

"I know so," Charlie said. Meghan smiled. Charlie so wanted to believe in miracles, wanted to be a part of one. She looked at Leslie and hoped she and Rich would one day be able to explain things to him. She pulled Charlie's face toward hers and gave him a kiss. He wiped it off.

"Why do you girls keep kissing me?" he said, rubbing his face.

I didn't know if we'd get any time alone on Christmas Day, so when Jim took Luke and Olivia home for the day and Allison slipped away to the cafeteria, I handed Meghan her gift.

"Yours is under the tree," she said. I found it: a small box covered with red paper.

"Open yours first," I said. She ran her finger under the tape and pulled at the wrapping. Her mouth opened when she saw it. "I saw it hanging in a store window."

I was walking toward Gunther's Sports in my hometown to pick up some new fishing equipment for Dad's Christmas present. It had just started to snow, and the wind had picked up, so I put my head down. I glanced up only a moment to say hello to someone in front of Wilson's Department Store when something caught my eye in the window. I walked closer and stared. *How did it get here of all places?*

I ran inside and a clerk lifted it out of the window and handed it to me. I tried to make out the name in the corner but couldn't. I flipped it over, hoping to find the information there.

"Who painted this?" I asked the clerk. She shrugged her shoulders. I kept staring at it. It was beautiful, painted to perfection down to the last detail: the giant oak, with snow clinging to every limb, the lake was frozen over, you could just make out footprints on the path surrounding it, and even the gazebo was there, decorated for Christmas.

"This park is an hour away," I said to the clerk. "Who brought this here to sell?" She shrugged again, mumbling something about how Wilson's didn't even sell paintings, let alone one by some unknown artist.

"It's so beautiful," Meghan said, holding the painting in her hands. She arched her brows and looked at the gift in my hand. I tore into the paper and opened the small box. There was a runner's wrist stopwatch inside. I read the card she had tucked under the bow.

*In case you can't find someone to pace yourself with.* I smiled and pulled out the watch, holding it in my hand. I leaned down and kissed her. "I found someone to pace myself with," I said.

It was there, in the quiet of her hospital room as she

held on to a painting of the park she adored, that I told Meghan I loved her.

On Christmas morning I watched as the Sullivans unwrapped one gift after another, and it seemed everyone, including Meghan, forgot she was ill. Jim waded through the sea of wrapping paper and pulled out the last of the gifts: coloring books that Santa left for Olivia, a remote-controlled car for Luke, and a lone gift sitting at the back of the tree with Meghan's name on it. "One more gift," he said, handing it to her.

"No name on it. This one must be from Santa," Meghan said, taking the gift from her father. She unwrapped the green foil, pulled back the tissue paper, and saw a beautiful silver frame with a stained-glass star on each side. She stared at the picture inside, one of the night sky twinkling with thousands of stars.

"Just in case you get too busy at Stanford or Georgetown to go out and look at them," Jim said, "you can hold this up and we'll still be looking at them together." Meghan smiled, holding the picture. "You're still my star," Jim whispered, kissing her. "You'll always be my star."

Leslie Bennett drove ten-year-old Matthew to her mother and father's house. They were supposed to spend the morning with her parents after opening gifts at their own house, but Charlie still wasn't awake at seven and Matthew could barely contain himself; he just had to get at those presents. At seven-thirty, Leslie checked on Charlie, and he was still sound asleep. Since they could no longer take Matthew's pleading, Leslie pulled on her coat and decided to drive Matthew to her parents' house; at least he could open a couple of gifts there. Maybe that would appease him until Charlie woke up. Matt was already beside himself over a gift Charlie had received yesterday at the hospital.

While Charlie was visiting Meghan, Denise had come down from pediatrics with a gift for him. His eyes lit up when he opened up an envelope with a certificate inside.

"Good for four tickets to the WWF in August," Charlie read, excited. "Is this real?"

"It's real." Denise squeezed his arm and turned to go.

"You didn't have to get him anything," Leslie said, moved by Denise's kindness. So many of the hospital staff knew that Charlie's medical bills had been a strain on the Bennetts and had been so kind over the years, giving him gifts on his birthday and Christmas.

"I know he loves it. I heard it was coming, so I just had to get them." Leslie felt a catch in her throat, but she managed to hug Denise and wish her a merry Christmas. Matthew was as excited about the gift as Charlie.

Rich rinsed out the dishes from breakfast and started to unload the dishwasher when he heard a knock at the door. Before he could dry his hands and get to the living room, whoever had knocked was already gone. He opened the door and saw a plain white envelope sticking to the door with a large red bow attached to it. He ripped it open and pulled out one thousand dollars in cash. Rich ran into the yard and spun around in all directions, looking for a car or anyone in the street. He bolted into the house to call Leslie, and as he was telling her what happened he heard another knock at the door. He threw the phone down on the counter and ran to the door. Again, no one was there but another envelope with a bow swayed in the cold air. Rich snatched it off and ran into the yard again, spinning on his heels. He opened it and breathlessly counted another wad of money as Leslie listened. "One thousand dollars," he shouted into the phone. Tears filled Leslie's eyes.

"What's going on?" she whispered.

"I don't know," Rich shouted. "I don't know!" Then there was another rap at the door. "There's another knock!" He threw the phone down and raced to the door, throwing it open and running to the yard before anyone could get away but again, there was no one there. He snatched the envelope from the door. His heart pounded as he picked up the phone. "It's another envelope, Les." His hands shook as he opened it and the money fell to the counter. "It's more money," he said, choking on the words. "It's two thousand dollars." Leslie cried on the other end. Meghan was right; Christmas was the season for miracles. There was just enough money to help them pay off bills that had accumulated over the past two months. Leslie sat down and held the phone to her ear, crying. They racked their brains trying to imagine who might have done such a thing. Everyone—people from the hospital to Charlie's school and their neighbors— had already been so good to them. They would never know who left the money so they could thank them, but sometimes giving is all the thanks that some people ever need.

Charlie visited Meghan in the afternoon, bringing a framed picture of the two of them together, taken after one of her cross-country meets. "I should have known the best gift would be from you," she said, making him smile. As they talked, Meghan drifted off to sleep; Charlie looked up at me, frightened. I led him down the hall, into the waiting room.

"It's the medications, Charlie," I said, trying to ease his mind. He was quiet for the longest time.

"Do you think she'd run through the gates of Heaven? Or would that be the wrong thing to do?"

"I think you can probably go through the gates any way you like." He thought for a moment.

"Then I'd definitely run through them." He smiled, looking at me. "It'd be the only time I ever ran without having to sit down and rest." I put my hand around his shoulder. We sat quietly, and I could hear the clock ticking on the wall in front of me. It's strange how deafening time can be when you want it to slow down.

Charlie waited for Meghan to wake up, then Leslie took another picture of Charlie sitting on Meghan's bed, Meghan's arm slung over his shoulder.

"Are you going to hover around my bed all day?" Meghan asked late in the afternoon. I threw my hands in the air.

"Are you trying to get rid of me again?" She reached for my hand.

"Please go be with your family for a while." I sat down next to her.

"They know I'm here."

"But it's Christmas! Please go wish your grandmother a merry Christmas in person. It's only an hour away . . . thirty minutes the way you drive. Please go see them. There's nothing for you to do here, anyway."

"She's stubborn like her mother," Jim said. "There's no reasoning with either one of them." He put his hand on my back. "Why don't you take a break and go be with your family?" Everything in me said I shouldn't go, that I should just stay put; but Meghan was adamant.

"You can go eat dinner with your family and be back here by ten."

"I'll be back by eight."

"You can't drive there, eat, open presents, and be back here by eight. Ten o'clock."

"Nine." I leaned down and I kissed her. "I love you," I said. She held my face and looked me in the eyes.

"I love you, too. Now leave."


When someone you love dies on a holiday, that day's never the same again. My father and grandmother did everything they could to make Christmas special for me and Rachel, and my memories of each Christmas are filled with lots of food and family filling the next several days with nothing but laughter and boisterous conversation. But in the middle of it all, I would catch my father holding his coffee mug and staring out the window. Even as a child I knew he was thinking of my mother. Or I could hear Gramma humming or talking to herself, but then the kitchen would grow quiet and I'd catch a glimpse of her staring at a bowl or the recipe box and I knew she was remembering working with Mom to prepare the Christmas meal. The kitchen would be silent for several minutes; then I'd hear her blowing her nose before the humming started again.

As we grew older, Christmas became a quiet celebration. Gramma would travel to visit her two remaining children, my aunt Kathy and uncle Brian, while Dad, Rachel, and I celebrated together. Because of medical problems, Gramma hadn't traveled the last couple of

Christmases. I had hoped Meghan would be part of our celebration this year. I shook my head. I couldn't believe I let her talk me into leaving the hospital. On the way to my father's house, I took a turn leading to the cemetery.

Our family visited my mother's grave every Christmas, but for whatever reason I decided to swing by there first before going home. I pulled onto the grounds and realized there was no way my little pickup was going to make it up the icy road that wound through the property. I parked and grabbed the sack off the front seat.

I hoofed my way up the road to my mother's tombstone and found it covered with ice. All the stones were sparkling from the most recent ice storm. I put the sack down and started clearing the leaves and debris from the stone. I caught movement in my eye and looked up to see a man carrying a wreath and poinsettias. We said hello to each other, and I think I wished him a merry Christmas, I don't know, I can't recall. He went about his business, carrying on with his work as I finished mine.

"I brought the shoes, Mom," I said, opening the sack and placing the glittery, beaded pair on her tombstone. "I know you don't need them anymore. Makes me feel better, though." The wind picked up, and I pulled my coat up around my neck and pushed the university hat I was wearing farther down on my head. "I've met a girl, Mom. And she's one of those girls you told me about; one I can't live without." My throat tightened, and I ran my fingers over the letters on the stone. "I can't imagine my life without her in it now."

The wind shrieked and drowned out my voice. I remembered my grandmother said she'd have dinner ready at 6:00. I looked down at my watch: 4:35. "I think I'm supposed to be eating Christmas dinner right now, but I'm not sure because the watch you bought for me doesn't work." I tapped the face of it and the second hand started to move. "But I can't get rid of it." I positioned the shoes so the light caught them, reflecting off the sequins just so. "I wish you were here with us, Mom. I'll wish that for the rest of my life."

Gramma pulled me inside the door, taking my coat from me. She held on to my face and studied my eyes before she gave me a kiss. "You didn't have to come," she said.

"Meg made me come." Her eyes filled with tears, and she kissed me again. After my mother died, words never had to be spoken to bring tears to Gramma's eyes.

I tried to eat my plateful of turkey and stuffing and mashed potatoes and peas, but I couldn't help but think I'd done something terrible in leaving the hospital. In my heart, I knew I should have stayed. We set the dishes aside and unwrapped our gifts by the tree. Rachel and I got Gramma a red silk wrap similar to the one she gave Mom on her last Christmas. Gramma had worn it when she was married and from the time she was a little girl, Mom had wanted it. Gramma pulled the wrap from the box and ran it through her fingers.

"What in the world will I do with something this beautiful? It looks like something the queen of England would wear."

"Then wear it while you and the queen are having lunch," Dad said.

"I wouldn't know what to feed the queen," Gramma said, fussing with the wrap. "I just can't imagine where I'd wear something like this."

"Wear it in the house," Rachel said. Gramma gasped at the thought.

"I couldn't wear this in the house! The neighbors could see me and think I was being uppity." Gramma was always afraid someone would think she was being uppity. Dad reached under the tree for an oversize gift with Gramma's name on it.

"Then go on a cruise and wear it there," Dad said.

"Good Lord, Jack! What would the neighbors think if they knew I was on a cruise wearing this? Lorraine would never let me hear the end of it." Dad put the present at Gramma's feet.

"Isn't anybody else having Christmas around here?" she asked, tearing into the wrapping. She waded through layers of tissue paper before finding an envelope at the bottom of the box. She opened it and her mouth dropped open. "What in the world?" Rachel laughed and scooted next to her on the sofa.

"It's a ticket for a seven-day cruise." For once, Gramma sat speechless. "Aunt Kathy and Uncle Brian and everybody pitched in." Gramma held the ticket in front of her as if handling the Hope Diamond.

"I can't go on a cruise by myself," she whispered.

"Lorraine's going with you," Rachel said. Dad opened the door, and Lorraine cha-cha'd her way through the living room, wearing a bright red sweat suit with a big smiling reindeer sequined to the back. Gramma laughed and sprang to her feet, grabbing Lorraine's hands in midair. They laughed and cried like young girls on their wedding day, planning when to go and what to wear. Watching them, I was grateful Meghan had made me come.

Robert Layton picked the phone up in his home office and dialed a number. "Paula, this is Robert." Paula Hurley had worked at the local paper for as long as Robert could remember. Her father, John Hurley, owned the farm that Robert's parents visited every year with Robert and his brother in tow as they searched for the perfect Christmas tree.

"It's Christmas Day, Robert. Don't tell me you need a favor today."

"I need a favor today."

"What is it?"

"I need you to look up a fifteen-year-old obituary for me for a woman named Margaret Elizabeth Andrews."

"Don't tell me you've got a client who's suing the dead."

"Nope. I think I just found an old friend."

I shoved the last of the wrapping paper and empty boxes that covered the floor into a garbage bag and was about to take it out the back door when the doorbell rang. A man around my father's age stood on the front porch wearing a brown leather jacket and holding a piece of paper in his hand. I assumed he was one of Dad's customers. I opened the storm door to speak with him.

"Are you Nathan?" I told him I was and motioned for him to come in. He stood at the door and looked at me before extending his hand.

"My name is Robert Layton. I think you and I know each other." When he heard a man's voice, Dad walked into the living room, and I thought for sure he would take over from there; but Dad looked at the man as if he'd also never seen him before. "I'm Robert Layton," he said again, shaking my father's hand. "I don't mean to disturb you but I wanted to be sure to catch someone at home and I was hoping it would be you," he said, looking at me. Gramma and Rachel walked into the living room, and Robert did his introduction for the third and final time. "I don't mean to interrupt your Christmas, so I'll make this quick. This is going to sound strange, but I met Nathan fifteen years ago at Wilson's Department Store."

My mind raced through the employees at Wilson's. "I bought him a pair of sparkly shoes." Gramma threw her hand over her mouth. I was stunned. Even as a child I remembered a man had bought the shoes for me, but I could never picture his face. I only remember grabbing the shoes and running.

"That was you," I said. "How did you find me?" He held up the piece of paper.

"We met again at the cemetery." In my mind I could see Robert holding the wreath and poinsettias. "I didn't know it was you until I was leaving and the shoes on top of your mother's tombstone caught my eye. I wrote down the information and called a friend at the newspaper. I hope that wasn't too intrusive but I'd let you get away one Christmas. I didn't want it to happen again." A small tear fell down my grandmother's cheek.

"Days after Maggie died Nathan told us how he got those shoes," she said in a whisper. "You showed up at that store just like an angel." Robert smiled and cleared his throat, laughing.

"I wasn't an angel, believe me. I was on the verge of losing my family when I saw Nathan that Christmas Eve." We were captivated as Robert told us the story of his marriage to Kate and about his two girls. Kate had told him that the marriage was over. Robert was in Wilson's that night buying gifts for the last Christmas they'd spend together as a family. "It changed my life when I met you. I still can't explain it. All I know is that nothing mattered to me more at that moment than my family, so I threw everything down and went home to my wife and kids— really went home for the first time in years." He stopped and cleared his throat again. "Anyway, I just wanted to thank you." He grabbed hold of me and wrapped his arms around me, pounding my back.

"Whose grave were you visiting?" I asked.

"My mother died that year, too—the day after Christmas. Christmas was her favorite time of year, so I decorate her grave no matter how cold it is, then I put a poinsettia on my father's grave. He didn't like decorations nearly as much as she did!"

Gramma told him how I had given the shoes to my mother that night. "Nathan was so proud," she said. "He put the shoes on Maggie's feet, and when her face lit up, Nathan just about burst, he was so happy. It's something I'll never forget." Dad jumped up to serve Robert a cup of coffee before we all dissolved into a puddle of tears. Gramma and Rachel went to clean the kitchen, leaving Robert and me alone. I noticed Robert's BMW parked on the side of the road.

"I bet you love that car," I said, pointing toward the window.

"That's only the second one I've owned. I had one the year my mother died, and I finally sold it six years ago. She did a lot of riding with me in that car, and I guess I had a hard time getting rid of it." I asked about Robert's work. "It's just a small practice," he said. "There was a time when I had dreams of owning a huge practice; you know, fourteen floors of associates and partners with a penthouse office overlooking the river. Now that dream seems absurd." He came equipped with pictures of his grandson, and several of Kate and their two daughters and son-in-law. Robert was obviously a man in love with his family. "I blew it for a lot of years," he said, rifling through the pictures. We touched on everything from football (he was a diehard Giants fan), to cable television: "Eighty-seven channels, and I can't find anything to watch!" He shuffled the pictures around; one of his mother landed on top.

"What do you miss most about your mother?" He didn't need to think about the answer.

"Her presence." He put the pictures back into an envelope. "I miss her presence to this day. Months after she died I was still picking up the phone to call her, or I'd catch myself driving to her house."

"I remember getting off the school bus and running into the house. I'd always run straight to the kitchen for something to eat. Sometimes she'd be in there, already making dinner, but other times she'd be doing laundry or be in the back changing Rachel's diaper. I never really knew what she was doing; I just knew she was there; she was in the house. After she died I'd come home from school and wander around the house, trying to feel her again."

"But you couldn't."

"No."

"At the cemetery you told me you're studying medicine," he said. I didn't remember telling him that. I made the conversation quick and told him I had just finished my last few days of school because it felt like the right thing to do. "You know, I love my job, but there are mornings when I sure don't feel like talking with another client. After I saw you on Christmas Eve I felt a passion for my family that I hadn't known in years but I didn't *feel* in love with Kate and I knew she didn't feel in love with me. If we were going to save our marriage we had to fuel up with something more than just feelings because the only ones we had between us were bitterness, anger, resentment, hostility, disappointment—feel free to stop me anytime." I laughed along with him. "All I'm saying is, you may feel different in a while, so don't pack it all in based on feelings alone." Robert was a man I wished I had known my whole life; and in a way it felt as if I had. I looked at Robert and knew he believed what he was saying.

"Do you have a girlfriend at school?" he asked. "I'm just wondering what she thinks." I looked down at my watch; I needed to go but for some reason I wanted to tell Robert everything about Meghan. I spoke quickly; there wasn't much time; it was already seven-thirty. I told him about the scholarship race she was organizing and recognition of some kind registered on his face, but Robert only nodded, letting me ramble on till he was certain I had finished.

We exchanged phone numbers with promises to stay in touch. "All of you need to meet Kate. I know she'd love to have all of you over for dinner one night."

I walked Robert to the door and shook his hand. He had parked on the street and I watched as he got into his car and backed it into our driveway. My eyes fell to the license plate: L8N LAW. He drove away, and I closed the door.

## ELEVEN

When I stand before God at the end of my life, I would hope that I
would not have a single bit of talent left,
and could say, "I used everything you gave me."
—Erma Bombeck

I pulled on my coat to leave for the hospital when the phone rang. It was eight o'clock. There are moments in life when you know who's going to be on the other end of a phone and what they're going to say and it's in that split second that you want to run. My foot was on the first step when my father stopped me. I looked at him. It was the same face I remember fifteen years ago when he told me my mother died. Dad ran to the truck and drove me to the hospital. He got there faster than I ever had.

In the course of only a few hours, Meghan's condition was deteriorating.

An hour earlier Dr. Goetz walked through the doors of the ICU and found Meghan's room. He stood at her side and brushed her cheek with the back of his hand. "You shouldn't have come in," she said. "It's Christmas."

"Do you think I'm going to let somebody else spend Christmas with my best girl?"

Meghan looked up at him. "Thank you, Dr. Goetz. Thank you for taking care of me for so long." He smiled and patted her hand. "I know what's happening." Dr. Goetz felt his heart quicken; it was the same feeling he had experienced throughout the years when a patient knew that what happened next was beyond the scope of medicine and technology.

"They're going to increase the antibiotics, Meghan, and . . ." She held firm to his hand.

"Will you tell my parents, Dr. Goetz?" She searched his eyes looking for truth, a recognition that he knew there was nothing more anyone could do. "Will you tell them what we know?"

Meghan opened her eyes and saw both her parents at her side. "I always knew what I had," she whispered. Allison stroked her face and put her ear closer to Meghan.

"What?"

"I always knew what I had. I always knew I was loved." Jim leaned forward and kissed her face. "I always knew you loved each other. So many kids never know that." Allison held on to Meghan's hand, letting her tears fall between her lips. "If we hadn't moved to this part of town I never would have run, or met Charlie or Nathan. That move was the best thing that could have happened.

Remember, you always told me that?" Allison nodded. Meghan looked at her dad and squeezed his hand.

"Remind Mom that it's okay to be sad for a while, but not forever." He struggled to smile and kissed her again. "I love you, Daddy. I always knew that there was no place on earth that you'd rather be than with us." Jim picked up her hand and kissed it again and again.

"You are the gift we always prayed for," he said, stroking her cheek. "You are more than we ever imagined." He looked at Allison. "A lot of people throw the word 'grace' around but they don't really know what it means. I saw it in your eyes every time you looked at me, and I hear it in your mother's voice when she lies down next to me every night and says she loves me. I never deserved any of you, but God gave you to me anyway."

"I know you always thought that you were nothing, Daddy—that you were just some guy who worked in a garage, but you were everything to me." Jim leaned down and pulled her to him.

"I'm not going to say good-bye," Jim said, his tears falling onto Meghan's shoulders. "I'm going to keep holding you and never say good-bye."

"Show the stars to Luke and Olivia, Dad," Meghan said. "Olivia will get bored but show them to her anyway." Meghan pulled away from her father and reached for Allison. "Tell them I love them, Mom. Will you tell them over and over for me?" Allison smiled and smoothed Meghan's hair. "And when Olivia asks why

I'm not home, will you help her understand?" Tears streamed down Allison's face as she nodded.

When I got to the hospital, Meghan was sleeping. I walked to her bedside and looked at her face; she was beautiful, too beautiful to believe she was ill. I held her hand and kissed it, holding it to my face.

*This is why Dr. Goetz left medicine,* I thought, looking at her. *And this is why he came back.*

Meghan opened her eyes and smiled.

"How was your family?" she said. Her voice was getting weak.

"I never should have gone." She held up her hand.

"Yes, you should have. Tell me how it was." I sat down and told her about Gramma's gift and how she and Lorraine acted like young girls again and Meghan smiled. She wanted to hear more so I told her about Robert and her eyes widened.

"That's the miracle, Nathan!" I couldn't imagine what she meant. "Robert came back into your life on Christmas. I told you there's always a Christmas miracle." Her eyes were dancing; she wanted nothing more than to convince me. "That's why you were supposed to be with your family today. If you hadn't gone, you would have missed your miracle."

"But what about your miracle, Meg?" She put her hand on my face.

"I have my miracle."

I shook my head.

"It was your love for me, Nathan. I couldn't leave without falling in love, so God brought you to me." A tear ran down my face. It was a heartbreaking, yet beautiful thought: Somehow, out of all the men in the world, I was chosen to love this extraordinary woman. "He brought you to me because you know how to love people, Nathan. You know how to care." My mother's letter sprang to my mind: *The pain you feel now will help you care for others.* Meghan ran her hand down the side of my face. "That's why you were meant to be a doctor. Because you listen from here." She touched my chest, resting her hand over my heart. "You were meant to work with children because they need people to listen to them from here. Not everyone can do that, but you can. It's your gift." She squeezed my hand and smiled; it was still the prettiest smile I'd ever seen. I tried to speak but felt a knot in my throat. She lifted her hand to stop me.

"You take the good with the bad. It's all part of the package. Remember?" I leaned down and held her face next to mine, feeling her breath on my cheek. *Please let her live,* I prayed. *Oh God, please don't let this happen.* We talked for as long as we could before Meghan grew tired and closed her eyes. Jim and Allison stood beside me and we watched her breathe, and waited. It was the only thing left to do.

. . .

It was a few minutes before eleven when Dr. Goetz ran into Meghan's room and told us a liver was available. Seconds later two orderlies came into the room and pushed Meghan's bed down the hall. The room was spinning; everything was happening so fast. We ran into the hall, prepared to follow the orderlies who were pushing Meghan to the OR, but Dr. Goetz stopped us. He told us about Meghan's donor: It was the miracle Meghan had been holding on to but it came at such a price.

It was late on Christmas night, and Charlie was on the sofa with Rich flipping through the picture book of Alaska he had unwrapped that morning. Charlie had already looked through it several times but was now going through it page by page with Rich. "Tell me about Alaska, Dad."

"Which part?"

"All of it. I want to hear about the birds with the colorful bills that sit on the water and about the dolphins and whales and the mountains. All of it."

"But we're going to go there someday, then you'll see it all for yourself."

"Tell me now, Dad," he said, whispering. "Tell me now so I can see it." Rich wrapped his arm around Charlie and pulled him closer, resting Charlie's head on his shoulder, and began to tell him one story after another till Charlie closed his eyes and slept. Death was quiet when it came that night. Several minutes into his story, Rich heard Charlie's breathing stop and screamed for Leslie. They called for an ambulance, but knew it was too late. His heart had stopped. Looking back, I was amazed at the strength my father and grandmother had as my mother was dying. Grieving parents were granted that same strength when they needed it most. An indescribable peace surrounded Rich and Leslie as they held on to Charlie, kissing him and thanking him for being their son.

Somehow, in the middle of their grief, Rich and Leslie made it known that Charlie wanted his liver to be tested to see if it could be a match for Meghan and that he wanted any of his healthy organs to help anyone who needed them. At first, Rich thought Charlie's liver might have been damaged from medications, but it was healthy and as close to an ideal match as possible.

We would not tell Meghan about Charlie until well after the transplant. It was an indescribable, bittersweet miracle that left all of us conflicted with feelings of loss and joy, grief and hope.

Soon after my mother died, my grandmother scribbled something on a pink notepad and taped it to her bathroom mirror. I read it again and again when I was a boy, never fully comprehending it. It read, *Now we see but a poor reflection as in a mirror; then we shall see face-to-face. Now I know in part; then I shall know fully . . . And now these three remain: faith, hope, and love. But the greatest of these is love.* It was the longer look my grandmother had tried to tell me about. One

day we'd know everything, but for now we would live
with so many unanswered questions.

It was Love that came down on Christmas, my mother said.
That is the greatest miracle of all. That is the blessing of Christmas. It is
love that requires us to do the hardest thing in impossi-
ble situations. It was love that compelled Rich and Leslie
Bennett to think of someone else's life during their greatest tragedy.

My heart broke for Rich and Leslie, for Meghan, and
for all of us who had been touched by Charlie's life. How
could Rich and Leslie think of someone else as they held Charlie in their
arms? But I knew. Of course I knew: And now these three
remain: faith, hope, and love. But the greatest of these is love.

## TWELVE

> The world is indeed full of peril, and in it there are many dark
> places; but still there is much that is fair, and though in all lands
> love is mingled with grief, love grows perhaps the greater.
> —J. R. R. Tolkien, *The Fellowship of the Ring*

I heard a knock on the door and opened it to see William. "Turn on the news," he said, brushing past me. He flipped on the television, and I sat on the sofa. Footage of Meghan winning a race in early fall was playing. I flipped to another channel and that station was running a story about her and Charlie as well. "How do you explain your ability to run so fast?" the reporter asked after a race. Meghan threw her arm over Michele's shoulder.

"I don't really know, but I think we've all been given something, you know? Some sort of gift that we're supposed to unwrap and give away. I think running was my gift." I leaned my head on the back of the sofa, listening to her.

"And how could you give that away?" the reporter asked. Meghan was embarrassed, and she looked down at the ground.

"I want to raise money for pediatric heart patients and help them go to college. I know it's nothing huge but I hope it can help in a small way because even the smallest ripple can change the shape of water." She squinted as she looked toward the camera. The reporter spoke of the scholarship race Meghan had been organizing and showed some of the tiny heart patients at the hospital. Pictures of Charlie flashed on the screen, and the reporter spoke about their friendship. I sat up and watched them replay the tape of Meghan running across the finish line, smiling.

William went with me to the funeral. We drove to the church but had to park several blocks away. We walked in silence with the rest of the crowd and saw Dr. Goetz helping his wife out of their car. William and I walked into the church together, which overflowed with members of the church, along with Meghan's team, who loved Charlie. They all wore running suits in honor of his relationship with them. Denise and Claudia and several of the pediatrics staff members sat in a row together. William and I sat a few rows behind Jim, Luke, and Olivia. Allison stayed with Meghan in the hospital. Charlie's teacher spoke at his funeral, along with Dr. Goetz and the minister. Charlie would have been embarrassed at the fuss everyone was making. I could see him cracking his knuckles in nervous anticipation of the whole thing just being over and done.

William and I stepped outside the church at the end of the service and the wind shrieked when I opened the door. I felt a little hand grab mine, and I looked down to see Olivia.

"It's so cold, Olivia," I said, leading her toward the door. "Why don't you go back inside?"

"My mom says Charlie isn't here. She said he's already in Heaven."

"That's right." The wind picked up her hair, and she closed her eyes. I pulled the hood of her coat over her head.

"Did God take Charlie to Heaven so Meghan could live?"

I sat down on the top step so I could look at her. "No," I said, remembering the words my mother had said to me. "God didn't take Charlie to Heaven. He received him: There's a big difference." She looked at me, trying to understand what I was saying. "Life took Charlie away from us."

"Why?"

"Because he was human."

After the funeral, I drove to my father's house, but he, Rachel, and Gramma weren't home. I noticed photo albums and the box of letters strewn on top of my grandmother's bed. It looked as if she was in the middle of cleaning out her closet. I sat on the bed and started rifling through the albums. There is a distinct break in one of the albums: The pictures go from the entire family together to ones that no longer include my mother. The rest of that album took over three years to fill. I reached for a letter that was sitting on top of another photo album and instead of discarding it back to the pile I opened it, recognizing my handwriting as a teenager:

Dear Mom,

I often wonder how those doctors treated you when you went to the hospital for tests. I wonder how they made you feel. Did they scare you or were they good to you, sitting by your side and making you feel safe? I wonder if they took the time to talk and get to know you. I wonder if they ever knew what a great mom you were or how you could make Dad laugh. I wonder if they felt bad when you passed away, or if they even knew. I wonder if they realized what the world missed when you died?

I miss you and love you every day,
Nathan

I held on to the letter as tears blurred my vision. It contained the reasons why I wanted to become a physician: Not because I thought I could save everyone but because I wanted each patient to know that he or she was being cared for to the very end. It was what my mother had tried to teach me before she died—the pain of living without her would help me care for others. It wasn't a weakness as I had thought for so long; it was my gift. Just as Meghan said.

## THIRTEEN

You gain strength, courage and confidence by every experience in
which you really stop to look fear in the face. . . .
You must do the thing you think you cannot do.
—Eleanor Roosevelt

Robert Layton cradled his grandson, Evan, with one arm
and picked the phone up in his den with the other. He
dialed a number written in his personal address book.
"Allen," Robert said, bouncing Evan up and down. "Are
you still in the Christmas spirit?" Robert hung up the
phone, wrote something on a legal pad, and dialed the
next number. "Larry, this is Robert. I need your help."
After several phone calls, Robert went to the kitchen and
fixed a bottle for Evan.

"I can take him, Dad," his daughter Hannah said.
Robert held the baby away from her.

"Don't even think about taking him. He's Grandpa's
buddy." Robert stuck the warm bottle in Evan's mouth.
"Aren't you Grandpa's buddy?" He whispered in the
baby's ear. "Come on, let's get back to work." He slipped
back inside his den.

"What are you working on in there, Dad?" Hannah said.

"Top-secret stuff," Robert said, holding the phone to his ear. "Gray, it's Robert Layton." He yelled into the phone. "Robert Layton! Can you hear me? Good. Do you have a second, Gray? I need your help with something." When Kate heard Robert shouting she stuck her head inside the den. He saw her and waved his hand, shooing her away.

He hung up the receiver, jotted something on his legal pad, and smiled before picking up the phone again.

I showered and reached toward the bathroom counter for the watch my mother had given me. I paused, then picked it up and looked at the time; it was running ten minutes behind. I didn't tap the face of it, but flipped it over to the inscription on the back: *With all the love in the world*, Mom. I ran my finger over the inscription and pulled out a piece of paper from my backpack and sat down at the table and began writing:

*Dear Mom,*
*I think it's time to put away the watch you gave me. It doesn't mean I don't love you; it just means it's time to move on.*
                              *With all the love in the world,*
                              *Nathan*

I put the watch and letter next to a picture of my mother and me on top of the chest of drawers and reached for the watch Meghan had given me. I put it on and finished dressing. My time at the hospital was done, but I went there anyway and lingered around a closed office door.

Dr. Goetz arrived a few minutes later with a cup of coffee in his hand. "Come on in," he said, unlocking the door. He looked tired; it had been a rough week. He offered me a seat, and I sat down, unzipping my coat. I knew he was wondering why I was there.

"Do patients know they're dying?"

"Some of them do."

"Do you think he knew?"

"I think he always knew. That's why he lived the way he did."

"Do you ever get used to it?"

He leaned back in his chair and sighed, looking at the ceiling. "No." He looked at me. "But you learn to accept it." He was quiet. "Sometimes it's just harder to accept."

Though I had gone over what I wanted to say several times in my head, I found myself stammering for the right words. "I would like to be part of your rotation again."

Dr. Goetz stirred his coffee and stared at me.

"Why?"

I had a feeling this wasn't going to be as easy as I'd hoped. "Because someone recently told me that you need to run with somebody better than you." Dr. Goetz smiled; he understood the reference. "That if I want to be the best, I have to run with the best." He sipped his coffee.

"That's good advice."

"Someone else said that we need to keep our eyes on the goal . . . if we take our eyes off the goal, we'll never make it to the end." He swallowed hard and looked at me, studying my face.

"It's not going to be any easier."

"I know that."

"What makes you think you can stick it out this time?"

"Because I can't just leave. If I could walk away, I would; but I'd never be happy." He leaned back and studied my face. I knew he believed me. "And, to answer your question . . . medicine is a calling." He nodded, and I could see the corners of his mouth turn up just a bit.

"There are things that I cannot tolerate from med students, Mr. Andrews. If you arrive late for a rotation, that shows me that . . ." I held up my wrist, stopping him.

"That will never happen again. I have a new watch." He smiled and cleared his throat. "Dr. Goetz, I need to apologize to you because I've made a lot of mistakes and—"

"So, are you here to waste my morning by telling me all the mistakes you've made, or are you here to start over?"

"I'd like to start over," I said, smiling.

Denise looked inside Meghan's room. Meghan had been moved out of ICU only days earlier into the step-down unit. "People are calling from all over about the scholarship run," Denise said, holding on to paperwork. "Two separate law firms alone have donated $5000 each." Jim and Allison sat in silence, listening. "Just within the last several days, $25,000 has been donated." Meghan gasped. Allison threw her hands over her face and cried. The scholarship fund would be bigger than what Meghan had ever dreamed.

My mind recalled a piece of conversation I had had with Meghan. "Some attorney in Jefferson gave $500," she said. *Could Robert Layton be that attorney?* I followed Denise into the hallway and looked over the donation sheets—there it was, Layton and Associates for $500. I called him, and Robert asked me to bring Dad and Gramma to his house that weekend for dinner.

When we arrived, Kate opened the door. She was a beautiful woman. I could see why Robert fell for her nearly thirty years ago. She threw open her arms and wrapped them around me. "You really do exist." Kate was as accessible in spirit as Robert. "For so many years I wondered what happened to you," she said to me. "Now look at you, sitting in our house and looking back at me!" Robert walked in through the garage door carrying an armful of firewood. Dad jumped up to help.

"Sit down, Jack," Kate said, springing to her feet.

"You're our guest. Robert can get it." Robert grunted as he bent to the floor, easing the wood into the bin on the hearth.

"When a man's arms are breaking, Kate, and another man offers to help . . . let him help." He greeted all of us with a hug, then said, "Can I bring out some hors d'oeuvres and drinks for everybody?" Kate moved toward the kitchen to help.

"Let me help with that," I said, following Robert into the kitchen. I wanted to ask Robert about the law firms and businesses that had donated money to the run, but didn't know how to bring it up.

"How's Meghan today?" he asked.

"She's great. Doctors see improvement every day."

"Does she know about Charlie?"

"Her mom and dad and Charlie's parents told her about a week after the funeral. She didn't take the news very well. How could she?" Robert didn't say anything. There was nothing anyone could ever say. I looked at Robert and tried to think of a way to ask him about the donations to the scholarship run. He gave me an opening.

"What's up?" he said.

"There's been this outpouring of donations for Meghan's scholarship run from lawyers and companies that the hospital hasn't heard of, people the Sullivans don't even know." Robert was listening with interest; he knew I was on to him. "It seems that someone is doing some staggering fund-raising for this run." Robert was nonchalant, impressed only with the scholarship run itself.

"Probably a friend of hers who wants to help."

"It seems to me that this friend is someone the Sullivans don't know, someone they've never met." Robert pulled glasses from the cupboard and began filling them with ice. "The Sullivans are trying to come up with a name for the race. I thought maybe they should name it after the person who's been so influential in fund-raising, what do you think?" Robert replaced the ice bin to the freezer and smiled.

"I think they should call it whatever Meghan wants."

"But maybe people should know that someone else was responsible for . . ." He held up his hand, cutting me off.

"This is Meghan's gift to someone. She should be the one giving it away." I watched him fill the glasses with ice before asking him what had been on my mind for so long.

"How'd you ever donate to the run in the first place?"

"She called my office one day and my assistant walked to my desk and said I should take the call. I knew it was important to Jodie; she's a runner, so when Meghan asked for a donation, I couldn't refuse that sweet voice."

"The Sullivans are going to need help with the money. They need someone to walk them through setting up a trust or something." Robert nodded.

"I know a few firms who would be glad to help. I'll

have Jodie get a package of info to you on each firm, and you can pass it on to the Sullivans."

There are some people who go through life seizing whatever they can for themselves; then there are others who, once their lives are touched, cannot help but leave others changed as well. Robert was such a person. No one would ever know who was working so hard behind the scenes for Meghan's run, and somehow that suited Robert just fine. Meghan was right: Robert's coming back into my life was one of the small miracles of Christmas.

I spoke with Robert's assistant about the package of info he'd pulled together for the Sullivans. "It's ready," Jodie said. "How do you want me to get it to you?"

"I can just swing by and pick it up."

"That'll be out of your way, though. Where do you live? Are you close to the university?"

"I live on the property, but it can be confusing for someone who's not used to all these little streets."

"I have to drive by Bryan Park on my way home every day. Do you know where that is?" We agreed to meet in the park at the end of the workday. I drove around the parking lot looking for anyone sitting in a car, but when I couldn't spot anyone I parked my truck and watched people ice-skating on the lake.

The runner with the neon ball cap made her way around the lake as I waited. I thought about getting out and talking with her, but I didn't want to miss Jodie, and since I saw this woman running here so often, I knew I'd get another chance. A car pulled in beside me, but a mother and her two young children got out and toted their ice skates down the hill toward the lake. Meghan's runner made another lap around the lake before she slowed down and walked the hill toward the cars. She banged her hands together and pulled the cap farther down on her head, swinging her arms. She caught me watching her, and I looked away, fidgeting with the buttons on my stereo. I jumped when I heard a small rap on my window. I looked up and saw the neon cap. I rolled the window down and looked at her, wondering what she wanted. "Are you Nathan?" *How did she know my name?* "Are you Robert's friend?"

"Are *you* Jodie?" I whispered.

"I am." She extended her hand through the window. "Nice to meet you." I reached up, grabbed her hand, and pumped it up and down, laughing.

## FOURTEEN

Where there is great love, there are always miracles.
—Willa Cather

In June, hundreds of runners lined up in front of the courthouse. A banner stretched high above the street, THE CHARLIE BENNETT SCHOLARSHIP RUN—Meghan wouldn't consider naming the run after herself. Hospital administrators and medical staff were out in force wearing matching yellow T-shirts with the name of the run on the front and the name of the department they worked in on the back. Denise and Claudia were busy corralling the pediatrics department, who were the noisiest by far. Dr. Goetz held on to a streetlight and stretched his quadriceps. "Don't fail me now," he said each time he stretched a muscle. "Just get me through this and I promise I'll take better care of you."

Dad, along with Lydia, Gramma, Rachel, and Lorraine (wearing a leopard-print sweat suit—she must have thought the print would at least make her look fast) lined up next to William, Robert and Kate, and Jodie, who was sporting her neon ball cap, of course.

"I'll stay with you, Gramma," Rachel said.

"Don't be ridiculous. You run alongside your father and Lydia. Lorraine and I will stick together and walk across the finish line at midnight if we have to."

"Midnight," Lorraine shouted. "You didn't say anything about being out here till midnight!" Gramma turned to her in a flash.

"We'll stay out here till dawn if we have to, Lorraine!"

"Well, I can't walk far, Evelyn. My knees will never let me."

"There's nothing wrong with your knees, and everybody knows it, Lorraine!" Lorraine stuck her hands in the jacket of her sweat suit and pouted, wishing she'd never answered the phone that morning.

I felt arms around my waist and looked down at Olivia; she was looking more like Meghan every day. Jim pushed Meghan through the crowd in a wheelchair. It was the only way doctors would let her participate. It would be well over a year before she would run again.

Earlier in the morning we had gone to Bryan Park, and Jim and I unloaded a bench from the back of my truck and set it under the oak tree by the lake. Rich and Leslie were there along with my family. Meghan tried to speak but couldn't. Every time she thought of Charlie she cried, and the day of race was especially emotional. She gripped my hand and looked at me for help, but I didn't need to say anything. Leslie read the plaque on the bench and tears flooded her eyes. It was for Charlie. Meghan had agonized what to put on it; she wanted it to reflect not only her heart, but Charlie's as well. It read:

IN MEMORY OF CHARLIE BENNETT
THE GREATEST MIRACLE OF ALL IS THE
LOVE OF A TRUE FRIEND

"I just wish I could thank him," Meghan whispered, holding on to Leslie.

"He knows," Leslie said, wiping tears from her face.

Jim pushed Meghan to the front of the line, and someone handed her a microphone. She welcomed the runners to the first annual Charlie Bennett Scholarship Run, then paused. I didn't know if she could get through the few words she wanted to say. "Many of you know that I am blessed to be here today," she said. "But I am more blessed to have called Charlie Bennett my friend." She put the microphone on her lap and paused. She had more to say but couldn't. She lifted the microphone to her mouth. "Let's run this for him," she said. She fired the starter's gun into the air, and the university band struck up a tune as the runners took off, running Meghan's dream.

We wound our way through town and into Bryan Park. Leslie had pushed her to the spot where we had positioned Charlie's bench earlier in the morning. They sat there together watching one runner after another make their way around the lake. I ran around it several times, just so I could kiss Meghan and see that pretty smile. I ran onto the path again with the other runners and grabbed Olivia's hand as the sun made its way from behind the clouds and shimmered off the water.

"Look at that," Olivia said, pointing to the water. "Heaven just opened up, and Charlie's smiling." Somehow, I think she was right.

I watched people cross the finish line, one by one, and I smiled, thinking of what Meghan told me while she sat in the cab of my truck—she had indeed changed her small part of the world. The money raised that day was $100,000, more than anything she had ever imagined.

. . . let us run with perseverance the race marked out for us.
—Paul of Tarsus

The wind has picked up, spraying a fine powder of snow along the lake's edge. Carolers are inside the gazebo warming up for a brief concert this evening. I stabilize the bench and shine the plaque that reads, *For Meghan Sullivan and all who believe in miracles.* I take a seat and look out over the frozen water. It is nice to see that the park hasn't changed in the three years I have been away, and the grounds are still beautiful, even in December. During the past four years, I finished up my fourth year of medical school with Dr. Goetz, then went to Rainbow Babies and Children's Hospital in Cleveland for three years of residency. I have moved back into town to take two months off before heading to Boston's Children's Hospital for three years of fellowship training in pediatric cardiology, keeping me closer to home. Then, hopefully, I'll come back and work in the hospital's cardiology department for a few years with Dr. Goetz before he retires.

Meghan went back to school on a part-time basis the fall after her transplant, but she chose not to go to Stanford or Georgetown; she stayed at the university and when she was able, she ran for them, "helping to put us on the map," as Michele Norris said. Meghan studied education with the hopes of teaching and coaching. She will be unbelievable at both.

Ice-skaters laugh as they attempt to make figure eights on the frozen lake. Two little girls, who look no older than three, run from the lake and climb up on Charlie's bench; the tassels on their knit hats bounce up and down. They look at me, and I see that they're twins. "Hi," one of them says.

"Hi."

"What are you doing?" the other little girl asks.

"Just leaving a bench here."

"For who?"

"For Meghan Sullivan." Their eyes light up.

"Our brother knew her," one of them says. I assume their brother was on one of the teams at the university. "He went to Heaven when she got her new liver." I snap my head to look at them. They are Rich and Leslie's twins. Soon after Charlie died, Leslie discovered she was pregnant. They had never planned for more children, so the news surprised them, to say the least. On what would have been Charlie's thirteenth birthday, Rich and Leslie laid flowers on his grave and Leslie felt one of the babies kick for the first time.

"That little kick brought such light to such a dark day," Leslie later said to Meghan. "These little girls brought nothing but joy with them when they were born." I watch them and see what she means. They are adorable, much cuter than the pictures I've seen.

"Come on, we need to get going," I hear someone say behind me. I turn to see a young man behind me who can't be older than fourteen but already he is as tall as I am. He motions for the girls to come to him. I look at him and can see the resemblance: the eyes, the nose, the jawline—it is Matthew, Charlie's brother. "Do you need help?" he asks me.

"No. Thank you." During the brief time I knew Charlie, I only met Matthew once, but he was a little boy. He doesn't remember who I am, and I had no idea he would have grown so much in four years. I open my mouth to tell him what an incredible person his brother was.

"I'm supposed to meet our parents in a few minutes, and I have to get them out of these clothes or else my mom will kill me," he says. I smile. They are headed to the same place I am. I shake his hand, and the little girls wave.

"Hey, what's your name," one of them asks, turning around.

"Nathan. What's yours?"

"I'm Abigail and she's Allie."

"Both of those names sound like the name of a princess. Are both of you princesses?"

"I am," Abigail says. "She's not." I laugh and look

down at Charlie's bench. I often wonder if he ran through the gates of Heaven like he wanted to. I smile. *He did. I know he did.*

During my training, there have been other children who have died since Charlie; children who entered my life for only the shortest time; but they have taught me, like my mother said, it's not about how long you live, but how you live, because before you know it, our time is up and we leave this place. Each of their lives was too short, but they all left their small part of the world changed, leaving this physician with the desire to be a better person, to change the shape of water; but to do that I have to jump into the water first. It's what my mother wanted me to learn.

I jump in the truck and drive through town, parking at the side of the road. I run inside the back of the building, and my grandmother and Rachel hurry to fix my tie. Tears are in their eyes as they kiss my cheek. "Thought you were AWOL there for a minute," Dad says, grinning. Lydia squeezes my arm. She and my father have been married nearly a year now and are very happy together. Lydia is a wonderful woman. She loves my grandmother; they cook together and go for walks and every now and then Lydia will sit down with Gramma and Lorraine and watch the Atlanta Braves play. She's even learned how to antagonize Lorraine, booing the Braves and cheering for the Indians during my time in Cleveland. For the first time in my life, Lorraine is wearing a skirt and jacket, not a sweat suit with sneakers, and there are no sequins in sight.

"No sweat suit, Lorraine?" I ask.

"I'm not trash, doll," she says, her laughter shaking the rafters.

Dad and I walk down the aisle toward the front, which has been decorated with red and white poinsettias and a Christmas tree covered with sparkling lights, gold ribbon, and red bulbs. Swags of spruce held together with strings of holly berries hang between each pew. As I pass, I smile at Robert and Kate, Dr. Goetz, Hope, who is now nine and beautiful, the Sullivans and the Bennetts, with Matthew and the twins at their side. The girls look at me, and their mouths open wide. One jumps on Rich's lap and begins to tell him something, but Leslie shushes her, fussing with her hair. I smile at them and take my place at the front, Dad by my side, along with William, who's flown in from his residency in Texas.

It's been twenty years since I stood on that windy hillside with my mother. "Time in the valley will teach you to be a man, Nathan," she had said. "It's where your character will form. I hope you go through the valley so that you'll learn how to love and feel and understand. And when life wounds you, I hope it is because you loved people, not because you mistreated them." It was a blessing of sorts; a blessing that forges love in the darkest places.

There have been times, especially during those early years without her, that I thought time in the valley was anything but a blessing, but now I know otherwise. As I grew, I began to understand what my mother meant: It is those times of struggle and pain that teach us how to live. It's not really living until you've thrown your heart and soul on the line, risking failure and suffering loss. And I have come to realize that we're never alone; everyone has been through their own valley or is walking through it now: A man fights alcoholism and vows his family won't live through the sickness and sadness of his own youth, a young woman contracts a disease and parents stand by her bedside praying for a miracle, spouses die, leaving brokenhearted widows or widowers behind, couples fight and separate, cars crash, a young boy dies, leaving a hole in the heart of everyone he touched. There were times when the grief in my life made it impossible to believe that God was alive and working, or the doubts were so great it seemed hopeless to believe anything at all, but as I look at the faces in the seats before me I know once again that we're all here for a reason, a purpose that is often beyond us.

The music swells, and I look up to see my bride standing at the back of the church. The wedding is small; many people couldn't make it into town for Christmas Eve. We knew that as we planned, but Meghan insisted we get married at Christmas, to honor both my mother and Charlie. "Even God's smallest plan is bigger than any dream we'll ever hope for," my father said, dragging our rowboat onto shore so many years ago. Glancing at him now, I still don't understand why God's plan couldn't include saving my mother, or Charlie; I know I never will. I smile as Meghan walks down the aisle and can hear the twins clap and giggle when they see her.

But I know that although we may never understand it, there is a plan, and though it may be traced in pain, in the end there will be joy, and it will be beautiful.